The Sea Stone Collection

To Brenda

Thank you —

Kathleen Martin

Kathleen Martin

ISBN 978-1-64515-036-7 (paperback)
ISBN 978-1-64515-037-4 (digital)

Christian Faith Publishing, Inc.
832 Park Avenue
Meadville, PA 16335
www.christianfaithpublishing.com

Printed in the United States of America

Dedications

I'd like to dedicate this book to my mother, Eleanor, who passed away in 2010. When I was twelve, I shared with her my desire to someday write a book. For years she encouraged me to "get started" before it was too late. However, raising my son, Michael, and working a full time job always seemed to take first priority. Then, in 2009, just 10 months before she died, she gave me that one nugget of advice that started me on my author's journey.

"Do not die with your book still inside you!" she told me. This book is for you, mom. Thank you for never giving up on me. I will forever love you!

Acknowledgements

The making of this book, The Sea Stone Collection, would not have been made possible without the help of the Weber and Robinson families. I would like to thank Marcia Weber for posing for the cover while on vacation in Ocean Isle Beach, North Carolina. And, to her son-in-law, Brian Robinson, who worked his artist's magic to take the perfect cover photo, as well as the photos used to promote this book. I would also like to thank Amy Weber, Marcia's daughter-in-law. As an avid runner, she generously shared with me her expertise and tips on running a marathon. Last, but not least, I'd like to thank my family. A heart-felt thank you to my husband, Darrell, who offered me his full support and graciously endured those days when I spent more time with my lap top than I spent with him. Also, kudos to my sister, Becky, for her love and encouragement. She was my cheerleader during the years I spent writing this book and graciously offered to help me promote it by accompanying me on my book signing tours. Thanks, Becky! With God's grace, everyone, we did it!

May 16, 1962
Sea Breeze Cottage

"Happy birthday, Kathleen," my Grandpa Jake whispered, as he lit the eleven candles on my small birthday cake. "Blow out your candles and make a wish."

"But, Grandpa, we just had breakfast," I reminded him. "Isn't it too early for a birthday party?"

"Perhaps," he said. "However, it's never too early for birthday wishes. Now pucker up and blow like you're the north wind."

Pulling a deep breath of air into my lungs, I aimed it at the tiny flames and released it. As I stood looking at the smoking wicks, I spoke my wish aloud.

"I wish Momma could be here for my birthday."

"That's a good wish, Button," said Grandpa Jake, using the nickname he'd given me as a toddler.

After carefully plucking each candle from the thick white icing, he picked up the knife. "However, it's been five years since your momma has been here to celebrate your birthday. I'd have thought you would be used to it, by now."

"Are you used to it?" I asked.

"No," he replied, cutting two generous pieces of cake and placing each on its own small plate. "She was my only child. I will never get used to her passing. She never smoked a cigarette in her life. How could she die of lung cancer? Not one doctor can give me a straight answer on that."

"Is Pappa coming to my party?" I asked, accepting the small plate of yellow cake.

"Maybe later, Button," he replied. "At the moment, he's out on the beach painting his pictures. He has to capture the light whenever it's available, you know. We'll save him some cake."

"He can have mine," I offered, pushing my plate away. After a moment, Grandpa Jake did the same. So far, turning eleven wasn't much fun.

"What do you say we go look for shells on the beach?" he offered, giving me a smile. "I'll go and fetch the cocker spaniels. Hector and Percy should be done with their naps by now and ready for a good run on the sand. We'll need a jacket, so run and fetch our slickers."

Gathering the dogs, we let ourselves out the kitchen door and stepped out onto the porch. Dead leaves and small branches, downed by the winter storms, littered the small yard, and Percy couldn't make up his mind which one he wanted to pick up first. The sound of the sea behind our small cottage beckoned to me, and I ran around the side yard, the dogs following at my heels.

"Wait on me, Child," Grandpa called out, stopping to zip up his worn yellow slicker against the spring chill.

As I waited at the edge of the dunes for him to catch up, I noticed the morning sun glinting off the windows of our house. I loved our home beside the sea. The house, known as Sea Breeze Cottage, sat on the edge of a slight rise, overlooking the Atlantic Ocean. I couldn't imagine living anywhere else.

When Grandpa joined me, we made our way down the sea path that led over the dunes and onto the beach below. To my right, I could see my father perched atop a small rocky outcrop, his easel before him. His faded artist's smock, spattered with a rainbow of oil paints, billowed out from the breeze making his slim frame appear larger. His dark, windblown hair, lay at odd angles. As he stared out to sea, he held his paintbrush poised over his canvas as if in deep thought. The painting before him was of a violent storm at sea, done in angry shades of gray and dark green.

"Smell the air, Kathy," exclaimed Grandpa Jake, filling his lungs. "I believe we've seen the last of the foul weather. That is the smell of spring in the northern climes, if I'm not mistaken."

As I sniffed the air, I thought there was little difference in the smell, no matter the season. The air always smelled of fish and seaweed.

"Shall we see what the surf has carried in?" he asked, throwing a stick toward the dogs. Hector, sensing a game, immediately picked it up and ran with it. "I'm sure we'll find something of interest on the beach after last night's storm."

I loved this time shared with my grandfather. Now as we stepped out onto the sand, he halted only long enough to light the end of his cigar. As he puffed, the smoke barely left his mouth before being whisked away by the ocean's breeze. His head of thick, curly white hair, hanging over the tops of his ears, was at the mercy of the wind as it blew around his face. Above his mouth, his thick white mustache blended into his beard and curled around his chin like dandelion fuzz. I loved the way his face crinkled when he smiled. Looking at him now, I wondered if he was old enough to die. The very thought struck terror within me.

"Grandpa, when will you have a birthday?" I asked, over the sounds of the rough surf.

"The end of September," he replied around his cigar.

"Are you old enough to die?" I asked, giving a voice to my fear.

"Not quite," he said, amused. "I'm only sixty-one."

"How old is Pappa?"

"Your pappa is thirty-eight," he said, turning left toward the pier, located a mile up the beach.

"Is that old?"

"It is when your heart has given up on life," he replied, sadly. "I just wish he could see that having you in his life is a reason to go on. I know you're the reason I look forward to each new day."

Pulling a handful of breadcrumbs from the pocket of his slicker, he began tossing them to a hovering flock of seagulls. Their high-pitched squawks grew louder as they dove greedily for the scraps. Knowing full well the dangers of standing beneath feeding gulls, I let go of his hand and stepped back.

Turning, I glanced back down the beach. My father, his paintbrush in hand, remained as still as the boulders surrounding him.

11

"How come Pappa isn't painting?" I asked, pushing the hood of my slicker off my head. "All he's doing is staring at the water. His picture still looks the same as it did yesterday. It's all gloomy and sad."

"He's an artist, Button," replied Grandpa Jake. "His talent is a gift as well as a curse. Your pappa's spark of inspiration has to come from within, from his heart. Oftentimes, it takes a long journey before making its way to the end of his brush. And lately, his memories of your mother are doing great battle with that inspiration. Some days she wins, and some days…he paints. Today, he thinks of her."

At that moment, Hector and Percival bounded up to us, calling our attention elsewhere. Leaving my father to his work, we walked on down the beach. When Grandpa Jake stopped and looked down, I made my way to his side.

"What is it, Grandpa?" I asked. "What do you see?"

"A sea stone," he replied in surprise. Bending, he scooped a small stone into his hand and held it out for me to see. "I haven't found one of these in a very long time. Heavens, I'd thought the magic had left me for good."

"What's a sea stone?" I asked, scrutinizing it. To me, it looked like an ordinary old rock. It was about the size of a hen's egg and appeared mottled with shades of brown and gray, its edges worn smooth by some unseen force. Small flecks of pink granite reflected the morning's sunlight as he rolled it in his hand.

"Hold out your hand, Button," he instructed. When I did so, he carefully placed the stone in my palm.

"Why are you giving me a rock?" I asked.

"Oh, this is not just any rock," he exclaimed, tapping the stone in my hand with his index finger. "It's a sea stone. Your mother collected them when she was your age. God rest her soul."

"What's a sea stone?" I asked, once again.

"Well, it's a magical gift from the sea," he replied. "I, myself, have collected them since I was a lad. Each one holds a mystery as old as time itself. This stone could very well be over a million years old. And with its great age, one must wonder, from where did it originate?"

"It came from the sea," I told him, stating the obvious.

"Yes. However, you must ask yourself, from where did the sea come by the stone?" he asked. "From what continent was it set adrift?"

"What do you mean?" I asked.

"Well, it could have come from anywhere," he replied. "It could have chipped off a cliff in Norway and rolled along the sea bottom for a thousand years before ending its journey here in Cutter's Cove. Maine is a long way from Norway, you know. How many years did the waves push it along the bottom of the ocean before depositing it at the water's edge just in time for me to find it?"

"What do I do with it?" I asked, peering at it. I was intrigued at the idea of holding a million-year-old piece of Norway in my hand.

"Why, you keep it of course," he stated. "I am giving it to you so you can start your own collection of sea stones. It's up to you to know which ones to choose. However, I must warn you, Button, once you begin to pick them up, you will be compelled to look for another and then another until you are as old as I."

"There are so many," I said, my eyes sweeping the sand around me. I quickly spotted several small dark pebbles bouncing in the rough surf. "How will I know which ones to choose?"

"The special stones will call out to you, beckoning you to choose them," he said, with a grin. "You must learn to listen for their invitation for that is the magic of the stones. And someday, you may be lucky enough to find that one special stone that sings to your heart. If you should find it, hold it tight, Button, for it will bring you true love. That is how I met your

Grandma Sarah. I found my singing sea stone a week before I met her and the rest is, as we say, history."

"Is that how Pappa found Momma?" I asked, curious.

"No. I'm afraid your Pappa never believed in the magic of the stones," he replied. "However, your Momma did. But alas, she was not one of the lucky ones. She never found her singing sea stone. Despite that fact, she thought your Pappa was her destiny and married him anyway. I'm afraid you are the only magic they found. Then your momma died and our lives changed forever. Oh, my sweet Paula, how I miss you still."

A far away sadness swept across his face and after a moment, he, too, stood staring out to sea. *He and Pappa must have loved my momma very much*, I thought.

Looking down at the stone in my hand, I felt its magic tug at my senses, urging me to tuck it away. Lifting the flap on the pocket of my slicker, I dropped it in and snapped the flap into place. Slipping my small hand into my grandfather's, I, too, stood staring out to sea, wondering if all my birthdays were going to be this sad.

Chapter 1

May 16, 2011
Forty-nine years later
Sea Breeze Cottage

"Come, Mussolini," I called from the sea path as my five-year-old cocker spaniel bounded across the yard. *There has always been a cocker spaniel at Sea Breeze Cottage*, I thought. "How about we have a nice walk on the beach before I leave for work? Today is my birthday, Pup. I'll bet you didn't know that?"

Mussolini, uninterested, barked twice and raced ahead of me down the path. Glancing down at my watch, I saw that I still had an hour before I had to be at my job at the antique bookshop in town. I loved walking in the soft sand and feeling small beside the ocean. Here I gained a real sense of how far eternity stretched out before me. The constant ebb and flow of the tides and the endless volley of waves hurrying in from the sea, reassured me that long after I was gone, they would continue their dance with the dunes and jutting rocks.

For years, I'd used my birthday as an annual opportunity to assess my life and future dreams. This birthday, however, I felt I was hitting a milestone— for I was turning sixty. This meant, of course, that I had more years behind me than before me. I most missed my mother on my birthday, and the little girl inside me still held the wish that she could be here to help me celebrate.

Looking out to sea, I watched as a fishing trawler lowered its nets to begin its morning run. Sensing an easy meal, the seagulls hovered like bees around the boat's exterior. As I walked, the breeze still held a hint of rain. Glancing down at my feet, I watched a small stone as it tumbled after the retreating surf. I smiled at the memory of that long-ago birthday when Grandpa Jake gave me my first sea stone. Since then, I'd spent my free time walking the beach in search of my precious pebbles. Years of scouring the beaches of Cutter's Cove now littered the windowsill of my bedroom. Each, had indeed called out to me just as my grandfather had predicted. However, despite my years of searching, I'd failed to find the coveted singing sea stone that granted me true love. As a result, I was turning sixty with no one to share my life. Of course, caring for my father until his recent death the previous winter, had consumed so much of that life that I had, by the time I was in my fifties, given up all hope of ever falling in love. Was it now too late for a woman my age to capture the eye and heart of that special man? I'd taken good care of myself over the years and was still considered a very smart-looking woman. However, the dark, shoulder-length hair of my girlish youth, had long ago faded to a soft gray. All was not yet lost. However, each birthday was a reminder that my chance for a family was going, going, gone. Was I to spend my last remaining years wondering what might have been?

I refused to allow the gray, overcast skies, a remnant of the storm that had raged during the night, to set my mood. Today was my birthday, and I was just happy to be alive. Suddenly, the sun broke through the thick cloud cover, and my mood immediately lifted. Peering down the beach, I called to Mussolini, who turned and started my way. I wondered just how many mornings I had left to walk on the beach now that I was sixty. I could just hear Becky scolding me for even thinking such a thought. As my best friend, she liked to think she was my conscience. I didn't mind, for she was as beautiful as she was smart. She was also a savvy businesswoman and owned and operated the town's only florist shop, the Posey Pot. Friends since kindergarten, we were there for each other through thick and thin. She stood beside me as I mourned the passing of my beloved Grandpa Jake and played the big sister through the worst years with my father. I, in turn, was there for her when Michael, her husband of thirty years, died suddenly seven years prior. Since we were both now alone, we established a regular lunch date every Tuesday at a small diner simply known as Della's, in the square of town. Although today was only Monday, I was meeting her for lunch to celebrate my birthday. She had better not forget.

As Mussolini made his way toward me, barking for my attention, I picked up a stick and tossed it ahead of me. As usual, something caught his eye, and he left the stick to the mercy of the waves. The early spring air was still cool enough to chill, so I pulled my jacket closer around me. The surf was rough this morning, and debris, swept in by the storm the night before, littered the beach. Reaching into the pocket of my jacket, I retrieved a handful of breadcrumbs and tossed them, one by one, into the air at a flock of seagulls. Hovering above me, they seemed to defy gravity as they floated in place above my head.

Noting the time, I started in the direction of the sea path that led to the cottage. As I made my way among the ropes of black kelp, a prune-size stone lying on the sand suddenly caught my eye. As I stood looking down at it, the urge to pick it up niggled at my senses. Was it calling to me? Yes, it was. Relief flooded over me for three years had passed since my last find. When Mussolini caught up with me, he butted his head in to see if what I'd found was something he could chase.

"Relax, Pup," I said, petting his head. "It's just a sea stone. Gracious, I'd thought I'd lost my touch." Brushing Mussolini aside, I leaned over and scooped the small stone up into my hand, anxious to add it to my collection. I didn't know it at the time, but I was about to receive the birthday present of a lifetime.

The moment my fingers encircled the stone, I knew this was no ordinary sea stone for I felt my heart flutter with joy. Music momentarily burst upon my brain, its tune vibrant but unrecognized. I had no doubt as to its meaning. I had, at last, found my singing sea stone! Clutching it to my breast, I wept at the knowledge of finally hearing the sea stone's song embrace my heart. Turning my face toward the sea, I felt the coolness on my face as the sea breeze dried the unexpected tears on my cheeks.

"Thank you, God," I whispered. "Thank you, for giving me the singing sea stone."

I quickly made my way up the sea path toward home, Mussolini leading the way.

In the stream from the kitchen faucet, I rinsed the salt and sand from my precious stone. It certainly wasn't what I had imagined it would look like. In my girlhood years, I'd pictured it as a beautiful smooth white stone filled with flecks of deep golden quartz that reflected the sunlight. Instead, the mottling of the stone was a mixture of different shades of gray. Turning it over in my hand, the light revealed the small pockmarks etched in its uneven surface. Fine lines resembling a spider's web wound their way among the blemishes. *Is this how fate now sees me?* I thought.

"Well, I guess it suits me as I am today," I voiced, aloud. "My girlish youth has indeed turned into cellulite and varicose veins. So what happens now, Pup?"

Mussolini replied by pounding his tail against the floor as he chewed on his bone. Becky was not going to believe this! Then again, she was another nonbeliever in the magic of the stones. She had, years ago, labeled the whole idea a childish fantasy. *Perhaps I'll just hold on to my secret for the moment*, I thought.

Now that I had my long-sought-after prize, I was unsure of what came next. Was my grandfather right when he predicted that the singing sea stone would bring me true love? Talk about your impossible odds. I knew of no one in Cutter's Cove that I'd want to fall in love with. In fact, I couldn't remember when I'd last went on a date. Questions began to bombard my mind. Did I really believe that a stone was capable of bringing true love to someone like me? Would I even recognize love, if it did manage to find me? What kind of man would turn my head? Someone tall, dark, and handsome? Well, that took most of the men my age off the table. Then a face came into my mind. Harrison Ford. Yes. He was not only very handsome, but intrigue hovered over him like starving gulls. In each of his movies, he was always the hero who wound up with the leading lady. *Yes, my dream man will look just like Harrison Ford*, I concluded. With my mind made up, I placed my precious stone on my bedroom windowsill with the others and went to get ready for work.

My job at Albert Bristol's antique bookshop on Main Street was my only escape from my father's thumbhold. For the past nineteen years, I was Albert's bookkeeper, shop attendant, and girl Friday. Albert, however, even at eighty, still handled the bulk of the buying and selling of his old and rare books now as dusty and outdated as he was. Bristol's Rare and Antique Books opened in 1954 and was a favorite retreat for the tourists during the summer months. In the winter, we now sold to the Internet auction houses in places like New York and London. For years, as I dusted and catalogued the old books, I'd see Albert hovered over his table, his thin wire-rimmed glasses perched precariously on the end of his nose as he examined the pages of one of his ancient tomes. His hair, now a thin white line encircling the back of his head, was as fine as a spider's web. Old fashioned to the core, he still arrived each morning wearing his brown three-piece suit and bowler hat, once popular in the fifties. Loved and respected by friends and customers, Albert was as much a part of Cutter's Cove as the beach. To me, however, he was a saint, and had literally saved my sanity.

I was forty-one when I spotted Albert's HELP WANTED sign in the front window of his bookshop. I immediately went in and applied for the job. To my relief, he hired me on the spot. He paid me a decent wage, which enabled me to contribute to the monthly budget of the cottage. This gave me eight blissful hours of freedom away from my father, thus restoring my sanity. From 8:00 a.m. until 4:00 p.m., Monday through Friday, I was free to be myself.

Over the years, I watched out for Albert's well-being, as he was without family. All I knew of his story was that he'd lost his young wife, Kathleen, in 1953, when she was barely twenty-one. To ease his loneliness, Albert opened the bookshop and tended it by himself for thirty-eight years until his age caught up with him and he found it necessary to hire help. I took over the everyday duties of running the shop, which left him free to concentrate on the business of buying and selling his rare books. A brisk business kept the shop going and made Albert a decent living. Although, I spent my days arranging and dusting the shelves of books, I rarely looked at their contents. Never having embraced the love of reading, my interest in the books lay only in cataloguing and arranging them on the shelves. I loved my job, and each day was a joy just to go to work.

"Good morning, Albert," I called as I stepped into shop, setting off the small bell above the front door.

"Very good, my dear," he said, as he sat hovering over his small table at the rear of the shop.

"Did something new arrive?" I asked him.

"My shipment of books from California came in just this morning," he replied. "I love this UPS invention. In the past, it would have taken weeks for my books to come by post. Now they can travel overnight. Amazing! Can you please unpack them for me?"

"I'll get to it right away," I said. "But first, I'm going to run down to the Crab Cake Deli and get us both a breakfast sandwich and a coffee."

"Perfect," he said, turning around to look at me. I nearly laughed aloud at the two huge brown eyes that looked at me through the magnifying glasses he wore. "However, at your age I think perhaps you'd better walk the distance. You wouldn't want to start tongues wagging, now would you?"

"You're right, as usual, Albert," I said, smiling at his little joke. "My word, what big eyes you have," I added as I left.

After a quick breakfast, I spent the remainder of the morning unpacking the books from California. By the time I placed the last book into its proper place on the shelf, it was eleven forty-five. The shop had remained quiet all morning so I'd finished in good time. Retrieving my purse from the bottom drawer of my desk, I was anxious to meet Becky at Della's. For us, birthdays were a reason to celebrate.

"Albert, I'm going to lunch," I called over my shoulder as I slipped on my jacket. Glancing toward his office, I was startled to see him standing in the doorway. "Do you need me to do something for you, Albert? I still have a few minutes before I meet Becky."

"No, no," he replied, a slight grin crossing his otherwise serene face. "This will only take a moment. Am I correct in assuming that today is your birthday?"

"Yes it is," I replied. "And we won't go into which one, thank you."

"Well, I guess a lady must have her secrets," he mused.

"Well, I'm not sure how much of a secret it is," I commented. "I believe the gray hair will reveal that I'm over the hill."

"Nonsense," he scoffed, holding out a small package wrapped in brown paper. "That phrase is overrated. You're still a fine-looking woman, Kathleen. Here, I have a small token for you."

"Thank you, Albert," I said, accepting his wrapped gift. "May I open it now?"

"Please do," he replied.

Lifting the paper free, I was delighted to see a small round music box, measuring about four inches across. Etched into its domed cream-colored lid, trails of embossed bright green ivy cascaded among the most delicate of pink roses. Its gilded edges caught the light, and I could tell that he'd recently polished it.

"Oh, Albert, how thoughtful of you!" I exclaimed, touched.

"It belonged to my late wife," he said. "I gave it to her the night before her illness took her from me. When my own Kathleen fell ill, I made her a vow that if death claimed her, I would take her back to Ireland to the bosom of her family. I never made the journey, as you know. Her ashes are still on my mantelpiece. Is the music box not a thing of beauty?"

"It is," I replied, examining it closer. I was speechless, as Albert had never given me an actual gift before. On past birthdays, he would always leave flowers on my desk.

"I have decided that it's time to part with a few of my Kathleen's belongings," he said. "Such beauty really should be shared, should it not? What good is a music box if no one enjoys its melody? For me, I am afraid the tune is like scratching open an old wound. Open it. I wound it for you."

"Yes, of course," I said.

The moment I lifted the small domed lid, the soft music drifted out. At first, I didn't recognize the tune. Giving Albert a quizzical look, I was shocked when he closed his eyes and began to softly sing to the music. His voice, slightly off key at first, quickly rose to a perfect baritone.

"I'll take you home, again, Kathleen,
"Across the ocean wild and wide.
"To where your heart has ever been.
"Since, first you were my bonnie bride.
"The roses all have left your cheek,
"I've watched them fade away and die.
"Your voice is sad when e'er you speak,
"And tears be-dim your loving eyes.
"Oh, I will take you back, Kathleen,
"To where your heart will feel no pain.
"And when the fields are fresh and green.
"I'll take you to your home, Kathleen."

As Albert sang, his furrowed brow told of the undying love he still carried within his heart for his beloved Kathleen. My own heart ached, as I witnessed the pain he still felt from losing her at such a young age. When he finished, I was awestruck.

"Albert, that was beautiful," I said, closing the lid to the music box. "I'm very touched by your gift."

"Well, I thought it was an appropriate gift, Miss Kathleen Jennings," he said with amusement. "My Kathleen was from a small village in Northern Ireland called Larne. Today, it's a tourist attraction. However, back when she was a young girl, it was a wee fishing village with stone cottages and fat sheep grazing on the moors. After I left the war in Korea in 1952, I found myself afraid to come home as I had such strong emotions from all the fighting. I had no family waiting on me here. A fellow comrade, David Myers, and I decided to do a bit of traveling, and we ended up in Ireland. The green lushness of the countryside was such a peaceful setting after the chaos of the war and we experienced a sort of healing of the mind. After some traveling, David and I found our way to Larne. It was there that I found my Kathleen. She was working in a small shop that sold fish and vegetables. She was so young and very beautiful. She had hair the color of a raven's wing and green eyes that would rival the new grass. She was barely eighteen the day I walked into her life, and for us both it was love at first sight. Three months later, I asked her to be my bride, and she acquiesced. We wed among the late-summer flowers blooming on the moors, and a week later, I sailed for home, bringing her with me."

"What a beautiful love story, Albert," I said, softly.

"Yes. Yes, it was," he said, sadly. "Oh, I should never have taken her from her family. But then again, how was I to know that she was destined to become an angel before the bloom had left her cheeks. Barely a year into our marriage, she suffered a ruptured appendix. She died, taking our unborn child with her. Oh, listen to me. How I go on. I'll not talk of death on your birthday. Enjoy the music box, Kathy, and take the rest of the day off. I'll see you in the morning." With a slight bow, Albert returned to his books.

I was the first to arrive at Della's. As usual, Becky was fashionably late. As I walked in the door, I glanced around at the patrons. Besides the usual crowd of locals, I saw a well-dressed older couple in a corner booth, sharing pie and coffee. *Tourists*, I thought. I caught myself watching them as they sat across from each other, smiling into each other's eyes as they ate. It was obvious that even in their eighties, they were still very much in love. The sight of two people sharing an intimate moment usually triggered within me a stab of jealousy. However, that was before I'd found my singing sea stone. I was sure that it was only a matter of time now before I, too, had someone to share in those intimate moments—hoping was still free for the taking.

Sliding into our usual booth near the back, I took out my mirror and attempted to repair the havoc that a morning of sweating over old books had wreaked on my hair and face. The black smear on the front of my white blouse, however, couldn't be camouflaged. It was the aftermath of an earlier attack by a first copy of *Ann of Green Gables* when it fell from a top shelf. Perhaps, I should send the heirs of Lucy Maud Montgomery the bill for having my blouse dry-cleaned, I mused.

When the bell over the door jingled, I looked up to see Becky heading my way. She looked refreshed despite the warmth of the morning. She hadn't changed much over the years. Tall and slim, she had great taste in clothes and was always well dressed. Her long strawberry-blond hair, pulled back into a tight chignon at the back of her neck, only served to accent the periwinkle pantsuit that hugged her slim figure. Perfect makeup and accessories should have made me green with envy, but I knew the great pains that she went through just to keep herself in top shape. An avid marathon runner, Becky was always willing to run for a good cause. At fifty-nine, she still looked like she did in her forties. Sliding into our booth, she greeted me with her usual friendly expression.

"What's up, girlfriend?" she asked. Oh, yes. Did I fail to mention her perfect white teeth?

"Same old, same old," I replied, handing her the music box. "Take a look at the gift Albert gave me for my birthday."

"Oh, Kat, it's beautiful," she gasped. As she lifted the lid, the soft tones of "I'll Take You Home

Again, Kathleen" filled the diner momentarily before she closed the lid. "This is a kingly gift. Doesn't he usually give you flowers?"

"That's been his practice in the past," I replied. "That's not everything. He actually sang to the tune as it played. Then he told me how he met his wife and how she died suddenly, taking their unborn child with her. I've never seen this side of Albert, Becky. In the nineteen years that I've worked for him, he's never once talked about his late wife in such detail."

"Well, I imagine it's still too painful for him to talk about," she said, handing me the music box. Pulling her glasses out of her purse, she slid them onto her nose. "I hate having to use these things. They make me look old and decrepit. However, I need them to read. Perhaps I'll have that new laser surgery done. Ditching the glasses will make me look twenty years younger, I'm sure. What do you think, Kat?"

"I think you're too old for such a dangerous procedure," I replied. "Besides, what good would it do to look twenty years younger? Everyone in town knows your true age. They'd think you are just being silly."

"Oh, perhaps you're right," she shrugged.

When the waitress approached our table, I was pleased to see that it was Patty, the owner's eighteen-year-old granddaughter. "What'll it be ladies?" she asked, her pad and pen at attention. "Today's special is the mushroom burger and fries."

"So your grandma has you working the diner again this summer," I commented.

Patty, I knew, was Della's pride and joy. Oh, to be young and beautiful again. Today, Patty's slim figure was poured into a pair of worn cut-off jeans and a faded red T-shirt advertising "Bali Skateboards". Her long straight blond hair fell down her back in a shimmering gold ponytail. She was tanned, long-legged, and had the full attention of the three teenage boys sitting in the booth behind us.

"I don't mind," replied Patty, smiling. "I'm leaving for college in the fall. This summer, I'm working here as well as modeling beachwear for a company out of Boston. Grandma is supplementing my tuition, so I'm helping her out by waiting tables."

"That's great, Patty," remarked Becky. "With your looks, you should get some great tips from the summer crowd."

"I hope so," she replied, trying her best to ignore the panting boys beside her. "What can I get for you?"

"I think I'll have the spinach salad and lemon water," replied Becky, closing her menu.

"Rabbit food," I remarked, shaking my head at her. "I'll have the mushroom burger and fries."

"I'll put your orders in right away," Patty stated, giving the boys a wink as she walked off. Moaning, they nearly melted into their seats.

"You really should eat better, Kat," remarked Becky. "Don't you want to live forever?"

"No," I replied, "Besides, I'm splurging. It's my birthday, remember?"

"Is that today?" she asked, eyes widening. "I thought it was next week."

"You know darn well it's today," I replied. "Now what did you get me? And it better be good."

Reaching into her purse, she pulled out a long white envelope with my name scrawled across the front in her sweeping handwriting.

"What's this?" I asked, eyeing it with suspicion. "It's either the deed to a new speed boat or an envelope full of money. Which is it?"

"Neither," she said, rolling her eyes. "It's a gift certificate to that wild new spa that just opened in Portland. Oh, Kat, I've been there. I'm telling you, it'll make a new woman out of you."

"Thanks, Becky," I said, looking at her over my glasses. "But I like this old woman well enough."

"Well, I'm your best friend, Kat, so this is best said coming from me," she said, looking serious. "Your 'old woman' is in bad need of a makeover. I hate to point out the obvious, but the only thing that has changed about your hairstyle since we were in high school is the color. Why not have it tinted and cut into one of those rad, new hairstyles we see on the magazine models?"

"I like my hair the way it is, thank you," I said, tearing open the end of the envelope and sliding out the gift certificate. "And please stop using words like *rad*. It scares me." She was right, of course. I'd worn my straight shoulder-length hair parted down the middle and swept behind my ears since I was fifteen. Perhaps I could do with a new hairstyle. But then again, this one has suited me for nearly fifty years. Why fix what isn't broken?

"We'll visit the spa on Saturday," Becky stated. "You'll thank me for the new and improved woman you'll see in your mirror."

"Or I'll never speak to you again for interfering," I chided.

"Whatever," Becky said, with a slight wave of her hand. "Have the mushroom burger, Kat. I'll give you a copy of my diet plan."

"No, thanks," I said. "I already have one." Why was she talking of dieting, anyway? She still had a great figure, and I certainly was not overweight. Well, perhaps I was a little. The last time I'd seen Dr. Ferguson, the local G.P., was just before my father died. At that time, he told me that I needed to lose a few pounds for my health. Of course, I would never tell Becky that. She would have me joining a fat farm and jogging to work.

"You seem a little down for someone who is having a birthday," remarked Becky. "What's up?"

"Oh, I wish my mother were here to enjoy the day with me," I replied. "Even after all these years, that still remains my only wish."

"I know how you feel," said Becky, softly. "I, too, miss my mother. Being raised by an overbearing grandfather ruined my childhood."

"We both missed out on our mother's love," I said. "Left with only my father to raise me, I might as well have been an orphan. The flowers were still fresh on my mother's grave when he made it painfully clear that he preferred his paints and easel to being with me. I shudder to think what would have become of me if Grandpa Jake hadn't moved in with us and took over the job of raising me. It was his love and attention that got me through the terrible years when my father scorned my affection with hurtful words."

"I remember your grandfather as a very kind and loving man," said Becky, sipping her water. "He possessed a quiet and gentle soul. That, I suppose, is why he loved the sea."

"Perhaps," I replied. "When I was little, he would take me for walks on the sand and hold me while I cried out my frustrations over my father's lack of affection for me. He also taught me to love the sea as much as he did. 'The sea is much like a gentle woman and will listen to your heart aches,' he'd say. 'However, she can turn into a ferocious tyrant when she's in the mood to argue.' He was as wise as he was kind, and I loved him beyond words. I miss my mother, but I mourn for my Grandpa Jake."

"How long has it been since he died?" asked Becky.

"I was barely fifteen," I replied. "I still want to weep when I think that he died all alone on the beach. Who wants to die alone, I ask?"

"Surely, not me," replied Becky, shaking her head. "I'm glad I was able to be with Michael when he passed after his heart attack. I just couldn't stand the thought of him dying without me there to hold him."

"I guess the hardest part of my Grandpa Jake's death was the fact that I didn't get the chance to say good-bye," I said. "I found him down by the old pier when I arrived home from school. He'd been dead for hours. After his funeral, I simply stepped into his shoes and took over the role of caring for my father."

"I remember," remarked Becky. "How did you cope all these years?"

"I had no choice, Becky," I replied. "He was my father. However, we were two unhappy souls living under the same roof. His death freed us both."

"I felt the same after my grandfather's death," said Becky. "Of course, the *Cutter Gazette* wasted no time informing the world that I was now an orphan. You wouldn't believe the phone calls I received from opportunists wanting to purchase the flower shop for mere pennies on the dollar. Outrageous!"

"Remember the morning after my father's death?" I asked. "I can still recall the bold headlines, 'Local Artist, Ellery Jennings, Dead at 87.' I, too, had those wanting to cash in on my father's death. The Bella House Gallery out at the mall contacted me in hopes of acquiring one or more of his paintings now that he was dead. Where was the Bella House when we needed to sell the paintings to survive? They were sorely disappointed to learn that there are no paintings. My father had to sell his seascapes to a gallery in New York, just to support us."

"What about the paintings of your mother?" asked Becky. "What became of them?"

"They disappeared soon after her death," I replied. "To assuage his grief, my father banished all that reminded him of her. He would have banished me, as well, if not for my grandfather."

"What a shame," said Becky. "What would drive a man to do such a thing?"

"Extreme grief, I guess," I replied. "I'd give anything to have just one photograph of my mother. I simply cannot remember her face. It's like missing a stranger."

"I, too, lack pictures of my mother," said Becky. "My grandfather thought taking pictures was a waste of money. I'd like to think I resemble her."

"I feel the same," I said as Patty approached, juggling a large tray holding our meals. "Our lunch has arrived. Listen, Becky, whether we resemble our mothers or not, let us visit your magic spa in Portland and allow the ladies to pamper our souls."

"Great idea, Kat," exclaimed Becky, lifting her water glass. "Here's to the two of us and our search for the fountain of youth!"

"Here, here," I said, tapping my glass to hers. "Do you think I should call ahead and warn them about the train wreck heading their way? I haven't had a facial in years."

"No way," said Becky, with a wicked smile. "Besides, I've heard they love a good challenge."

The next few days brought the first wave of early summer tourists, and the store windows dressed for the occasion. Even Albert's bookshop enjoyed a few more customers than usual. Although I was busier, my singing sea stone, and what it meant, was always in the back of my mind. Each time the bell above the door announced another customer, I'd glance up to see who walked in. One of these days, I was sure, Harrison Ford, or his double, was going to walk through that door and sweep me off my feet. I still hadn't told Becky about finding the sea stone. Loaded with practicality, she didn't believe in anything she couldn't see and touch.

Chapter 2

On Saturday, Becky and I drove the forty miles into Portland to visit the new spa. Seeing the beautiful and stylish women using the facilities made me feel frumpy and outdated. I'd have run for the parking lot if I could have managed to do so without being noticed. Becky, reading my thoughts, erred on the side of caution by placing herself between the door and me. I wasn't ready for any big changes in my appearance, and it took her and three spa beauticians to finally talk me into having my hair cut short and styled. Afterward, though, I was surprised with the results. Looking in the mirror, I decided that the new hairstyle made me look like Jamie Lee Curtis. Becky thought I looked "chic", and for once, I agreed with her.

"You look like a movie star, Kat," she said, nodding her head with approval.

"Jamie Lee Curtis, right?" I asked, turning my head in the mirror.

"No, not really," she said, with a straight face. "I was thinking more of Betty White."

"Okay, that's it!" I exclaimed. "For that remark, you're buying lunch."

Giggling, Becky decided that with just a few tweaks, I could look like Lucille Ball.

"No way!" I said, crossing my arms for emphasis. "You are not talking me into dying my hair red."

"Why not? Lucy was famous for her red locks," she remarked. "She managed to catch the eye of a hot-blooded Cuban, remember?"

"And she was still a redhead when she died at age seventy-seven," I stated. "How was that possible?"

"She wanted to make a beautiful corpse," remarked Becky. "An actress must always think of her last glamour shot."

Laughing ourselves to tears, we enjoyed the rest of the morning, which included a massage, a sea-mud mask, a manicure and a pedicure. After a short class on how to apply makeup, I indeed felt like a new woman. When finished, we strutted our way to the parking lot, giggling like a couple of high school girls skipping class. We then dined at a fancy French restaurant before heading home. It was the most fun I'd had in years.

On Monday, I carefully applied my newly purchased makeup to my eyes and lips. After dressing in my usual dark slacks and cotton blouse, I drove my ten-year-old red Cavalier to work through a light rain. I couldn't believe I'd let Becky talk me into wearing makeup! It was nothing short of false advertising, if you asked me. But as Becky so boldly pointed out, if you want to sell a house, a bit of sprucing up doesn't hurt. And after finding my sea stone, I needed to be prepared for anything.

The day, however, passed uneventful, and I spent the evening enjoying a glass of iced tea and the last rays of the sun on the front steps of the cottage. The rain over, the evening was warm with a clear sky. Mussolini sat begging me for a walk on the beach, so I finished my tea, grabbed a handful of breadcrumbs for the seagulls, and headed for the sea path. I was lonely, yes, but never alone. This evening, I felt the spirit of my Grandpa Jake beside me as I walked along the surf. Was I really willing to give up my solitude by allowing another person into my life? Why not? The thought of falling in love intrigued me. Of course, I gave up any hope of having a family of my own years ago. However, a bit of male companionship would be nice. I also knew that it was the thought of the unknown that now led me to doubt. At my age, however, I was even willing to trust in a magic stone if it could bring me happiness. God, alone, knew how precious little of that I'd had growing up.

The following day, at noon, I met Becky for our regular Tuesday lunch date at Della's. When I arrived, she was already seated and looking over her menu. Sliding into the booth opposite of her, I gave her a weak smile. I was hungry, and my clothes were sticking to me. Looking at her, I just shook my head in wonder. She looked like she had just stepped out of a magazine. She was wearing her hair down this morning, and it fell like a shimmering blond wave down past her shoulders. The deep pink of her silk blouse accented the pale pink rouge on her cheeks, and her eye lids were tinted the perfect shade of blue. It was obvious that her day at the spa was much more productive than mine. An attractive silver chain attached to her eyeglasses held them perched on her nose as she looked over the menu. I glanced down at my gray cotton blouse and dark slacks and winced. I looked like a storm cloud about to dump its load of rain. I shuddered to think what my makeup looked like after a morning of unpacking dusty old books.

"What's up, girlfriend?" she asked, smiling at me as she handed me a menu.

"Same old, same old," I replied. "Look, today's special is creamed chicken over biscuits. Care to join me in a plate of cholesterol and carbs?"

"Not on your life, Kat," she replied. "I'm running in the Founder's Day 5K marathon. Did you forget?"

"Founder's Day isn't until July the twenty-third," I pointed out. "You can splurge a little, can't you?"

"Not if I'm in training," she replied. "A pound of fat equals a pound of flesh, and my body is a machine that runs on lean fuel. I have goals."

"Becky, you're fifty-nine," I reminded her. "I thought you were going to start taking it easy. Remember what Doc Ferguson told you? He said that your heart is in good shape but your legs are trashed."

"You don't have to remind me of how painful shin splints are," she said, wincing. "However, this marathon is for a good cause. It's to benefit juvenile diabetes."

"They're all good causes," I said. "If you were fifty, I'd think nothing of it. However, you, my friend, will turn sixty in August. I'd say it's time to think about donating money if you want to support your causes. I'm going for the cholesterol and carbs."

"Oh, Kat, you're going to wreck all our hard work," she said, shaking her head. "Besides, creamed chicken and biscuits is not on our diet plan.

"What diet plan?" I asked, eyeing her over my menu. "Listen, Becky, I've already allowed you to talk me into getting my hair cut ridiculously short. Now you want me to lose weight as well. You'll have me needing therapy if you keep this up. I gave poor Albert the scare of his life when I walked into the shop yesterday morning. He thought I was a burglar letting myself in. At eighty, he can't take such a fright."

"Oh pooh!" she scoffed. "Albert could use a good shaking up once in a while. It keeps his heart young. You know, you should have allowed them to dye your hair red. Gray makes you appear ghostly."

"I am a ghost," I said, sighing. "I passed on years ago. I'm here only because no one has yet informed my body that I'm dead."

"Very funny," said Becky, glancing around the diner. "Now where is Patty? I have to be back at the shop soon. I've hired Mr. Preston to make my flower deliveries to the hotels out on the beach. It's only on Tuesdays and Thursdays, so it's nothing too strenuous. However, I have to be there to let him in as he refuses to take a key."

"The same old Mr. Preston who raises and lowers the flag every day in front of the courthouse?" I asked. "He must be eighty. I would think that he'd be too old to work a job."

"He's actually eighty-one," said Becky. "And he came to me asking if I had anything to keep him busy. His wife is gone, and there's no one else in his life. So as long as he's working for me, he's out and about two days a week doing something he loves."

"True," I said, thinking of my own situation. I, too, was all alone. When I'm eighty-one, will I still be trudging to some part-time job somewhere simply because I've nothing else to do?

"You need to get out more, Kat," said Becky.

"Oh, I'm just feeling old today, I guess," I said, sighing heavily. "Perhaps, you're right. I have been a bit unsociable as of late."

"As of late?" asked Becky. "Kat, you haven't been anywhere but Albert's bookshop in years. When was the last time you attended any of the town's social functions? For years, I've been asking you to help with the children's Halloween party and Christmas pageant and you've declined. And you haven't been to the annual Founder's Day picnic since we were at Cutter High."

"I've been taking care of my father, Becky," I said, attempting to defend my antisocial behavior. "That left me little time for carving pumpkins or singing Christmas carols."

"Well, your father is gone," said Becky softly, placing her hand over mine. "The time has come for

48

you start thinking of yourself. After all, you're sixty. If you don't start living soon, it'll be too late. There is life beyond Sea Breeze Cottage."

"I know what you're saying," I told her, recalling the bygone memories of my now deceased biological clock. "It's just that you're about forty-five years too late if you're thinking of throwing me a debutant ball."

"It's never too late for a woman to have a coming-out party," said Becky, grinning.

"Becky, please don't do anything I'm going to regret later," I warned her.

Memorial Day brought the summer renters out in droves. Vacationers flocked to the public beaches, and soon the sand resembled a field of wildflowers as a hundred multicolored umbrellas burst into bloom. Carl Wyndom, a tall, well-built man, a year ahead of me in school, opened the doors on his ice cream shop, a true sign that summer had officially opened for business. A sign announcing his fifteenth year of serving the summer crowd, offered a Memorial Day special on the wares of his trade. His arrival back in town meant I now had the daily luxury of walking across the street for a sweet treat before heading home after work. I prided myself on being a true ice cream aficionado.

With the days getting warmer, the bookshop's ancient air conditioner struggled to keep up. My early morning walks on the beach, however, did much to prepare me for the heat of the day. It was already in the seventies as I let myself into the bookshop the morning following Memorial Day. After my usual breakfast sandwich from the Crab Cake Deli, I glanced over at the morning's UPS delivery. Stacked beside the front door, four medium-sized boxes from a book auction house in New York awaited my attention. I knew the routine well. Each box needed to be unpacked, and the books catalogued and placed on a shelf.

"Even a journey of a thousand miles begins with the first step," I said, picking up a box and retreating to the back room.

Soon the sweat was running down my back and my hair lay damp against my forehead. When the bell chimed above the front door, I stood, straightened my crumpled yellow blouse, and stepped out into the shop. A man of medium build, wearing a starched white dress shirt and brown trousers, stood looking around the shop. He looked to be around my age, as his short, dark, slightly wavy hair held highlights of silver. His salt-and-pepper beard and mustache, I noted, were neatly trimmed. *This is a hand-*

some man, I thought. However, he was no Harrison Ford. Despite my disappointment, I stepped forward and pasted on a smile.

"Hello," I said, forcing my voice to sound light. "May I help you?"

"Yes," he replied, his face breaking into a smile. He had great teeth. "I'm looking for a book." His voice was strong and manly, and I detected his slight accent.

"Well, you've come to the right place," I told him, now giving him by business voice. "Albert Bristol, the owner of the shop, has books on every subject. However, they're old. So if you're looking for a current author, there's a bookstore located inside the Sand Dollar Mall at the edge of town. The store's called the Book Emporium, and they carry all the best sellers."

"Oh, the book I'm looking for isn't a new one," he said, glancing over at the nearest shelf. "I'm looking for one dealing with the art of engineering in ancient Egypt. Do you have such a book?"

"I'm not sure," I said. Did we have such a book? I, alone, had catalogued every book in the shop, but I couldn't recall seeing one on engineering in ancient Egypt. Not wanting to show my ignorance as to the inventory of the shop, I again gave him my business voice. "Do you know the author? Perhaps if you could give me his name, I could look him up."

"Well, I'm afraid you have me there," he said, looking slightly embarrassed. "I read the book back in my college days, and all I can recall is the book's title, *The Art of Engineering in Ancient Egypt*."

"Well, that's a start," I said, squirming as I felt the sweat trickle down my back. "You can access the Internet to find the author's name. Do you have a home computer?"

"I'm afraid I don't," he said. "Darn complicated contraptions."

"Okay. Well, you can also access the Internet on your smart phone," I suggested.

"Smart phone?" he asked, now appearing slightly puzzled.

Oh brother, I have a real green one here, I thought. "You mean you don't have a cell phone, either?" I asked.

"A cell phone?"

"Yes," I said. "A mobile telephone that you can use to place calls when away from home."

"Oh, yes," he said. "No. I'm afraid I don't have one of those, either. I thought of purchasing a mobile telephone a few years ago. However, it looked too complicated to operate. Besides, I have no one I wish to call."

I thought of telling him that I didn't have one for much the same reason. "Let me guess," I said, beginning to like this man. "You don't own a DVD player, either."

"A DV what?"

"I thought so," I said, genuinely smiling now. "I'll tell you what. I'll research the book on the shop's computer and let you know what I find."

"That would be most helpful…Miss?"

"Jennings," I offered. "Kathleen Jennings."

"How nice," he said, giving me a full smile. Yes, he was a very handsome man, indeed. "Is it miss or missus?"

"It's Ms.," I replied, with just a tad too much emphasis. *Now where did that come from,* I asked myself. I never referred to myself as Ms.

"Oh, well, I see," he said, his smile now fading a few shades.

Just then, the bell above the door jingled and Becky walked in. "What's up, girlfriend?" she asked, looking fresh as a daisy. How did she do it? "I finished up early so I thought I'd come over and collect you."

"For what?" I asked, trying to sort through my jumbled thoughts. Did my confusion have anything to do with the handsome man in front of me?

"It's Tuesday, remember?" she said. "Della's. Lunch."

"Oh yes," I said, finding my brain. "I'll only be a moment."

"Well, who's this nice-looking gentleman?" she asked, turning her attention to my customer. "I'm Becky Porter. I own the Posey Pot flower shop over on Juniper Street."

"What a wonderful occupation," he said, offering her his hand. "My name is Marcus Stone."

"Well, Mr. Stone, please don't tell me you're into stuffy old books," she said. "There are too many talented new authors out there for you to be in here digging up old bones."

"Hello," I said, raising my eyebrow in her direction. "He came in here to buy an old book. I sell old books for a living."

"Sorry, Kat," she said, looking apologetic. "I hope I didn't just ruin a sale for you."

"Forget it," I said. "We first have to research the book. I have to—"

"Dig up old bones?" she asked, finishing my sentence.

"Access the Internet," I said. "Tell me, Mr. Stone, does your wife have a smart phone? Perhaps she can—"

"Oh, I'm afraid I don't have a wife, either," he said. "I never married. And I believe the odds of my finding a wife are about the same as finding a book on the art of engineering in ancient Egypt. Especially, since I've no access to broadband."

"I like him, Kat," declared Becky, hooking her arm into his. "Sophisticated yet witty. That's a rare breed in these parts."

"So you sell flowers?" asked Marcus, turning his attention to Becky. "Now there's something that will never go out of style."

"True, but they do go out of season," she offered, releasing his arm. "Are you new in town, Mr. Stone?"

"I am," he replied. "And please call me Marcus. I recently bought the old Clausen place over on Sandpiper Road. A bit of a fixer-upper, but it has great character."

"I know the place well," said Becky. "I provided the flowers for old man Clausen's wake. He died about a year ago."

"How sad," said Marcus.

"Nonsense," said Becky. "He was nearly one hundred years old. The poor old dear had outlived three wives, both of his children, and was the last surviving member of the Cutter High School class of 1930. Only a handful of folks attended his viewing.

And I suspect most of them were only there to look over the property."

"Well then, I guess it was a good time for him to turn up his toes," Marcus mused. "Anyway, I was just asking Ms. Jennings here—"

"Ms. Jennings?" asked Becky, now raising an eyebrow in my direction. I shook my head slightly, imploring her with my eyes, not to make a scene.

"Yes," said Marcus, not missing the exchange. "I'm searching for an old book, and Ms. Jennings has been gracious enough to do a bit of research for me on her electronics."

"It might take a day or so," I told him. "But if I do find out anything, Mr. Stone, how do I contact you? Do you have a landline?"

"A landline?" he asked.

"It's a telephone in your home," I explained.

"Alas, a home telephone is not one of my options, either," he replied, with a slight shrug of his shoulders. "You can, however, reach me through young Douglas down at the Food King. He delivers my groceries to me. You can leave word with him, and I'll return to town at my earliest convenience."

"In what?" I asked, glancing out the front window. "Don't tell me that you actually own a car?"

"As a matter of fact, I do," he said, finding my question most amusing. "You don't expect me to walk the three miles into town at my age do you?"

"You'll have to excuse Ms. Jennings," said Becky, with emphasis on the word Ms. "She's thinking like a sixty-year-old these days."

"Becky!" I exclaimed. "Don't give away all of my secrets."

"What secrets, my dear," she said. "You're an open book. At least you're in better shape than those old tomes you lug around."

"As a matter of fact, I have recently passed that milestone myself," said Marcus. "Sixty is the new fifty, I'm told. And being in the presence of such charming ladies, I am feeling younger. Well, my dears, I'm keeping you from your lunch date. Parting is such sweet sorrow. Till we meet again?"

Giving us a slight bow, he left the shop. The atmosphere seemed to dim a little after he was gone. I felt an excitement race through me, something I'd never felt before. My hands were shaking as I lifted my purse from the drawer of my desk. *I'm just in need of food*, I decided, hoping that Becky wouldn't notice. As I locked the shop door, I couldn't get the handsome stranger off my mind. However, I wasn't about to let Becky know how badly he'd rattled my senses.

"I'm starved!" I announced, as I slid into the booth across from Becky. Della's was always busy now that the tourist season was in full swing.

"You're always starved," remarked Becky. "I, on the other hand, try to control my animal instincts."

"Which means what?" I asked, picking up the menu.

"Self-control, girlfriend," she replied. "Something you lack. You eat like a truck driver."

"I do not," I said, rolling my eyes. "I simply have a healthy appetite. Look, today's special is chipped beef over toast."

"I'm having the strawberry and walnut salad with a light Italian dressing," she said, scanning the menu. "I'm running, you know. I have to eat light. I've read that strawberries give your eyes a certain sparkle. Something you'll need if you're hoping to turn that man's head."

"What man?" I asked.

"Marcus Stone, of course," she replied, looking serious. "Kat, please tell me you're not going to discourage that delightful man's attention. I know when a man is interested in getting to know a woman. He smiles a lot and finds some subtle little way of informing you that he's single. And Marcus has done just that. I'm telling you, he's got his eye on you."

"What makes you think I'm putting him off?" I asked her.

"You told him your name was Ms. Jennings," exclaimed Becky. "You do know what the Ms. means, don't you?"

"Not really," I replied.

"According to *Vogue*, it means that you're not interested in finding a mister," replied Becky. "Using the title tells a man that you don't want a relationship."

"I'm not sure where the Ms. came from," I admitted, hoping she would drop the subject. "He's a customer, Becky, not a suitor. End of story. So let's order, I'm starved."

After Patty took our orders, we sat sipping our lemon water in silence for a few moments. However, I could tell by the way that Becky was fidgeting that she had something else to say. Somehow, I was sure she had not yet exhausted the subject of the handsome stranger.

"You know, Kat, Marcus Stone is the most sophisticated man to come into these parts in ages," she began. "How could you not be interested in him?"

"Simple. He's not my destiny," I said, without thinking. "I'm supposed to marry a man who looks like Harrison Ford." I knew the moment the words left my mouth that I was going to get the third degree.

"What does Harrison Ford have to do with whom you marry?" asked Becky, "Confession time, Kat. What's going on in that head of yours?"

"I don't know what you're talking about," I told her, pouring a sugar packet into my lemon water. What was I doing? I was drinking water, not tea. I'd said too much and I was about to pay the price.

"You said that your destiny was to marry a man who looks like Harrison Ford," she reminded me. "And this is according to what source? You can't keep any secrets from me, Kat. I'm your doppelganger, remember? Wait, this doesn't have to do with your silly sea stones, does it? Look, you'd better spill your guts or I'm going to send Marcus a big bouquet of flowers with your name on it."

"You wouldn't!"

"I would," she said, leaning back in her seat and giving me a wicked grin. "And I'll even make you pay for them."

"I don't want to tell you anything," I said. "You'll just make fun of me."

"Oh, Kat, I wouldn't," she said, softening. "It's just that you've wasted your whole life waiting on some singing sea stone to tell you that it's okay to fall in love. It's not real, Kat. It's just a silly idea that your grandfather put into your head when you were eleven. Think of all the eligible men you've ignored over the years because they weren't heralded by a silly rock screaming out 'Name That Tune'!"

"I don't recall sidestepping any eligible men," I said, fiddling with my silverware. "And the singing sea stone is not some silly idea of my grandfather's. He believed in it, and so do I. Besides, the reason I've never fallen in love before was that I wasn't ready."

"Well, I hate to point out the obvious, girl-friend," she said, crossing her arms over her chest for emphasis.

"Which is?" I asked, not really wanting to hear her answer.

"That if you don't deem yourself ready soon, you'll be falling in love with a male orderly in some nursing home as he adjusts your oxygen tube. Besides, Harrison Ford is already married. So if your sea stone is suggesting him, you'd better have it reprogrammed."

As Patty delivered our food, the distraction offered me a moment to think. How much should I tell Becky about finding my sea stone? Now that I'd let the cat out of the bag, I was going to have to explain myself. How was I going to make her understand that the magic of my sea stones was real? Becky, however, was not one to believe in such things. She was practical to the core. When Patty walked away, I did a bit of damage control.

"I didn't say the man had to be Harrison Ford," I said, folding my napkin into my lap. "I merely suggested that he resemble him."

"You're living a fantasy, Kat," said Becky, shaking her head. "This is the real world. You're missing out on so much of life because you're out walking the beach searching for magic rocks. The magic isn't real, Kat!"

"Well, for your information, I have found my singing sea stone," I announced. "And the magic is real, Becky. I've felt it touch my heart."

It took a moment for my words to register with her. When they did, she lowered her fork. "What? When?" she stammered.

"I found it on my birthday," I said, now giving her a look of triumph. "And the moment I picked it up, it sang to me, Becky."

"And you kept this from me?" she asked, looking hurt. "I'm crushed. I'm your best friend. Why didn't you tell me?"

"Because I knew you wouldn't believe me," I replied. "You've never believed in the magic of the sea stones."

"Kat, honey, I'd believe there's a hotdog stand on Mars if it would bring you the kind of happiness that I shared with my Michael."

"Was it magic that brought you and Michael together?" I asked.

"Not really," she said, filling her fork with lettuce. "It was more like my grandmother's cannolis."

"I suppose you think it's too late for me now," I said.

"Not at all," she replied. "However, there's nothing like being young and in love. The magic, to me, is two hearts sharing the same dream of mortgages and parenting. But, in your case, if you don't hurry, it'll be more like pensions and pacemakers."

"I believe it is too late for me, Becky," I said, sighing. "I'm not twenty."

"Love is ageless," she stated. "Seriously, Kat, where did you find your singing sea stone? I promise I won't make any more jokes."

"I found it just below the rocks where my father painted his seascapes," I replied. "It literally begged me to pick it up. And, when I did, it—"

"Let me guess," Becky mused. "You heard Elvis Presley singing 'It's Now or Never.'"

"No jokes!" I reminded her. I didn't mind, though. I'd confessed to her, and she was still speaking to me.

"Sorry," she said, stifling a giggle. "It was too good to resist. Now what happens?"

"I'm not sure," I replied. "I guess I wait."

"Wait for what, Kat?" she asked, throwing up her arms. "You've been waiting for forty years. Wait a minute. You aren't destined to fall in love with the first man you see, are you?"

"Gosh, I hope not!" I exclaimed. "If that were so, I'd be walking down the aisle with Bob Wiles down at the Lug Nut Garage. And we both know that he hasn't changed the oil under his fingernails in thirty years."

Upon returning to the shop, I spent a good two hours searching the Internet for Marcus Stone's book on the art of engineering in ancient Egypt. I put the title into every search engine I knew, and still I came up empty. Exhausted, I made a few notes and gladly put the matter into Albert's capable hands. He knew his books like a fashionable woman knew her shoes. If the book existed, Albert would locate it.

At four o'clock, I left for home, via the ice cream shop, of course. As I entered, Carl Wyndom waved at me.

"Hi, Kathy," he said, from behind the counter. "Today's special is tutti-frutti sherbet. Two scoops for $2.95."

"That sounds wonderful, Carl," I said, digging three ones out of my wallet. "Have you been busy today?"

"No more than usual," he replied, scooping my sherbet into a cup. "However, it'll get busier as the days grow hotter. By the way, I've been asked to chair the events for the Founder's Day picnic this year. Mac Freeman finally called it quits at age eighty-nine. You wouldn't want to help me out with a few good ideas, would you?"

"I'm afraid I'm fresh out of ideas, Carl," I said. "Actually, I haven't attended the picnic in years. I've been caring for my father."

"Oh, yes," he said, handing me my sherbet. "I was so sorry to hear about your dad. I missed his funeral, as I live inland during the winter months. He was a bit of a recluse in his last years, was he not?"

"He was," I replied, handing him my money. "I kept his funeral very low key. Dawson's Funeral Home arranged a small service in the sitting room at Sea Breeze Cottage. Of course, only a handful of mourners attended, more so out of curiosity, I'm sure."

Just then, a family of five came in and immediately lined up in front of the counter. Everyone spoke at once as they scanned the ice cream flavors. I took it as a sign to move on.

"Well, Carl, I'll leave you to your customers," I said, heading for the door.

"It was nice seeing you again, Kathy," he said, before turning his attention to the brood pressing their faces against the glass of his ice cream cooler.

After a light dinner, Mussolini and I headed for the beach. As I sat on the rocks below the cottage, my thoughts drifted to Marcus Stone and his book. *Albert simply must find it*, I thought. Without the book, there would be no reason for me to contact Marcus again. Did I want to? Yes. Yes, I did. I wondered if sending him a progress report on my search would be too forward of me? And if Becky was wrong in assuming that he was interested in me, I'd be making a fool of myself. He did say that he was unmarried. Perhaps at his age he wasn't looking for a relationship. Was I expecting too much from this latest sea stone? No. This stone was very different from the ones I'd found in the past. With the others, nothing had changed in my life. Now suddenly there was a hope that wasn't there before.

Chapter 3

As the days passed, I couldn't seem to get my chance meeting with the handsome stranger out of my thoughts. Each day, I found myself watching the door, hoping he'd drop in to inquire about his book. The following Tuesday, I met Becky for lunch as usual. The beautiful day invited us to leave our cars at our respective businesses and make our way to the diner on foot. As we slid into the booth, I noticed that the walk had winded her. She looked exhausted, and there were dark circles under her eyes. Her fair complexion looked slightly yellowed and I grew concerned.

"What's wrong, Becky?" I asked, reaching for her hand. It felt cold for such a warm day.

"Nothing's wrong," she said. "I'm just a little tired from the walk. I've been fighting a bug for the past week, and I think it's winning."

"Well, promise me you'll go see Dr. Ferguson," I said. "Now order something healthy."

"I'm not really hungry today," she said, laying her menu on the table. "Perhaps, I'll just have a diet soda."

"You should eat something, Becky," I said. "You're simply getting too thin for your bone structure. And a little sun wouldn't hurt you, either. Look at you, you're as pale as butter."

"Oh, quit worrying, Mother," she said, with a wave of her hand. "I haven't shaken off the effects of winter yet. I'll get some sun and be tanned in no time."

This, I thought, was not like Becky. She never skipped meals. She was all about healthy eating and staying in shape for her running. I thought about ordering the meatloaf, but not wanting to eat in front of her, I too settled for a diet soda. When my attempts to pull her into a conversation failed, I suggested we take a walk in the morning air.

"I have to kick this fatigue soon," she said, as we walked. "I've been running these past couple of weeks, getting ready for my 5K run. It's only a little over six weeks until Founder's Day. That doesn't give me much time to improve my game."

"Becky, perhaps you should let the younger crowd run this year," I suggested. "You don't look well."

"No way!" she exclaimed, trying to muster up strength she didn't have. "I can do this. I'm just a little out of shape from being lazy over the winter months. Don't fret. I'll soon be running rings around that younger crowd. You wait and see."

When we reached Becky's flower shop, she hesitated.

"If I didn't have flowers to prep, I'd almost think about going upstairs to my apartment for a nap," she said, rubbing her lower back. "I've got a terrific backache. Perhaps I am pushing myself too hard. I'm running five times a week, and my time isn't getting any faster. Oh well, those flowers will not arrange themselves. See you later, Kat." After a quick hug, she slipped her key into the door.

"Call the doctor!" I reminded her as she disappeared inside.

As I made my way to the bookshop, my mind was reeling. What was going on with Becky? She was actually thinking of taking a nap in the middle of the day. She never talked this way. She was always the wind beneath my wings. She was probably coming down with the flu. Yes, that had to be it. I was so preoccupied with my thoughts that I failed to notice Marcus Stone waiting on the wooden bench in front of the shop.

"Ahh, here is our Ms. Jennings," he said, rising to his feet. "I just dropped by to check on your progress in locating my book."

"Hello, Mr. Stone," I said, hoping that he didn't pick up on the excitement in my voice. *He's only a customer*, I reminded myself, pulling the keys from my purse. "Please, come in."

As I opened the door, he stepped past me into the shop, and I felt a surge of excitement go through me at his closeness. His aftershave gave off a musky scent, putting me in mind of a deep forest.

"How have you been, Ms. Jennings?" he asked, giving me his best smile. "How goes the book search? When young Douglas failed to bring me word of your success, I thought perhaps I'd better drop by and inquire myself."

"Albert is still searching the Net," I offered, glad that I'd taken such pains with my appearance that morning. The day was cooler, and for once, the air conditioner was keeping up. "Please, Mr. Stone, feel free to look around. Perhaps you'll find another book that will tide you over until we find the one you're searching for."

"Please, call me Marcus," he said. "Mr. Stone sounds so formal, does it not?"

"Then you must call me Kathy," I said, warming to his quiet presence. "You can drop the Ms. as well."

"I will," he said, stepping over to the nearest bookshelf. "You know, I've always had a passion for reading. Adventures are hard won on their own."

"True," I said, watching him. "But I'd rather ride in a hot-air balloon than read about it."

"Oh, I agree," said Marcus. "However, my adventures go much higher and deeper than hot air balloons. I want to walk on the moon and spelunk Krubera Cave, the deepest cave in the world. And ever since I was a young man, I've wondered what it was like to stand on the pinnacle of Mt. Everest and look out upon the frozen world below. Books allow me to do just that but spare me the dizzying heights, oxygen deprivation, or utter darkness. In what do your interests lie, Kathy?"

I thought for a moment then shrugged. "I've never been any farther from home than Portland," I replied. "And I'm afraid of heights, as well as being slightly claustrophobic. Just thinking about caves and mountains makes me nauseous." Good heavens! My statement sounded so lame! Was I really so boring? I had never before put it into words.

"Well, how about a good love story?" asked Marcus, pulling a book from the shelf in front of him. "No truer tragedy was ever penned than that of *Romeo and Juliet*. Shakespeare was a true master. Have you read any of his works?"

"No," I said, now feeling embarrassed. "I'm afraid my interest in books lies only in their care. I'm embarrassed to say that I've never actually read any of them. I've been so busy caring for my father these past years that I never gave reading much thought."

"Oh, you still have your father?" he asked, surprised. "How remarkable."

"Well, actually, he died this past winter," I said.

"Ahh, then you are now left with an abundance of that precious commodity known as free time," he said, handing me the book. "May I suggest you fill it with a classic? Try *Romeo and Juliet*. I guarantee it will stir your heart."

Accepting the book, I smiled up at him. When our eyes met, I felt a shock wave course through my body that traveled from my head to my toes at hyperspeed. As I looked into his deep brown eyes, I felt as though I were about to topple over into their depths. My body suddenly felt hot and cold at the same time, and my hands began to shake. Gripping the book to my chest, I stepped back and looked away, breaking eye contact.

"I...ahhh...thank you," I stammered, not daring to look at his face. "I'll read it tonight and let you know what I think of it tomorrow."

"Please, Kathy, take your time reading this story," said Marcus, with a serious look. "Shakespeare should be sipped, not gulped. It's the only way to enjoy its full-bodied flavor."

"Okay," I said, unsure of what to do next. If he felt the electric between us, he gave no sign. Braving a glance at his face, I raised my eyes. He stood looking at me with a slight grin on his face as if he alone knew a great secret, he wished to share with only me. When the bell above the door sounded, we both jumped, breaking the spell. A short, heavyset woman, stepped in and glanced around the bookshop. I thought she was alone, until I noticed the small boy, hiding behind her.

"Well, Miss Kathy, you have a customer so I shall be on my way," said Marcus, with a slight nod of his head. "I'll be in touch with you very soon."

As he walked toward the door, I almost cried out for him to stop. A feeling of sadness swept over me, for I felt he was taking the magic with him. I wanted to savor the way he made me feel for just a moment longer.

I was surprised, however, when he reached the door, stopped, and turned around to face me. Watching my face, he stood still as though in deep thought, before retracing his steps. As he stood before me, his closeness rattled me and my palms grew moist. My breathing paused with the sheer anticipation of what was to happen next.

"Miss Jennings," he said, lowering his voice. "If I may be so bold? Will you do me the honor of having dinner with me this evening? There is an excellent restaurant out at the mall that is known for its wonderful Italian cuisine."

I nearly dropped the book in my hands. "I… yes," I stammered, trying to form my words. My thoughts were bouncing around inside my head like the silver ball in a pinball machine. Willing my emotions to slow down, I took a deep breath. "Yes, Marcus. I'd love to have dinner with you." Phew! That wasn't so bad!

"Excellent," he said. "I'll pick you up at eight."

"Don't you want to know where I live?" I asked him.

"Sea Breeze Cottage," he replied. "Out on Pebble Bay. On the beach. Correct?"

"Correct," I replied, impressed.

"Until this evening, then?" he asked. Taking my hand into his own, he gave it a quick squeeze and released it. A moment later, he was gone. Regaining my senses, I remembered my customer.

"May I help you?" I inquired, giving the woman a huge smile. With no need to pull out my business smile, she got the whole enchilada of my happiness in one viewing. The knowledge that I had an actual date left me feeling on top of the world! I was so happy, I was ready to sell this woman anything she desired. However, when I informed Mrs. Customer that my most current book was written in 1956 and cost forty-nine dollars, she looked at me as though I'd just told her that I was thinking of burning the shop to the ground with her in it. With a look of disgust, she grabbed her child by the hand and fled the store.

A moment later, I heard Albert entering the shop through the back door, and I went to meet him.

"How was your lunch, Albert?" I asked him, my excitement barely concealed.

"I had bagels and lox at the Crab Cake Deli," he said. "A lox is a fish, you know. Was that Marcus Stone I saw leaving the shop?"

"It was," I said, my smile beaming.

"Well, from the jubilant look on your face, Kathleen, may I assume he just purchased his weight in books."

"Albert, Marcus has asked me out on a date for this evening," I said, keeping my excitement in check.

"Ahh, and you are in need of a chaperone. Is that it?" The look on my face must have tickled his funny bone, for he chuckled.

"Actually, I need to go out to the mall and buy a dress," I said, realizing that he was pulling my leg.

"Oh yes. A new dress indeed," he said, looking at me over his gold-rimmed spectacles. "You must have the proper attire for your outing. Very well, you may leave at three. I'll tend to the shop. And, if you'd like, you may come in late tomorrow. I'll be here all day. Don't let him keep you out too late, Kathy." Albert was like a father to me, and I took his concern as such.

"Thank you, Albert," I said, hurrying to finish cataloging a stack of old books.

At three, I stepped into the back room to inform him I was leaving. "I'll see you tomorrow after lunch," I said.

"I am still available as a chaperone, if you should still have a need," he said, chuckling.

I was walking on cloud nine as I hurried up the street to the Posey Pot. Becky was not going to believe me. For the first time since third grade, I was going to knock her socks off.

"You did what!" she exclaimed, when I told her my news.

"I accepted a dinner date with Marcus Stone for this evening," I repeated.

"Well, you certainly knocked my socks off, Kat," she said. "This is the biggest news since third grade when you informed me that you'd just kissed Douglas Appleby behind the monkey bars."

"And that was the last time I kissed a boy," I admitted, giggling. "Oh, Becky, what am I going to wear?"

"You'll need a new dress, girlfriend," she replied. The fatigue from earlier seemed to have vanished, and she now sounded more like herself. "After I close, we'll run out to the mall and see if we can find you a little black dress—one that will catch his eye."

"A little black dress, you say?" I said, thinking of the meager contents of my closet. "Well, I believe I can save us time and money. I already own a black dress, remember? I purchased it last December."

"You bought that black dress for your father's funeral. I forbid you to wear it on a date with Marcus!" stated Becky, horrified. "I believe in recycling, but there I put my foot down. Just leave it to me, Kat. I know just where to take you."

"Are you sure you're up for this?" I asked her, concerned.

"Absolutely," she replied. "Besides, my best friend has her first date in what, forty years? I'm up for it."

"Actually, I went on a double date with you and Michael," I said. "Remember?"

"Oh yes," she said. "It was with Merle Peterson. You should have married him, Kat. He's now a big-time lawyer in Portland."

"Yes, and on his third wife," I stated.

Thirty minutes later, we were standing outside the classiest dress shop in Cutter's Cove. Simply Elegant was, in Becky's opinion, the Pizza Hut of dress shops. Only the latest styles were on the menu here. Whether you were looking for glamorous or casual, Glynis O'Malley had it in stock. A retired runway model from New York, she truly knew her stuff when it came to knowing what a woman needed to please her man.

"Shall we dine on only the best?" asked Becky, linking her arm in mine.

"We shall," I replied, as we swept through the doors to begin our search.

Glynis, still slim and glamorous at sixty-three, greeted us as we entered the shop. Her fiery red hair, obviously still maintained with a bit of help, hung down over her shoulders like molten lava. Her complexion spoke of just a hint of makeup to hide the fine lines that revealed her age. All of this was wrapped up in a plum-colored midi dress and matching slouch boots. She had that timeless beauty that women like me, could only admire from afar.

"Becky Porter!" Glynis exclaimed, holding out her arms for a quick embrace. "How are you doing, my darling?" Her voice was low and sultry, and I imagined that she could have easily played the role of an actress from the forties.

"I'm good, Glynis," replied Becky, returning her hug. "I'm on a mission. You remember Kathy Jennings, don't you?"

"Yes, I do," replied Glynis. "I was so sorry to hear about your father, Kathy. He was such a talented man. I purchased one of his seascapes for my dad, a few years back. I found it in a Bronx gallery. The painting reminded him of the storms he'd encountered at sea, as a young naval officer. He loved it."

"Thank you, so much," I said. "Unfortunately, I no longer possess any of my father's paintings."

"What a shame," said Glynis. "I bet they'd be worth a fortune now that he's gone."

"I suppose so," I replied.

"What can I do for you, ladies?" asked Glynis, getting down to business.

"Kathy needs a dress," replied Becky. "She has a date tonight with a very distinguished gentleman. What do you have that will knock him off his feet?"

"First or second date?" asked Glynis.

As she spoke, I made a quick inventory of my surroundings. Dresses in every color of the rainbow and in every style adorned the racks and walls. Slacks, blouses, jeans, and casual tops dominated the center racks. She'd dedicated one area alone to accessories, such as shoes, belts, purses, and lingerie.

"First date," replied Becky, when I failed to answer. "He's taking her to that new Italian restaurant near the mall. I think it's called the Olive Branch."

"I'm sorry, Becky," I said, realizing that I was leaving her to answer for me. "I'm just a bit overwhelmed with it all. How does one choose from such a variety?"

"That is why I am here," said Glynis, beckoning me to a nearby rack. "For the first date, you'll want to wear something subtle. You don't want to overwhelm him. And with your hair color, I'd say you need something in a bold shade. I have this dark-blue polyester blend. If you'd care to try it on, the dressing rooms are in the back."

"Yes. Thank you," I said, accepting the dress. Stepping into the small dressing room, I removed my slacks, blouse, and shoes and slipped the dress on over my head. It felt like heaven as it floated down over my body. It clung to my curves like a second skin. It was a very pretty blue with three-quarter sleeves, V-neck and midcalf length. I was amazed at how it accentuated curves that I didn't know I had.

"Well, don't keep me waiting, Kat," I heard Becky call from the other side of the door. "Step out and let's have a look."

The moment I stepped out the door, I heard her gasp. "Kat, you look wonderful!" she exclaimed. "Blue is a good color for you."

"I agree," said Glynis. "However, let's not settle on the first dress. Here, try on this forest-green wraparound. It'll bring out the hazel in your eyes."

"Kat, are you ready to shop till you drop?" asked Becky.

"Bring on the dresses," I replied, feeling like Cinderella getting ready for her first ball.

Two hours later, I stepped from Glynis's shop carrying a huge bag. Inside was a dress and appropriate shoes guaranteed, by her, to be subtle yet alluring. I was ready for my evening with Marcus. Becky, however, looked totally exhausted.

"I think I'll drop you off at your car and head home to the apartment," she said. "I have a run that starts at 5:00 a.m. The kids I run with are half my age, and they'll not put up with my being tardy. They'll call me old, and I'll have to retaliate."

"Why don't you skip your run tomorrow, Becky," I said, as we reached her car. "Just until you're feeling like your old self again. You admitted that you needed to take it easy."

"We'll see," she said.

Arriving home, I found Mussolini waiting at the door. I knew what he wanted, and for once, I was about to disappoint him.

"Sorry, Pup," I said, opening the door for him to go out. "No time to walk on the beach tonight. Cinderella has a date with Prince Charming."

He gave me a look that said, "I'll let it slide this time. However, you will owe me one."

Glancing up at the small clock above my kitchen stove, I was relieved to see that I still had ample time before Marcus was to pick me up, and I was going to need every minute of that time. After a long hot shower to wash away the day's stress, I blow-dried my short hair and carefully applied my makeup. Satisfied with my efforts, I lightly misted with a soft musk fragrance and pulled my new dress over my head. Nervously, I stepped in front of the full-length mirror in the corner of my bedroom, anxious to see the results. The mirror had belonged to my mother and had often stood in her place when it came to approving her daughter's appearance. In my early years, it had offered its unbridled opinion on bell-bottoms, flowered shirts, and love beads. It bravely saw me through the age of big hair, tight pants, and sequined blouses. By my forties, it grew less critical as my apparel grew less rambunctious. By the time my fifties rolled around, I imagined it growing bored as loose-fitting slacks and a sensible blouse became the norm.

However, tonight, I could have sworn I heard it burst into an excited applause. What I saw in the glass now truly mesmerized me. Is this beautiful woman really me? Her short silver hair held a sheen that matched the sparkle in her hazel eyes. Light makeup and just a touch of rouge gave a healthy glow to her cheeks. Her full lips, painted subtly in a perfect shade of soft pink, made her mouth appear just a bit pouty yet inviting. From her tanned shoulders, a burgundy spaghetti strap dress, fell to her knees like liquid icing on a cake. A buttonhole neckline gave only a hint of skin without being too revealing.

Its beaded waist gave it a slimming effect that accentuated the curve of her hips without seeming too outspoken. On her feet, she wore a pair of burgundy strap sandals with just a hint of heel.

"Yes, it really is me," I whispered, feeling beautiful for the first time in years. My only wish was for Marcus to see the same woman I was now looking at. What was it Becky had said? *Be captivating and he'll be captivated.*

Stepping over to my windowsill, I picked up my singing sea stone. It now lay cold and silent in my hand. Was I expecting an encore?

"You, my friend, are my special stone," I whispered. "Thank you for this night." Smiling at my own silliness, I dropped it into my small clutch bag. *Just for luck*, I concluded.

At ten minutes until eight, I stood waiting in the sitting room for my prince to drive up in his magic pumpkin coach. The ticking of the clock on the mantle sounded like small bursts of laughter. What was I doing? I didn't even know this man, and here I was about to go on a date with him. What if he changed his mind or was delayed? How was he to reach me when neither of us had a telephone? I hated to think that I'd done all of this prepping for nothing. As the clock on the mantle struck eight, I imagined the gods were laughing at me. "S-i-l-l-y-y-o-u," it chimed out. I startled when the sound of brisk knocking on the kitchen door, broke into my thoughts. Mussolini jumped to his feet and, barking madly, ran for the kitchen door.

"Who's there?" he seemed to ask, barking out his warning. "State your purpose!"

"It's okay, Mussolini," I said, tugging on his collar. "It's a friend."

The calmness in my voice seemed to relax him and he sat back on his haunches. However, the sound of his tail thumping against the tile floor, told me that he was prepared to attack, if only I gave the command. Steeling my jumbled nerves, I took a deep breath and opened the door.

"Hello, Marcus," I said, giving him a welcoming smile. "I was expecting you. Please, do come in."

"Thank you," he said, stepping into the kitchen. "Okay, who's the attack dog with the hungry stare?"

"Relax," I said. "This is Mussolini, the brave knight who guards the damsel's ivory tower. He's a gentle soul who likes anyone that I do. Mussolini, say hello to Marcus Stone." Hearing his name, Mussolini stepped forward and offered Marcus his right paw.

"Well, I'm impressed with his manners," said Marcus, accepting the dog's offered paw. "I once owned a cocker spaniel of my own. Her name was Cassiopeia. She traveled with me for years. Alas, old age caught up with her, and I was forced to do the right thing."

"My Grandpa Jake brought the first cocker spaniels to Sea Breeze Cottage," I said. "Their names were Hector and Percy. In fact, Mussolini is a direct descendent of Hector. A woman, who lives alone, needs a faithful guardian to be her champion."

"You look lovely tonight, Kathleen," Marcus said, smiling at me. Then addressing Mussolini, he stated, "I will bring her home safe and sound, Sir

Mussolini. She will be back before the stroke of midnight, I promise." Mussolini gave off three loud thunder claps as if to say, "You'd better, pal!"

I allowed my taut nerves to relax as we made our way to the Olive Branch. I was impressed with Marcus, who was handsomely dressed in a three-piece suit in a dark slate gray. My magic pumpkin coach turned out to be a sporty-looking Mustang in a deep metallic red. The engine beneath the hood purred like a kitten as he smoothly shifted the gears.

"When you said that you owned a car, I wasn't expecting this," I said, glancing around the car's interior. "I am impressed, Marcus."

"Madam, you are riding in a true classic," he said, showing obvious pride. "This is a vintage 1969 Ford Mustang."

"I love the color," I commented. "It reminds me of a candied apple."

"Precisely, my dear," he said, smiling. "Its true name is Candy Apple Red. Wait a minute. Just what were you expecting me to drive up in?"

Put on the spot, I didn't know what to say. I surely didn't want to insult him by naming something boring or plain.

"A magic pumpkin coach?" I replied, watching for his reaction.

"Well, for you, anything!" he exclaimed, laughing aloud.

The evening was warm and pleasant, and before we knew it, we were pulling up to the front of the restaurant.

The Olive Branch was truly living up to its reputation for Italian ambience. Its exterior design of sand colored Venetian plaster and red-tiled roof, reminded me of pictures I'd seen of the quaint streets of Italy. Surrounded on three sides by towering spruce trees and rosebay rhododendrons, it sat protected from the blustery Nor'easters that ravaged the coastal areas during the long winter months. Tonight, however, the warm night was alive with overhead strands of small lights that gave off a soft welcoming glow. Large stone urns filled with dianthus and day lilies, graced the portico leading to the front door. The sound of a soft violin played out over the PA system, and I couldn't wait to see what awaited us inside.

A true gentleman, Marcus hurried around the car to open my door. He even offered me a hand as I got out, and I immediately stuck another feather into his cap. I, indeed, felt like a princess. Never having eaten at this restaurant, I didn't know what to expect. Marcus, on the other hand, greeted the valet like an old friend.

"Hello, Thomas," he said, tossing the young man the keys to his car. "Treat her like you would your grandmother."

"Will do, Mr. Stone," said the young valet, saluting Marcus before sliding in behind the wheel of the Mustang.

Taking my elbow, Marcus steered me through the glass doors and into the restaurant. It took a moment for my eyes to adjust to the low light and when they did, I smiled in appreciation. It was like walking into another world. Huge sweeps of grape-laden vines, covering the walls and ceiling, gave one the impression of strolling through a vineyard in Tuscany. The atmosphere was lively with the sound of violins playing a selection of Baroque classical music. The green, white, and red decor evoked the colors of Italy, complete with red and white checked tablecloths. A small candle burned on each, lending a romantic ambiance to the room. We were approached by the maître d' who instantly recognized Marcus.

"Good evening, Mr. Stone," he said, with a friendly smile. "Would you like your usual table, or would you care to dine on the veranda this evening?"

Glancing over at my bare shoulders, Marcus thought a moment then replied, "I believe we'll stay indoors tonight, Steven. And will you please have Enrico bring us a bottle of your best fruit cordial."

"Very good, sir," replied the maître d' before leading us to a table near the back. After seating us, he handed us each a menu and hurried off.

"I can't believe I didn't know about this place," I remarked, glancing at my menu. "But then again, I really don't get out much."

"Actually, it opened its doors about a year ago," replied Marcus. "Arriving in town, I was deeply grateful, as I love Italian food. And the owner is actually Italian, unlike some restaurants where the owner purchases the place but doesn't know his cuisine from his cheeseburgers. Every town should have a good restaurant if it is to cater to the tourists."

As I scanned down the list of dishes on the menu, I knew I was out of my league. The names were all in Italian, and the only thing I recognized was a dish involving snails. And since eating bugs was not an item on my bucket list, I knew I was in trouble.

"I must confess to you, Marcus, that I don't speak Italian," I admitted. "Therefore, I have no idea what I'm ordering."

"It's perfectly understandable, Kathy," he said, taking my menu. "If you will allow me, I'll order for the both of us."

"Go for it," I exclaimed, before remembering where I was and with whom I was dining. "I mean, yes, Marcus, that would be lovely."

When Enrico brought the cordial, he carried it as if it was a priceless vase. After popping the cork, he filled our wine glasses about half-full and placed the bottle in front of Marcus.

"Suspecting that you don't drink, I chose a non-alcoholic cordial that will go with any dish with red sauce," remarked Marcus. "Just in case, you are a lover of spaghetti."

"Well, that's about as close to Italian as I get," I said. Sipping from my glass, I was impressed with its unique flavor. "This is very good."

"Ahh, here comes our waiter," said Marcus, picking up his menu.

"Is the gentleman ready to order?" asked the young dark-haired waiter. I noticed that he didn't carry a pad and pen. I had never eaten in a restaurant, where the server didn't write down my selection. Classy.

"I am, indeed," replied Marcus. "The lady and I will start off with the pasta fagioli and a small salad with house dressing. For the main course, we'll have the linguine with olives and shrimp. Then check back with the dessert menu."

"Very good, sir," replied the waiter, before taking our menus and hurrying off.

We made light conversation until the first course of our meal arrived. I realized that, having not eaten lunch, I was starved. However, I also remembered Becky's comment about curbing my animal instincts and so restrained from blurting out my condition.

The soup they served was delicious. It had a light tomato base with tortellini pasta, Italian chickpeas, beans, garlic and fresh rosemary. It came with a small loaf of Italian bread that we tore and dipped. By the time the main course arrived, my appetite was more under control.

The Linguini with olives and shrimp was remarkable. I was very grateful for Marcus and his familiarity with Italian cuisine. And, thankfully, my meal didn't contain snails.

"This is wonderful, Marcus," I commented. The dish consisted of savory green and black olives and succulent shrimp nestled on a bed of linguini pasta smothered in a marinara sauce. The fruity taste of the cordial only served to enhance the flavor of the meal. We sat quietly for a few minutes, each lost in our own thoughts as we ate. Then Marcus broke the silence.

"Have you always lived in Cutter's Cove, Kathy?" he asked, taking a sip from his glass of cordial.

"I have," I replied. "My mother was born here as well. My father, on the other hand, migrated here from Western Canada and married her soon after he arrived. My mother died when I was six. I was born in Sea Breeze Cottage, and the thought of living anywhere else is terrifying for me."

Now whatever possessed me to tell him that? I wondered. Did I really feel this way? Afraid that I would say something else revealing, I decided to skip over all of the unpleasant details and leave it at that. "What about you, Marcus?"

"I was born in Torquay, England," he replied.

"You're British?" I asked, surprised. "I thought I recognized a slight accent. And your manner of speech is somewhat old worldish. How did you find your way to America?"

"I came here when I was twenty," he replied. "My parents had me quite late in life so they were both dead by the time I was in my late teens. My father died of a heart attack when I was nine, so the father figure in my life was my maternal grandfather. My mother, rest her soul, passed when I was nineteen. A year later, I moved to Boston, where I lived with an elderly aunt until she died. When I entered college, I paid my way by working in an upscale Italian restaurant as a waiter."

"So that is how you are so familiar with the menu?" I said, nodding.

"Yes," he replied. "When I was twenty-five, I went to work for a large publishing company in New York."

"New York!" I exclaimed. "However did you stand the traffic? My friend Becky went to New York years ago, and she said the traffic was nonstop and that everyone was out to run you over if you hesitated for only a moment."

"Well, it's not quite as dangerous as it sounds," said Marcus, sipping his drink. "However, it's no place for an English country boy. It took me years to get used to the noise and just about that long to tone down my British accent."

"Did you say you worked for a large publishing company?" I asked. "Did you enjoy it?"

"I loved it," said Marcus, stopping to wipe his mouth on his napkin.

"How long did you work in publishing?" I asked.

"Thirty-seven years," he replied, leaning back after replenishing his glass from the bottle of Cordial. "One never gets lonely in New York, Kathy. You are surrounded by 8.3 million souls."

"Outrageous!" I exclaimed. "How could you live among so many people? If there's five people in Tucker's Grocery store, we considered it crowded. However did you cope?"

"I escaped the city whenever I got the chance," he replied.

"Your job must have agreed with you for you to keep it for nearly forty years," I said.

"Oh, it did," replied Marcus, smiling slightly. "I've handled thousands of manuscripts over the years. Several, that would amaze you."

"Real best sellers, huh?" I said, thinking of the authors that I'd dealt with over the years. Mine, of course, were all dead by the time their books made it to the shelves of Albert's bookshop.

"Well, not all," said Marcus. "Some were about as boring as it gets. I recall one author in the late nineties who sent me his manuscript, begging me to publish it. I had to turn him down. I did so politely, of course."

"What was his book about?" I asked, curious.

"It had to do with the failing of the dot-com industry," replied Marcus. "It nearly bored me to death, and I'd only just read the introduction. However, there were those that piqued my interest greatly for they were books about travel, real-life situations, and, of course, one cannot resist a good romance."

"Were there any books that stirred your heart?" I asked, recalling the book of Romeo and Juliet he'd bid me to read.

"Plenty," he replied. "And, there were those that stirred the proverbial pot. In 2000, we received the manuscript for a tell-all book about a certain New York socialite. When the press got wind of it, it nearly got the author killed. He wisely decided not to publish it at that time. Smart move on his part. I, of course, advised him to wait until she was dead to release it. In my calculations, she should have about six more good years left in her."

"Do tell!" I exclaimed. "Who is this socialite?"

"I'd rather not divulge her identity at this time," said Marcus, shaking his head. "If the author ever decides to come out of hiding and publish it, I wouldn't want to spoil his big moment. You'll just have to wait, my dear."

"Buggers," I muttered, as the waiter approached our table.

"Excuse me, sir," he said. "Would you and the lady care to see the dessert menu?" Handing Marcus a small leather-bound menu, the waiter waited patiently for him to make his selection.

"We'll have the salted caramel and chocolate Tiramisu and a carafe of black coffee, please," said Marcus.

"Wonderful choice, sir," said the waiter, collecting the menu and the remainder of the bottle of Cordial. When he'd gone, I glanced at Marcus as he adjusted his napkin in his lap. He was such a handsome man. *How did I, Miss Plain and Simple, ever manage to turn this man's head?* I wondered. I was, after all, a sixty-year-old spinster whose only claim to fame was having a famous artist for a father. When Marcus suddenly looked up at me, I felt the familiar excitement course through me. The light of the burning candle accentuated the tiny gold highlights of his brown eyes. When his right eye winked at me, I was horrified that he'd caught me staring. Lowering my eyes, I felt a flush of heat envelop my neck and cheeks. My mind searched for something to say— anything to break the thundering silence.

"So, Marcus, how did you find your way to Cutter's Cove?" I asked him, now fidgeting with my own napkin. "It must have been quite a change from the hustle and bustle of New York."

"Oh, it was indeed, madam," he replied. "A few years ago, I came here to meet with an author and I liked what I saw of the town. It was quiet and laid back and, off peak, the entire town couldn't host enough people to staff a good Manhattan restaurant. So, when I retired, six months ago, I settled in Cutter's Cove. I thought of returning to England to live, however, too many years have passed. In coming here, I found a simpler place and time, and a chance to live near the sea as I had in my childhood."

"May I ask? Was the author you came here to see Howard Francis?" I inquired.

"It was," replied Marcus, sounding surprised. "I so enjoyed his work that I wanted to personally hand him the contract to publish his manuscript. His novel was called—"

"*The Silence of the Deep*," I offered. "Howard Francis was my mother's uncle. He never married nor had any children of his own. My father always said Uncle Howard was a strange duck. He wrote *The Silence of the Deep* when he was in his early eighties, you know. When the book topped the best seller's list, he killed himself. He simply arose one morning and, after a hearty breakfast, walked into the sea. I had always feared that my father would suffer that same fate."

Confessions. *Why was I telling this man, whom I barely knew, my deepest fears?* Thankfully, the waiter delivering our dessert, saved me from having to explain myself.

As the young waiter served our tiramisu and coffee, I took the time to collect my wits. What other secrets was I recklessly going to divulge this night?

Even after a full meal, I was surprised to discover I still had room for dessert. My first bite of the sweet mocha taste of the multilayered confection brought a smile to my lips. I didn't want to think of the calories it contained.

"This is extraordinary," I said, before placing another bite into my mouth. Wanting to savor each bite, I placed it on my tongue and allowed my taste buds to absorb the unusual flavor. "Do I detect coffee?"

"You do," replied Marcus, with a knowing smile. "It's made from layers of sponge cake soaked in espresso coffee, Marsala, mascarpone cheese, and chocolate. My grandmother used to make it for me when I was a lad."

"I believe I've just discovered my new favorite dessert," I said, silently wishing that the kitchen had been just a tad more generous with its portions. "And the fact that it contains chocolate only seals the deal."

"I'm glad you approve," said Marcus, sipping his coffee. "You'll get a good dose of caffeine this evening. I hope it won't keep you up tonight."

"I'll be fine," I replied, knowing that the memory of this evening, alone, would make sleep impossible.

After enjoying our dessert and two cups of coffee, Marcus paid the check and we set out for Sea Breeze Cottage. The night was warm so we rode with the windows down. As we neared Pebble Bay Road, the smell of the sea permeated my nostrils, welcoming me home. Climbing the steps of my front porch, I was pleased that Marcus was acting the part of the perfect gentleman. My nerves tingled as we stood in silence on my front porch. I was grateful that I had remembered to leave the small overhead light on, as it now bathed us in a soft light.

"I had a lovely time tonight, Marcus," I said, nervously. "Thank you."

"You're quite welcome, Kathy," he said, taking my hand in his. I felt his warmth engulf my fingers. "I'd love to do it again very soon."

"I'd like that too," I said, feeling my body tense as he looked at me. "However, this time, I'd like to take you to one of my favorite places. It's just down the beach a couple of miles. It's a place called the Sea Shanty, and they serve the best steamed crab on the east coast."

"That sounds most inviting," he said. "I grew up beside the sea, and steamed crabs were the main staple of our diet."

"Have you ever eaten snails?" I asked him, curious.

"No, and I don't wish too," he said, grinning. "You're not planning on cooking them for me, are you?"

"Not unless you're willing to catch and clean them," I said, enjoying his playful bantering.

Suddenly he leaned in and lightly touched his lips to mine. I was stunned. I hadn't kissed anyone since third grade, and I was sorely out of practice. Marcus, sensing my hesitation, took matters into his own hands. Pulling me into his arms, he pressed his lips firmly against mine. It was pure heaven. I felt the electricity course through my body, sending my senses reeling. His lips were soft and warm, his cologne musky and smelling of the outdoors. I felt his hand press lightly against my back, and I leaned into his embrace. When he pulled away, I was breathless.

Looking deep into my eyes, he smiled. "You have beautiful hazel eyes, Kathleen Jennings," he said, softly. "I will lose myself in them if I'm not careful."

"My mother's eyes were hazel," I said, unsure of how to react to his romantic words.

Stepping back, Marcus took my hand and planted a light kiss on my fingers. "I will be in touch, Miss Jennings," he said, allowing my hand to slide from his. "Parting is such sweet sorrow. Speaking of Shakespeare, have you begun your adventure with the Capulets and the Montagues yet?"

"Who?" I asked, wondering of whom he was speaking.

"Romeo and Juliet," he offered. "When next I see you, my love, hopefully their fate will be bound up with your own. Read the first chapter, Kathy, and you'll see what I mean. Till we meet again?"

With a slight bow, he smiled and walked to his car. As he drove away, I leaned back against the doorframe. *So this is romance*, I thought. My head was swimming with the sheer joy of my evening with Marcus. With our first kiss still fresh on my lips, I found myself wondering if this was falling in love? Oh, what cruel fate would have me fall in love so near the end of my life? What joy I've missed all these years by not believing in myself. Reaching into my purse, I fumbled for my keys, and my fingers curled around my sea stone. It had indeed brought me good luck.

"Thank you," I whispered, "for allowing me to feel love before it's too late." Hearing Mussolini bark from within, I pulled out my keys and let myself in.

After a quick shower, I donned my pajamas and crawled into bed. Mussolini, his breathing a rhythmic lullaby, lay curled up on the rug beside my bed. As I reached to turn out the lamp, my eyes fell on the worn copy of *Romeo and Juliet* lying on my nightstand. Feeling as though I could, at last, know their emotions, I lay back, opened the cover, and slipped into their world.

Chapter 4

I rose with the sun, and took Mussolini for a walk on the beach. The memory of the night before seemed to infuse me with abundant energy, and I was forever grateful to Albert for giving me the morning off. Feeling as I did, I simply needed to be somewhere else besides among the dusty old books. I needed sunshine to match my singing heart. When I returned to the cottage, I collected my cleaning supplies. Housework was always a task that helped when something huge occupied my mind. Whistling a merry tune, I set to work.

Starting with the kitchen, I scrubbed the tile floor until it gleamed. Grabbing a bottle of spray cleaner, I set to work on the kitchen windows, finishing with the glass panes in the panels of the kitchen cabinets lining one wall. In minutes, they too sparkled. The cupboards still held the rose dishes that my father had given my mother on their wedding day.

The small wooden table in the center of the room revealed the worn evidence of thousands of cups of coffee and nearly seventy years of meals. Stepping over to glance out the window over the porcelain kitchen sink, I saw Mussolini chewing on his bone in the small side yard.

Reaching for the dust mop, I next tackled the living room. I soon sent an army of dust bunnies sailing across the scuffed wooden floors and into the corners to regroup. Straightening the doily on the back of the red and gold brocade sofa, I felt the old tug of familiarity. This sofa had sat in this same spot for over six decades. The same four gold throw pillows I'd played with as a child still sat propped up against the arms. Now glancing around at the other outdated furnishings, I shook my head. Once a week for the last fifty years, I'd dusted this room without ever using it. The last gathering this room witnessed, I was certain, was sometime in the early sixties when Grandpa Jake had used it to entertain a few of his army friends. Still, the room had a past. My father had purchased the furniture when he and my mother were first married, and she'd decorated the room herself. After she died, my father closed it off like a memorial tomb. *My mother loved this room*, I thought. Why change it? Fluffing up the pillows, I closed the drapes and moved on.

Stepping into the sitting room, I walked over to stand in front of the bay window. This room faced the sea and therefore was the room most used. It now held for me, a lifetime's worth of memories as it was here, in this very room, that I'd spent my evenings playing cards with Grandpa Jake and listening to the radio. Here, I shared with him my childhood dreams and he encouraged me to keep searching for my sea stones. After his death, the room seemed to lose its magic. For the next forty-five years, it served as my father's sitting room, where he spent all his days. Once filled with laughter, it became a tomb, his very presence resembling that of a living corpse. His dark moods were like a black cloud blotting out the sun as he sat brooding in front of this very window, mumbling to himself and cursing God for not allowing him to die. I'd sit with him each evening, hoping he would acknowledge me and draw me into conversation. That day never came.

Loneliness consumed my evenings, even in his presence. He wanted no reminders of the past and refused to talk of the early years with my mother. He even forbade me to place any pictures of myself out where he could see them. The old red easy chair, where he'd spent his last days, still sat before the bay window, where I found him on that fateful day last December.

Next to it, on the end table, his reading glasses waited as if he'd just stepped out for a walk on the beach and would return momentarily. His last painting, left unfinished, leaned on the easel near the window where he'd abandoned it. On the 2 x 2 1/2 foot canvas, the sea's angry waves rode nearly to the edge, where they hung suspended as if waiting for the artist to return and complete their journey. Unfortunately, their journey ended here, for the artist was dead.

My father's death, I had to admit, brought relief to both our souls. Growing up in his shadow he'd always seemed immortal to me. However, when he hit his eighties and was no longer able to navigate the sea path to the beach, I saw him finally grow old. Unable to sit on his beach rock with his easel, he turned to painting here, facing the sea in front of the sitting room bay window. For him, though, it just wasn't the same as feeling the sea winds and salt spray on his face. Taking this as the final blow to his tortured soul, he abandoned his craft altogether. This final painting sat as a cruel reminder of all that he'd lost. He spent his final days sitting in his old red easy chair, silently staring out to sea. I once asked him what it was that he saw when he stared at the ocean.

"Eternity," he muttered, before retreating, once again, into his silent world.

When I felt my sunny mood begin to match that of my father's picture, I shook off the feeling of despair and returned to the task of house cleaning.

Falling into my usual dusting routine, my cloth skimmed across the tabletops, lamps, and windowsills. Pausing only long enough to replenish my dusting spray, I continued on to my Grandpa Jake's favorite ashtray, the broken hall tree near the unused back door, and my father's old Philco radio. I took a moment to catch my breath on one of the two ladder-back chairs that graced either side of the room's small stone fireplace. Dominating the wall to the left of the bay window, it too sat unused. Looking now at the cold and blackened grate, I was saddened with the realization that it hadn't held a fire since my grandfather's death. *What a shame*, I thought, remembering the cozy fires we enjoyed on cool evenings. He and I would sit within its warm glow and make up stories of ghosts and one-legged pirates. Oh, how I missed those long ago days. Once more shaking off the depressing thoughts, I rose and set my cloth scurrying over the oaken mantelpiece. I smiled when my eyes fell on the small rose and ivy music box, my gift from Albert. The old clock in the mantel's center was, I knew, a family heirloom. However, unsure of its past, to me, it was just an old clock. I wound it and moved on.

Stopping to survey my progress, I was struck with the sudden realization, that I was still dusting the same items that I'd dusted when I was ten. Why was I still fluffing pillows on a sofa that no one had used in decades or dusting off a radio that hadn't played since I was fifteen? And what use did I have for a broken hall tree that held no coats? *All I'm doing is caring for ghosts*, I thought. I was stunned at the realization that my beloved Sea Breeze Cottage had turned into a mausoleum, full of useless "things," occupying the rooms like so many inanimate corpses awaiting someone to lay them to rest.

"What this place needs is a rummage sale," I muttered.

Looking around the room, I mentally checked off the items that needed to go. Some things, however, I couldn't bear to part with, like the tiny white tea set that had belonged to my mother now displayed on a corner table. I'd found it when I cleaned out Grandpa Jake's bedroom after his death and had placed it on the small table near the sofa, just daring my father to say something. When he loudly demanded that I remove it from his sight, I ignored him. For me, it made me think of my mother, although her face was now a vague image. After my father died, I waited only a month, before bringing my Grandpa Jake's large, black, leather-bound Bible out of hiding and placing it in the middle of the coffee table. It now lay open to the last page he'd read before he died. I knew this for he'd marked his place with that Sunday's church bulletin. Seeing his Bible every day now brought me a comfort that I hadn't known since his death. Taking a moment, I sat down on the overstuffed gray sofa and allowed my finger to rest on the verse he'd underlined in red, Psalm 27:1: "The Lord is my light and my salvation: Whom shall I fear? The Lord is the strength of my life; of whom shall I be afraid?"

I thought about that verse for a moment. I really had no fear of God. I simply ceased to believe at age fifteen that He had my best interest at heart. I kept the Bible only because it had belonged to Grandpa Jake. Glancing around the room, I realized that everything in this room had belonged to someone now deceased. How could love possibly flourish in such a stagnant environment? A brisk knocking on the kitchen door drew me from my thoughts, and I hurried to answer it.

I was surprised to find old Mr. Preston standing on my front porch. He was dressed in a baggy pair of overalls that greatly accentuated his rail thin frame. Beneath a pair of red suspenders, he wore a wrinkled blue dress shirt that I was sure he'd pulled straight from the dryer. His wind-creased face wore a worried look that gave his mouth a downward turn. Despite the heat of the day, he wore a dark stocking cap on his head, which left small tufts of white hair protruding above each ear.

"Mr. Preston," I said, stepping back so he could enter into the kitchen, "what brings you out this way?"

"Oh, Miss Jennings, I've bad news to bring ya," he said, wringing his bent and gnarled hands. Remembering his manners, he quickly slid the stocking cap from his head. "It's Mrs. Porter, ma'am. She collapsed this morning while running near the park. She's been taken to the hospital in Portland. I'm afraid she's poorly, ma'am."

"Becky collapsed?" I asked, letting his words sink in. "Thank you, Mr. Preston. I'll go to her at once."

Seeing him to his car, I dressed quickly and drove into the bookshop to inform Albert of the situation. Frantic, I drove the forty miles to Portland Memorial Hospital in record time, just slightly over the speed limit. When I arrived at the emergency room, the receptionist informed me that Becky was undergoing tests.

"I'm her best friend Kathy," I told her. "Becky's husband died a few years ago, so I'm really the only family she has."

"I'll tell the doctor you're here," she said and directed me to the waiting room.

Hours passed as I watched the shadows lengthen on the walls. Finally, the doctor came out to talk to me. In my opinion, he was much too young to be a doctor. But then again, anyone younger than forty was much too young to me. When he smiled at me, I returned his friendliness. Darkly tanned, he sported a full head of black unruly curls, which gave him a certain boyish charm. He wore a pristine white lab coat over his washed denim jeans, with a nametag that listed several letters after his name. On his feet, he wore a pair of scuffed sneakers. Under different circumstances, I would have thought his attire unprofessional. However, at the moment, he was treating Becky and my only hope of finding out how dire the situation.

"Miss Jennings, I presume?" he asked, sliding into the chair beside me. "I'm Dr. Sheffield, Becky's doctor. She has given me permission to speak with you. Becky is suffering from exhaustion, and we've run numerous tests to find out why. Her white blood cells are up, and that could mean an infection. The person who found her said that she was unconscious for a few minutes, and that concerns me. Can you tell me anything?"

"Well, yesterday, she said she was a bit tired," I replied. "That's not like her, Doctor. She's always upbeat and full of energy. She's a runner, you know."

"Yes, she told me," he said. "The tests we've run will hopefully tell us what's going on."

"So what happens now?" I asked, feeling helpless.

"Now we wait on the results," he said. "That may take a couple of days. In the meantime, I'm keeping her overnight for observation. We'll send her home tomorrow."

"Can I see her?" I asked, standing.

"Of course," he said, getting to his feet. He thrust his hands into the pockets of his white lab coat. "Be brief, though. She's been through a lot."

When I walked into Becky's room, it was deathly quiet. A small light above her bed dimly lit the area around her, leaving the rest of the room in shadows. Approaching the bed, I saw that her eyes were closed and her breathing shallow. Not sure if she was sleeping, I quietly slid into the chair next to her. I was shocked at her appearance. Her skin was the color of parchment paper, and dark circles defined her eyes.

"Is that you, Kat?" she asked in a wee voice. "I knew you'd come. You're my best friend, you know." Her validation of our lifelong friendship warmed my heart, and I took her hand in mine. It was cold as ice.

"How are you, Becky?" I asked, with genuine concern. "What happened?"

"I'm not sure," she replied, opening her eyes. "I was twenty minutes into my run when I suddenly felt light headed. Before I knew what happened, I found myself on the ground and one of the other runners was asking me how many fingers he was holding up. I kept telling him three, but he just kept asking. Why do they do that by the way? It was my legs that gave out, not my eyes."

"What does the doctor say?"

"Not much," she replied. "They never tell you anything until they've run all their tests. I'm convinced that it's nothing, Kat. I simply skipped breakfast and my blood sugar was low. If my knight with the three fingers would have given me a soda, I would've been fine. Instead, he called an ambulance."

"Becky, you were unconscious," I pointed out. "Low blood sugar does not render you unconscious."

"Wait. How did you find out about me?" she asked.

"Mr. Preston told me you'd been taken to the hospital," I replied. "The poor old dear had to drive all the way out to my place to tell me. He was frantic. By the way, I'm calling the telephone company in the morning and having a phone installed."

"Good idea," she said. "They're discharging me in the morning. Will you come and get me? I can't afford to spend my day lying in bed. I have a business to run. Besides, I don't want to lose my momentum. I'm attempting to keep up with the young bucks, you know."

"You need to get better first, Becky," I said. "And yes, I'll be back in the morning." When the nurse came in to take her vitals, I took my leave.

Driving back to Cutter's Cove, my mind was in turmoil. I couldn't bear to think of Becky being sick. I thought of driving out to see Marcus, but it was after six o'clock. That, in my opinion, was too late to show up unannounced on someone's doorstep, friend or foe. When I got home, Mussolini was waiting on me. I had left for Portland in such a hurry that I'd forgotten to fill his bowl with kibbles. However, he was very forgiving once his belly was full.

Needing to feel the cool ocean breeze on my face, I took Mussolini for a walk on the sand. I was worried about my friend, and the beach was a great place to take my concerns. After our walk, I took a hot shower and settled into my father's chair with a restorative cup of tea. My life was suddenly beginning to accelerate, and I wasn't sure in what direction it was going.

When the mantle clock chimed ten thirty, I made my way wearily down the hallway toward the bathroom. After brushing my teeth, I stopped and pulled a pair of pajamas from my old dresser that sat in the hallway across from my bedroom door. As I pushed the drawer closed, my eyes fell on the attic door directly behind it, and an old fear niggled at my senses. Was that a noise I heard on the other side? *Don't be silly*, I admonished myself. *You're a grown woman, for Pete's sake. This fear you have of the attic is old business. Then why did just looking at the door still give me goose bumps?* I thought.

My fear of the attic stemmed from a story told to me by Grandpa Jake when I was a small child. His tale of meeting a black creature on the narrow attic stairs still made no sense to me. Why would my sweet, gentle grandfather feel the need to frighten me so badly? What was his purpose in keeping me from a room filled with old dusty boxes and unused furniture? The small room under the eaves was always a favorite childhood playhouse for Becky and me on rainy days. After my grandfather's tale of encountering the creature on the steps, I never set foot there again. His tale so terrorized me that even after fifty years, I still could not bring myself to move the dresser and fully expose the door. The fact that it had sat there, unmoved after all these years, still caused Becky to raise an eyebrow. But then again, after Grandpa Jake's funeral, it was her idea to drag my dresser out of my bedroom and to place it in front of the attic door. It was the largest thing we could find. And here it remained still in place, a sad reminder that even as an adult, I still felt the boogeyman's presence lurking behind the door. When something brushed up against my leg, I nearly jumped out of my skin. Discovering that it was just Mussolini gave me a momentary burst of bravery.

"One of these days, Pup, I'm going to march right up those steps and see what's up there!" I said, reaching down to scratch his head. "However, it won't be tonight. It's bedtime." Giving the dresser a reassuring shove, I hurried Mussolini into my bedroom, where I felt safe.

The next morning dawned bright and full of sunshine. After my walk on the beach, I drove into the bookshop. Albert was there waiting on me as I came through the front door.

"Kathleen, how is Becky?" he asked, with a worried look. "I do hope it's nothing serious."

"As do I, Albert," I replied. "I didn't return from Portland until dinnertime."

"How long will she be in the hospital?"

"They're discharging her this morning. They'll phone here when she's ready. I'd like to go and bring her home, if you don't mind. She has no one else."

"Please do!" he exclaimed. "And see to it that she gets some rest. I'll take care of the shop while you're gone. Oh, by the way, I found the book that your Marcus Stone has been searching for."

"That's wonderful, Albert!" I said, surprised. "By the way, I'm having a telephone installed at the cottage as soon as possible."

"Now it's my turn to show surprise," he said, smiling. "I've only been suggesting that very thing for years. What changed your mind?"

"This emergency with Becky has changed my mind. If I'd had a telephone, Mr. Preston could have simply called instead of driving all the way out to the cottage. I could have been there for Becky much sooner."

"How can one not have a telephone?" asked Albert, shaking his head. "It's a necessity these days."

"It was actually my father who insisted we not have a phone," I remarked, now laying blame where blame was due. "He wished to cut himself off from the world. I shudder to think of what could have happened had there been an emergency. And now that he's gone, I'm going to make a few changes."

"Good for you, Kathleen," said Albert. "That is a sure sign that you're ready to move on. For me, it was giving away a few of my late wife's things. I'm sad to say that it took me fifty years to reach that point."

"Better late than never, Albert," I said, switching on the OPEN sign in the front window.

The call from the hospital came in around nine thirty, informing me that Becky was being discharged. The drive back to Portland was uneventful, and I made good time. When I walked into Becky's room, I found her dressed and waiting on her bed. After a night's rest, she still looked tired, but her color had improved.

"Well, I'm glad to see you're feeling better," I said, giving her a quick hug.

"I'm right as rain," she said, smiling. "And I'm ready to blow this popsicle joint."

"Not so fast," I said. "You still need the doctor's word of approval."

"And the word is given," declared a male voice from the doorway. Becky smiled as the young Dr. Sheffield sauntered into the room. "I am happy to say, Becky, that your vitals are good and you can indeed go home."

"Thanks, Doc," she said, getting to her feet.

"Not so fast," said Dr. Sheffield. "I have a few instructions for you, and the nurse has to officially discharge you. And there are a couple of tests that are still being processed, so I'll call you when the lab is finished."

"I'll bring the car around, Becky," I said. "I'll meet you downstairs. Thank you, Dr. Sheffield, for taking such good care of her. She means a lot to me, you know."

"I do," he said, giving me a smile that would have melted a younger woman's heart. As for me, it triggered a hot flash, and I hurried out into the air-conditioned hallway.

On the drive home, I filled Becky in on my date with Marcus. She sat quietly listening, which was not like her. I expected her to bombard me with questions, such as what did we have for dinner, how late were we out and, yes, did he kiss me before he left. Her very silence spoke volumes on just how much the last twenty-four hours had cost her. Finally she spoke.

"I'm so happy for you, Kat," she said. "You've waited your whole life for someone like Marcus to come along. And you can believe it's all because of your silly sea stone, if you'd like. However, I believe in the power of true love and destiny. All I've ever wanted was for you to be happy and to find the special enduring kind of love that I shared with Michael. The kind that transcends even death."

"Thanks, Becky," I said, touched by her words. "However, Marcus and I have only had one date. I doubt if either one of us is thinking about true love and destiny."

"You will," she said. "You have that sparkle in your eyes."

When we reached Cutter's Cove, I pulled up in front of the red brick building housing the flower shop and her small upstairs apartment.

"I should work on my flower arrangements for tomorrow's deliveries," she said, sighing heavily.

"Not today, sister," I said, sternly. "The doctor said for you to rest." In a millisecond, I saw her face go from defiance to compliance, and I knew she would heed his advice.

"I will do so only because I lack the energy to argue with you," she said, climbing out of the car.

After settling Becky on her sofa, I returned to the bookshop. Entering by the back door, I was surprised to find Marcus and Albert bent over an old book, discussing its properties. They were so engrossed in the pages that they both failed to see me come in. Quietly, I walked over and leaned in to have a look for myself. I just caught the book's title, *The Art of Engineering in Ancient Egypt*.

"This book, for its age, is in better shape than I imagined," Marcus remarked, examining the book's spine. "Wherever did you finally locate it, Albert? I've looked for this book for years with no success."

"I've got people," Albert replied, proudly. "After nearly sixty years in the book business, I've made quite a few connections. I've a friend in Canada who knows someone in Wisconsin, who knows someone in Texas, and so forth."

"I see what you mean by connections," said Marcus, grinning. "I'll take the book, of course, once you've decided on a price. I shall have to thank Kathy, as she was the one to start the ball rolling."

"You're welcome," I said, surprising them both.

"You're back," said Albert, stepping back from the desk. "And how is Becky doing?"

"She's resting, I hope," I replied. "She's had enough excitement for a while."

"Forgive me for asking," said Marcus. "But what happened to Mrs. Porter?"

"She collapsed while training for her 5K run," I replied. "She spent the night in Portland Hospital while they ran some tests. I'm afraid at this point the jury is still out on the cause of her collapse."

"Perhaps, we can send her some flowers to cheer her," suggested Marcus.

"She's a florist," I pointed out. "Flowers are her business. It would be like sending a bag of mulch to an ailing landscaper. Besides, flowers will only make her think of getting back to running her shop."

"Good point," said Marcus.

"We could send her an interesting book to read during her confinement," suggested Albert. "I'm sure we can find her a nice romance or an adventure somewhere on these shelves."

"Another good suggestion," I said. "However, if we send her a book, it'll have to be something more recent than *The Cain Mutiny*. Perhaps a nice Danielle Steele would interest her. She's a romantic at heart, you know."

"Do I have a Daniel Steele in house?" asked Albert, glancing around the shop.

"Albert, your authors passed on years ago," I said, grabbing my purse. "I'll run out to the mall and pick her up a book. You know, Albert, I've had this idea that perhaps we could start stocking a few paperbacks. I could arrange a section just for the latest best sellers. At the present, if someone is looking for a beach read, they're forced to drive all the way out to the mall. I turn away customers every day who are looking for a simple paperback. What do you think?"

"Well, I suppose," said Albert, shrugging his shoulders. "Perhaps the market for books such as *Moby Dick* and *War and Peace* is waning a bit. Go ahead and pick up a couple of dozen paperbacks, and we'll give your idea a try. What is the world coming to, I ask? Folks today want books involving fast cars and superheroes. They're no longer reading the classics."

"Sad but true," said Marcus. "However, there's nothing I love more than a good book about vampires and medieval castles. I'm a sucker for Count Dracula, no pun intended. What can I say? I'm British."

"Count Dracula was Romanian," I pointed out.

"Yes, but Christopher Lee was the greatest actor to ever play the good count," said Marcus. And—"

"Let me guess," I said, rolling my eyes. "He was British."

"Bingo!" exclaimed Marcus, smiling broadly. Returning his smile, I left them to deal with ancient Egypt and its dead engineers.

Chapter 5

Arriving at the mall, I parked my car in a shaded area and made my way into the building's cool interior. It was alive with bustling tourists, all seeking relief from the heat outside. Some lounged at the food court, while others browsed the many shops lining the main thoroughfare. Shouldering my purse, I stopped to admire a rack of tie-dyed T-shirts in front of the Cutter's Cove Gift Shop. Although it was early in the season, the store was busy with kids and adults alike. I was pleased to see the multitude of people all poring over the shelves of knickknacks bearing the logo of Cutter's Cove, Maine. These folks, lovingly known to the locals as "souvenir hounds," were the bread and butter of the town's merchants. Leaving them to their bargains, I made my way to the center of the mall, where I grabbed a coffee from *Jitters*, the mall's coffee shop, before heading for the bookstore.

The *Book Emporium* was a candy store for readers of all ages. Its huge glass-enclosed front held numerous posters announcing the works of new as well as well-known authors. Their motto, etched above the door, read, "Read Em' and Reap. Every Book Holds A Treasure" Their claim of having one hundred thousand books in stock, I was sure, was no exaggeration. Shelves, some as high as eight feet, crisscrossed the store, creating a definable maze filled with books of every subject and color. Customers, young and old, milled about the shelves like ants on the move. As I sipped my coffee, I browsed the aisles to see what was drawing them in. Having worked the past nineteen years with writers such as Michener, Tolstoy, and Woodward, I was truly amazed by the many new genres now available for the avid reader. Spotting a table filled with bargain hardbacks, I hurried over to examine them.

"Could it really be this easy?" I asked myself, glancing over the many titles. It didn't take me long to learn why these books were a bargain. Someone by the name of Marilyn Sconce had written a book entitled *The Many Faces of Today's Elderly*. How many faces could the old folks have for heaven's sake? After the age of eighty, they all wore the same wrinkled expression in my opinion. *Too boring*, I decided.

The next title was even more mundane. "*The Art of Choosing Good Sensible Shoes,*" I read aloud, rolling my eyes. "Now there's a book that would keep me up all night!"

The elderly woman, standing next to me, gave me a strange look and quickly moved to the other side of the table.

"Can it get any worse?" I mumbled. Yes, it could. The next book title proved it. "*Cooking Pasta Dishes in the Nude,*" I read aloud. Catching the eye of the woman across the table, I leaned toward her. "Now why, I might ask, would I want to cook noodles while naked? I don't know about you, ma'am, but some things are better off not exposed to hot steam!"

Giving me a shocked look, she scooped up the book on sensible shoes and scurried off.

When I spotted a thirtyish-looking male sales attendant arranging books on a shelf, I raised my hand to gain his attention. As he approached, I had to hide my smile. In his attempt to blend in with the tourists, he was dressed in a bright red-and-white Hawaiian shirt that hung out over a pair of faded blue jeans crudely cut off just above the ankle. On his feet, he wore a pair of worn beachcomber sandals. To complete his islander look, he'd pulled a white bucket hat down over his dark Beatle-style haircut.

"Excuse me, Gilligan," I said, barely containing my amusement. "I'm looking for a couple of thrilling books. Something with a bit more zing than wrinkles, sensible shoes, or naughty noodles."

Totally missing my little joke, he gave me a blank expression and pointed to the name printed on the store badge pinned to the pocket of his shirt. "My name is Skippy," he said, smiling. *Same thing*, I thought.

"Well, Skippy," I mused. "What is selling these days?"

"If you're looking for an exciting read, ma'am, then look no further than the paperback section," he replied, pointing toward the back right corner of the store. "We carry all the latest kills and thrills on the market. I'm sure you'll find one that will definitely get your adrenaline pumping."

Wondering why a woman my age would want to pump adrenaline, I thanked him and headed in that direction. "Why did I think this was going to be easy?" I muttered, as I stood gazing at the back wall filled with row after row of colorful paperback books. "Well, let's see what's hot," I said, stepping forward.

As my fingers flew over the book titles, I came across a book with a dark and sinister-looking spine. Pulling it out, I read the title, *The Ghoul Feasts at*

Midnight. The cover featured a ferocious-looking creature in a dark forest setting. Two large yellow eyes with black slits glared out at me from a face covered in black shaggy and matted fur. Its wide mouth displayed huge canine teeth, dripping with the blood of its last victim. I imagined that this was what my grandfather's creature in my attic might look like and I felt a chill course through me. The last thing I needed to do was to put a face on my fears. "Now this is a book that would definitely keep me up all night!"

Replacing it, I pulled out the one next to it. The cover featured an innocent-looking eighty-something woman leaning on a silver walker. She was standing in the doorway of a retirement home. Lounging in the background, three fellow residents all appeared to be napping. I would have thought she was advertising sensible shoes if not for her face. A deranged expression had distorted her sweet grandmotherly features, as she stared at the reader through two angry yellow eyes that reminded me of a wild animal. Her evil smile revealed two large bloody fangs that dripped blood down the front of her old-fashioned paisley print dress. It was then I noticed the two bloody fang marks in the necks of her fellow residents. They were not napping.

"*My Grandmother Was a Vampire*," I read aloud. "Good heavens! Just when you thought it was safe to get old! Who would read this rubbish?"

"I would," replied a heavy-set, middle-aged woman to my left. I immediately pegged her as a tourist, as she was shopping in her bathing suit. "Honey, don't waste your money. It wasn't that good."

"The title is a dead giveaway to that opinion," I said, sliding it back into place. "What will they think of next? Let me guess. The old lady had a set of fanged dentures."

"How did you guess?" she said, laughing. "The story is about a grandma vampire that lived in a nursing home on the outskirts of New Orleans. It doesn't end well, though. The only blood she could find comes from her fellow residents, and in the end, she dies from malnutrition. Not enough Geritol, I guess."

"Perhaps we could team her up with the ghoul who feasts at midnight," I suggested. We both had a good howl over that one. After she walked off, I continued with my search. The other choices were not much of an improvement over the elderly and anemic vampire.

To narrow down my search, I decided that for a book to be a good "beach" read, it should take place in a beach setting. I was now on a roll. An hour later, I headed to the checkout counter with an armload of the best that *The Book Emporium* had to offer me. After combing through at least a half dozen shelves, I settled on two dozen books about finding love at the beach, murder and mayhem at the beach, and even one involving an alien abduction at the beach. Spotting the display announcing Jewel Taylor's newest book, *Love at High Tide*, I added it to the pile as well. On my way past the bargain books, I grabbed the book on *Cooking Pasta Dishes in the Nude* for Becky. In my opinion, one is never too old to learn new culinary techniques.

When I saw that Skippy was now working the register, I dumped my armload of kills and thrills on the counter in front of him and pulled out my wallet. As he rang me up, he scanned the titles and nodded his approval. When he came to the one about the alien abduction, he leaned in and quietly informed me that he'd recently been abducted by aliens out near the old pier and would I like to hear about his experience over a drink?

"What? You're just a boy!" I declared in a loud whisper, giving him my best "horrified" expression. I left him, wallowing in his wounded pride as my ego and I, soared happily out the door with our purchases. By golly, I still had it! I just prayed that "it" didn't abandon me before I had a chance to use it on Marcus Stone.

The next day, I spent the better part of the morning arranging my "beach" books into an eye catching display. An old shelf lined with light brown paper, a few well-placed seashells, and a small beach ball gave me just the look I was after. After placing a similar display in the front window, I waited to see if anyone would notice. I wasn't to be disappointed. By lunchtime, I had sold eleven paperback books and made a new friend. Greta Farnsworth of the Portland Farnsworths purchased five books and in the process, gave me a brilliant idea for a new sales gimmick.

"I just love a good beach story," she said, adjusting her rhinestone-encrusted sunglasses perched in the front of her hair. As I rang up her purchase, I marveled at the way her silver-blue hair reflected the fluorescent light from the fixtures above her head. "And I love your window display," she added, patting an imaginary loose strand of hair back into place.

"Thank you," I replied, handing over her change.

"I've never been in here myself, as I'm not much of a reader of old books," she commented, glancing around the shop. "I much prefer the newer authors myself."

I wondered if she was here for the sights or the sand. Her freshly painted nails, huge diamond ring, and expensive-looking peach pantsuit screamed upper class. She was, in my opinion, a little over-dressed for the beach. But then again, who was I to judge?

"Thank you for your compliment," I said, handing her the bag containing her books. "I do hope you'll enjoy these."

"Oh, I'm sure I will," she said, picking up her huge multicolored beach bag. "As I said, I love read-ing. However, my problem is what to do with the books after I've read them. I'm forced to toss them in the rubbish simply because we've no room to store them at the condo."

It was at that moment that I had an epiphany. "I've got an idea," I said, leaning on the counter. "Why don't you bring the books back to the shop after you've read them and I'll buy them back? This way you can purchase a different book."

"Why, that's sounds like a stupendous idea!" she exclaimed, clapping her diamond-studded hands together. "I'll do just that."

When the word got out that Bristol's Rare and Antique Bookstore had a best seller's paper-back-exchange program, the books began flying off the shelves. To my surprise, most of the paperbacks returned just days later like literary carrier pigeons. Within hours, those same pigeons left the store in the bag of another reader. My idea was a brilliant success. Jewel Taylor's newest bestseller, *Love at High Tide*, had been bought and sold three times before finally flying the coop. When the selection grew slim, I made another trip to *The Book Emporium* to browse the paperback section. Skippy, however, was nowhere in sight. *Darn it. My ego could have used a healthy tweak.*

Albert, who at first was less than enthusiastic with my idea of selling paperbacks, was soon in agreement with my logic. His smile grew when the husbands began accompanying their wives into the store. Not interested in romance novels, the husbands began browsing through Albert's selection of older books. To his delight, the classics were making a comeback. Soon his book sales rivaled my own.

"Kathleen, you're a genius," he remarked on Monday afternoon as the last husband-and-wife team left with their purchases. She bought a copy of *Love at High Tide*, and he was thrilled with his copy of *The Carpetbaggers*.

"Thank you, Albert," I said, turning on the CLOSED sign. "By the way, I now have a telephone. My new number is filed in your Rolodex."

"Excellent," he said. "I'll keep it safe."

When the shop telephone jingled to life, I hurried to answer it.

"Oh good, I caught you before you left for home," exclaimed Becky. "Oh, Kat, the doctor just called me and has asked me to come to Portland in the morning. He wants to give me the results of my tests in person. That's never good. When I asked if he couldn't just tell me over the phone, he refused."

"Now, Becky, I don't want you upsetting yourself," I said, in an attempt to calm her frantic voice. "He most likely doesn't want to violate the HIPAA law or something. What time is your appointment?"

"I have to be in Dr. Sheffield's office at 9:00 a.m.," she replied. "I'm afraid to go alone, Kat."

Covering the phone with my hand, I turned to Albert. "Becky needs me to go to the Portland Medical Clinic with her in the morning, Albert." His nod of approval was all I needed. "Yes, I'll go with you," I said, silently mouthing "thank you" at him. "I'll drive my car. I'll pick you up at seven thirty. And, Becky, calm down. It doesn't have to be bad news."

The following morning, I was up before dawn. When Mussolini discovered that I was not taking him for his usual walk on the beach, he seemed a bit put out with me. After promising him an afternoon picnic on the rocks, I headed for Becky's apartment. She was unusually quiet on the drive to Portland. She seemed listless and tired even after a night's sleep, and her skin had a slight sallow look to it. When we arrived at the clinic, I let her out at the huge double glass doors and parked the car. The building was huge for a clinic. It resembled more a small hospital. However, across the front of its red brick face, huge letters spelled out Portland Medical Clinic.

"Come on, Becky," I said, joining her. "Put on that gorgeous smile of yours and let's go talk to the doctor. Then I'll take you out for tofu pancakes, powdered eggs, and chicken bacon." When she laughed at my joke, I felt her relax a bit.

Finding our way to the third floor, we stepped into the realm of Drs. Sheffield, Barker, and Twain, medical wizards. I was relieved to find the waiting room empty. Becky was a nervous wreck, and a crowd would have made her more so. When the nurse called her name, Becky grabbed me by the hand.

"Please come back with me, Kat," she said, desperation filling her voice. "I don't want to be alone."

"You're never alone, my friend," I assured her, as we walked arm in arm in to see Dr. Sheffield.

We found the good doctor waiting on us in his office. Today, he was dressed more professional in black dress slacks, a pressed white shirt, and black tie. He'd replaced his worn sneakers with a pair of shiny black paten leathers. His dark curly hair, however, was not to be tamed.

"Mrs. Porter, I'm glad to see you again," he said, rising to shake her hand. "I've got the results of your tests and I'd like to go over them with you. I'm glad to see you again, Miss Jennings. Please, take a seat, both of you." The look he gave me silently thanked me for accompanying Becky. I knew then that it was not going to be good news.

Taking our seats across from his desk, Becky and I sat rigid, waiting on him to begin. The soft rustle of the papers in his hands sounded like cymbals in the still room.

"Mrs. Porter. Becky," he began, folding his hands on the desk in front of him. He looked at her through eyes that, I was positive, had seen this scenario many, many times. "The results of your tests are as I feared. The CT scan shows us that you have stage 4 pancreatic cancer."

Cancer! Tears sprang to my eyes, and I swallowed hard. No! I felt like screaming, but I had to be strong for Becky. With no reaction, she sat still as a stone.

"What exactly does this mean?" I asked, fearing his answer.

"It means that she has a tumor in her pancreas," he replied. Stepping around his desk, he took the empty chair beside Becky and chose his words carefully. "Becky, the cancer has spread to your liver as well. This is why you're slightly jaundiced. I'm sorry, but there are few options at this stage."

"Wait," said Becky, looking at him. "If it's a tumor, why can't you simply remove it?"

"It's what we refer to as a nonresectable," he replied, reaching for the papers on his desk. "This means that the tumor has spread too far to remove. We can, however, try chemotherapy drugs, and there are some excellent ones on the market. Radiation is also an option."

With these words, the room grew deathly still as Dr. Sheffield gave Becky time to digest all that he'd thrown at her. A long moment passed in silence. Then in a wee small voice that could have belonged to a child, Becky spoke the very question that I could not put into words.

"Am I going to die?"

"I can't promise you that you won't, Becky," replied Dr. Sheffield, using the papers in his hands to steady their shaking. *His job had to be the worst job in the world*, I thought. The fact that he could still feel the impact of his own words told me of his caring nature. "What I can promise you is that we are going to do everything in our power to give you...time." I could tell he was choosing his words with caution.

"What are my chances?" asked Becky, her gaze dropping to her shaking hands in her lap. "And, please, don't tell me what I want to hear. I need you to be straight with me now, Dr. Sheffield."

"Becky," he said her name and waited until he had her full attention before speaking. When she made eye contact, he leaned toward her and took her hands into his. "In my honest professional opinion, your chances of being cured are...very slim if not impossible. The cancer has spread too far. We can try the chemo and radiation, but it will only make what time you have left unpleasant. The side effects are devastating, as you'll experience fatigue, vomiting, hair loss, as well as a risk of infection. The treatments will require days of recovery between sessions."

"And if I choose not to undergo the treatments?" asked Becky, softly. "What then?"

Dr. Sheffield hesitated a moment, and I could tell he was still struggling with his words. How do you tell someone, even a stranger, that death was imminent?

"At this point, my advice would be to go home and put your affairs in order," he said, softly. Standing, he carefully pulled her to her feet. "Look at each day as a great gift, Becky, and live it to the fullest. Surround yourself with friends and family. Go sailing. Take a drive to the mountains and revel in their timeless beauty. Don't hesitate to tell those important to you, that you love them. Don't dwell on your death, Becky Porter. Instead, dwell on your life and what time you have left."

"Isn't that like giving up?" asked Becky.

"No, it is not," he replied. "It's more like taking your life in your own hands. Most people depend on others around them to dictate how they should act, feel, and live. You must work because you have bills to pay. You have to mow your lawn or the neighbors will complain. You, being in the business of flowers, cater to the needs of your customers. Your bouquets help them to feel better, to have a beautiful wedding or to please someone they love. What I'm suggesting here is that you begin to think about yourself now. What does Becky need to make her happy? What does Becky want to do today that is fun?"

I felt like an intruder, a peeping tom, spying on an intimate moment between doctor and patient. At that moment, I wanted to bolt for the door. However, I stood my ground, for fear of distracting Becky. She needed to hear the doctor's precious words. When he'd finished, she stood in silence as if mulling over his lengthy answer. After a moment, she put into words the huge question hanging over the room like a ravenous vulture.

"How much time do I have?" she asked, steeling herself for his answer.

"Well, the answer to that question is never set in stone," he replied. "It depends on the patient. Each case is different. However, given the progression of the cancer, I'd say perhaps a month. You've kept yourself in great shape, so that may buy you a little extra time."

"Thank you, Dr. Sheffield," she said, picking up her purse from beside her chair. "Thank you for being honest with me. You've given me a lot to think about. I'll be in touch."

"You're stronger then you think, Becky Porter," he said. "I'll await your decision on what options you choose, if any. The nurse will give you a couple of prescriptions that will help with the pain, as well as some informative literature. Call me if you need anything."

"I will," said Becky, making her way to the door. "And please don't worry about me, Dr. Sheffield. I have Kathy to lean on. We've been friends since kindergarten, you know. She'll catch me should I fall."

"You know I will," I told her, my heart breaking in two. "We've always been there for each other."

"Till the end?" she whispered.

"Till the end," I whispered back.

Chapter 6

The ride home was long and silent. As I drove, Becky sat quietly staring out her window at the midmorning landscape. When we neared the square of town, I spotted the sign for Della's and slowed down.

"Becky, are you hungry?" I asked her, fully expecting her to berate me for thinking of food at a time like this.

"Surprisingly, I am," she said, turning to look at me. "Are you?"

"Always," I replied, turning into the nearest parking spot near the door.

As we slid into our usual booth, Patty spotted us and headed our way. "Hey, ladies," she said, smiling. "What can I get for you? Today's lunch special is the meat loaf and mashed potatoes. We also have our strawberry and walnut salad."

"I'll have the meatloaf and mashed potatoes, please," replied Becky, without hesitation. "And I'll have a slice of cherry pie with vanilla ice cream."

I was shocked. The Becky I knew would have deemed such a meal, a plate of cholesterol and carbs with wasted calories for dessert. But then again, she'd just been told that whatever she ate no longer mattered.

"I'll have the same," I said, handing Patty the menus.

"I've always loved this place," remarked Becky, smiling as she glanced around the diner. "I can remember when my parents would bring me here as a child. After they died in the car wreck, I stopped coming. My grandparents thought eating out was a waste of good money. Do you remember when you and I would come here after school? It's funny how you remember things when you're facing eternity."

"What do you remember?" I asked her, knowing her need to reminisce was good therapy.

"I remember, in high school, how we'd both flirt with Ronny Billings, hoping he'd come and sit with us," she giggled. "He never did. This is also where Michael brought me on our first date. Did you know that? Of course, you did."

As she spoke, I watched for any sign of a breakdown. Listening to the gaiety in her voice, I could have almost deemed the last three hours a bad dream. Was this denial on her part? If it was, I certainly didn't blame her.

When our meals arrived, Becky ate a few bites of the meatloaf and sat back. My appetite failed as well.

"Do you want me to just take you home, Becky?" I asked her, softly.

"Would you mind?" she said. "We can take this to go. I suddenly don't feel like eating. I just want to go back to the shop and tiptoe through my tulips."

"Sounds like a plan," I said, waving Patty over to our table.

"Kat, may I ask a favor of you?" asked Becky. "Can we please keep my...bad news, our secret for the moment? I'd like a chance to come to grips with my illness before our friends start asking me questions that I'm not yet prepared to answer."

"Absolutely, Becky," I said. "Mum's the word."

After paying the check, I drove her home. Pulling up in front of the flower shop, I offered to stay with her, but she declined.

"I just need to be alone now," she said, sighing heavily. "I have some tough decisions to make, and I need to think. And I do my best thinking while arranging my flowers. Thank you, Kat, for going with me to see the doctor."

"I'm afraid I wasn't much of a help, Becky," I said. "I wish I could have done more."

"You were beside me," she said, squeezing my hand. "You have always remained by my side, in times of great loss. You were here when I lost my family, and you held me together when Michael died. And, my dearest Kat, you're here now when I'm told I'm dying. You're a true friend, Kathleen Jennings. Now don't you go worrying about me. I'm going to be okay."

With that said, she retreated into her flower shop to work her way through yet another blow to her fragile heart. When I saw the OPEN sign blink to life, I knew she was indeed going to be okay, and I turned my old Cavalier toward the bookshop.

Becky Porter and I, have been best friends since 1956, when we both walked into Mrs. Walker's kindergarten class at the Cutter's Cove Elementary School. We played together as children, defended each other on the playground, and cried on each other's shoulder when the boy of our dreams turned out to be a jerk. When Becky was twenty-two it was me she asked to be her maid of honor when she walked down the aisle with her beloved Michael. Over the years, our friendship only deepened. In her middle twenties, I held her as she mourned the loss of her two unborn babies. She, in turn, stood by me when I lost my Grandpa Jake and kept me afloat through the difficult years of caring for my father, when he refused to love me only because I reminded him of someone he'd lost.

I never begrudged Becky for having the kind of love and happiness that I only dreamed of, for I loved her as a sister. She and Michael ran the flower shop together and made their living making people happy. Since I remained single, the three of us often did things together, yet I respected their need for privacy. As the decades silently slipped by us, Becky and I found ourselves leaning on each other's quiet strength. Then seven years ago, Michael died unexpectedly and I quickly became the strong one. I literally held Becky up at Dawson's Funeral Home, as the entire town showed up to pay their respects to a man they loved and to the woman who had stood beside him for thirty years. Now as we faced yet another crisis, I realized that the one constant in Becky's life, the one thing that had held steady through all of the storms she'd weathered, was her beloved flower shop. It still stands on the corner of Juniper Street as a monument to her family.

The Posey Pot flower shop, had been in Becky's family for three generations. Her maternal grandparents, Ernest and Eileen Stoker, had opened the shop in 1923 and there, in the small two-bedroom apartment over the shop, raised their two children. Cora Ann was born in 1926, a healthy and inquisitive child. Two years later, in 1928, her parents gave her a baby sister, Hannah, who brought sunshine and laughter to the dreary lives of the Stoker family. Cora loved Hannah with the heart of a protective big sister and watched over her whenever they left the safety of the flower shop. However, in 1932, while Cora was at school, tragedy struck their small family.

On a warm May morning, Cora's father had propped the shop door open to allow the breeze to cool the rooms. Four-year-old Hannah, left unattended, wandered out into the street through the open shop door. Spotting a traveling organ grinder and his pet monkey performing on the other side of the busy street, tiny Hannah went to investigate. With her attention focused on the funny little monkey, she failed to see the horse-drawn milk wagon making its rounds. The man atop the wagon pulled hard on the reins of his moving horse, but was unable to stop in time. Little Hannah, the sunshine of Cora's life, was trampled to death beneath the huge hooves of the frightened horse. Cora was devastated and blamed her father for her baby sister's death. He, in turn, clamped down on young Cora's activities, out of fear of losing his only remaining daughter.

When Cora graduated from high school in the spring of 1944, her father still maintained his firm grip on her, allowing her no freedoms. And, although she was eighteen, he forbid her from moving into her own place. As the years passed, young Cora worked the long hours demanded by the shop and dreamed of one day making her escape. Finally, on her twenty-seventh birthday, she revolted against her father's iron grip. Behind her parents back, she married a traveling shoe salesman named Arthur Fraser, whom she had only known a week. Now a married woman, she promptly quit the flower shop and went to live with her new husband in a small, two-bedroom saltbox style house at the edge of town. Here Cora and Arthur raised their own two children, Rebecca Ann, born in August of 1951, and Richard William, born in the spring of 1955.

Arthur's job as a traveling shoe salesman grew more difficult as the wave of new department stores opened up in the state. This eventually forced him to expand his territory to include the whole of the Eastern seaboard, often putting him on the road for weeks at a time. Cora, in her husband's absence, struggled to care for her home and two small children. When Richard turned three, he began suffering from terrible seizures, and Cora, fearing for her son, sought the advice of several specialists in brain disorders. Having no insurance, the medical bills soon began to pile up. Unable to pay them and remain in their home, she had no recourse but to take her children and return to the home of her parents above the florist shop. Her father, welcoming her back, promptly fired the hired help, and Cora filled the vacancy.

When Becky turned five in 1956, she entered kindergarten where we met for the first time. That same year, the shoe company that employed her father went out of business, and he returned home to join his family above the flower shop. With no skills other than selling shoes, the only job Arthur could find was working on a local fishing trawler making far less than what he'd earned as a salesman. Cora, now living once more under her father's strict rules, grew resentful and bitter at life's cruel turn.

When Richard's doctors failed to find the cause of his seizures, they released him with the prediction that he would "grow out of them." When three years passed with little change in Richard's condition, Cora doggedly held out hope of someday finding a cure. What Richard needed was a miracle. Then in the early spring of 1961, Cora read of a doctor in Boston who claimed he could treat the terrible seizures that kept Richard, now six, from starting school. A week later, Cora and Arthur left Becky in the care of her grandparents and took their son to meet his miracle.

The day of the appointment dawned cold with freezing rain, making the journey difficult. Once in Boston, they waited all afternoon before finally getting in to see the doctor. The weather outside only worsened as the hours passed. No one would ever know if Richard found his miracle that day, for tragedy struck just after nightfall as the family was leaving the city. The police report stated only that a large delivery truck, sliding out of control on the black ice, had slammed into the Fraser's ancient pickup truck, crushing them against an embankment. When the state police informed Becky that her family was dead, she was inconsolable. Knowing her pain after the death of my own mother four years earlier, we mourned our losses together, thus cementing our friendship. Over the years, we came to depend on each other's strength to navigate the storms of our youth and beyond. She was my rock, and I, in turn, was hers. Now Becky was in need of my strength once more, and I was determined to be there for her until the end.

Returning to the bookshop, I spent the second half of my day packaging up books to be mailed to online customers. By the time I left for home at four, my clothes were sticking to me and my feet felt as if they were encased in cement. Turning on the car's radio, I caught the tail end of the weather report for the rest of the week. They were predicting unusually warm weather with a chance of thunderstorms. This was bad news for Ricky Taylor, the boy who mowed my yard every Wednesday. He was a good kid, and I hated to see him get behind. For him, a thunderstorm meant lost revenue. He'd recently graduated from Cutter High and was heading for college in the fall. The money he earned mowing lawns, I knew, would ease his burden of purchasing his textbooks. If a success, Cutter's Cove would be getting another dentist in a few years. *Now this is a cause I can get behind,* I thought as I turned onto Pebble Bay Road.

Arriving at the cottage, I was surprised to see that Ricky had taken care of business a day early. He'd mowed the yard, and the bushes were neatly trimmed. He must have listened to the same weather report. Climbing out of the hot car, I longed for a cool glass of the iced tea I knew awaited me in my ancient refrigerator. Before going inside, I walked over to the edge of the yard to peer out at the ocean.

The predicted storm was already brewing out at sea, and the waves were raging inland and breaking on the rocks below. The sea always seemed to know how I was feeling and matched my moods. Gauging the distance of the thunderhead on the horizon, I decided there was time for the picnic on the rocks I'd promised Mussolini, if we hurried.

The rest of the week seemed to fly fast, and before I knew it, the weekend had arrived. I awoke early on Saturday and drove over to see Becky. I respected her need to be alone, and for the past three days, it was hard not to live on her doorstep. My concern, that the news of her diagnosis had sent her into a spiraling funk, had me on edge. After making my way up the back steps, I knocked on her door.

Getting no answer, I had a sneaking suspicion where I'd find her. Retracing my steps, I let myself in the back door of the flower shop, nearly frightening her out of her wits when I suddenly appeared in the doorway. She was just closing the door to the cooler when she saw me.

"Yikes!" she screeched, clutching her chest. "Kat, you nearly sent me into the unknown!"

"Sorry," I said, steadying her. "I didn't find you upstairs."

"No, I'm downstairs," she said. "I need to keep busy."

She was, in my opinion, taking it on the chin, as only Becky would.

"Well, I had hoped you were taking it easy today," I said, leaning on the counter. Buckets of fresh cut flowers littered the floor. "I was worried about you, despite your telling me to do otherwise. And not talking to you for three days was not easy, my friend."

"I needed the time to think about all that the doctor heaped onto my plate," she said, blowing a strand of blond hair away from her face. "Thank you for giving me that time. I know how hard it must have been for you."

"It was excruciating!" I exclaimed. "You're not open, are you? It's Saturday."

"No, I'm not open," she replied. "I just need to do a little catch-up, that's all."

I so wanted to ask what she had decided to do, but I also knew that she would tell me when she was ready.

"I have a surprise for you," I said, handing her a scrap of paper.

"What's this?" she asked.

"It's my new telephone number," I said, smiling. "I finally had a phone installed."

"Well, it is about time, Kat," she said, pinning it to her message board behind the counter. "It's time you stepped into the new millennium."

"I'm about to make quite a few changes in my life," I said.

"I'm glad to hear that," she commented. "It's never too late to start something new. Now when are you going to get a cell phone?"

"One step at a time, please," I said, dropping my nose into a large bouquet of white roses, sitting on her counter. "White roses are my favorite."

"Kat, are you only checking up on me, or are you free for the morning?" Becky asked. Stepping away from the counter, she reached for a large white bucket filled with day lilies. "My order of fresh flowers just came, and Mr. Preston is out sick. I have to get them into the cooler as soon as possible. If you help me, I can take it easy in half the time."

"You are amazing, Becky," I said, picking up a bucket of large daisies with faces as wide as a dessert plate. "I'm here as long as you need me."

"Good," she said, leading the way to the cooler. "I also have to make a large delivery to the new hotel out on Gull Road this morning. You can drive the van."

The delivery on Gull Road took us most of the morning, and we chatted as if the dire news of Becky's illness never existed. At noon, we stopped at Della's for lunch and a tall glass of iced tea. The lunch special was a cheeseburger, fries, and a drink. Becky, feeling a bit tired, wasn't hungry, so she drank her iced tea and took her cheeseburger to go. When we returned to the flower shop, she pulled her large book containing pictures of her flower displays from under the counter and spread it out on the table.

"Surely you're not going to work after this morning's errands," I commented.

"Relax," she said. "I have a couple coming in at two to pick out the flowers for their wedding. After they leave, I promise I'll retreat upstairs to rest. Will that please you?"

"Immensely," I said. "If you need me, just call me. I'll be here before you can say Jack Robinson."

"Who is that, by the way?" she asked.

"I haven't a clue," I replied, heading for the back door. "Get some rest."

Leaving Becky to her business, I stopped at the Food King for milk, bread, and a #50 bag of kibbles for Mussolini. After a morning of manual labor and shopping, I decided to treat myself to a large cup of chocolate ice cream with sprinkles, so I stopped at

Carl Wyndom's ice cream shop to pick up my reward before turning for home.

As I unlocked the cottage door, I heard the telephone ringing in the kitchen. It felt like an intrusion, and I hesitated to answer it. But then again, it could be Becky. Dropping my purse on the table, I ran to pick it up.

"Hello," I said.

"Hello, Miss Jennings," said a low male voice with just the hint of an accent.

"Marcus, how are you?" I asked, with genuine warmth.

"I'm good," he said. "And you?"

"Never better," I replied, slipping out of my shoes to quiet my aching feet.

"I just happen to be calling you from my recently installed wall telephone," he said, proudly. "I felt it was time that I embraced the modern era. My dependency on young Douglas to deliver any messages to you at this point in our relationship could be construed as awkward, would it not?"

"It would indeed," I said, laughing. "Wait. How did you get my new number?

"I had to do a bit of finagling to acquire it, I assure you," he said, chuckling. "Actually, I noticed Becky was in the flower shop, so I stopped in to inquire how she was feeling today. She just happened to mention that you now had a telephone. Of course, I had to promise her the moon and stars before she would divulge your phone number to me."

"I'm sure you did," I said. "But knowing Becky as I do, I'm more inclined to believe that she flagged you down in the middle of the street and insisted that you take it."

"You're close," he chuckled. "The reason I called was that I was wondering if you'd care to have dinner with me this evening. Can you meet me at Della's at seven? I have something to tell you."

"That sounds wonderful," I said, his invitation coming like a balm to my soul. "I'll see you there. And, Marcus, thank you for asking. I've missed you."

"I've missed you too, Kathy," he said. "Time for me will indeed stand still until we meet again. The minutes are but tokens that vanish into eternity like frightened birds. Until tonight?"

"Until tonight," I replied, smiling to myself as I replaced the receiver.

I wandered into the sitting room and stood looking out of the bay window at the sea. It was calm today, and I felt my jumbled nerves settle. My heart wanted to soar with pure happiness with the fact that Marcus wanted to see me again. But how could I allow it to do so when my best friend was dying? I felt like my heart was becoming the prized object in a game of emotional tug of war. Who would win? Sorrow or happiness? *Why can't I have both?* I thought.

At six, I dressed for my dinner date with Marcus. Since it was at Della's, I chose a red silk blouse and a pair of casual black slacks. Sliding a pair of gold hoops through my ears, I dropped its matching chain around my neck and stood back. I smiled at my reflection in the oval mirror. Classy but casual, Becky would say. After stepping into a pair of black comfortable pumps, I hurried to the kitchen and dialed Becky's phone number. When she took a moment to answer, I grew concerned.

"Hello," she said, in a weak voice. "Who is this?"

"It's Kathy," I replied, thinking she sounded far off. "Are you okay? Did you rest?"

"I did," she said, brightening. "I feel much better."

"Have you eaten?" I asked.

"I'm not really hungry at the moment," she said. "I have the sandwich from lunch at Della's should the mood hit me."

"Please eat, Becky," I encouraged her. "You have to keep up your strength."

"Perhaps I'll eat it later," she said. "I guess I'll have to start pacing myself now."

"That'll be a first," I said, smiling. "What are your plans for this evening? Something low-key, I hope."

"I'm planning on writing a couple of letters," she replied. "And you?"

"I'm actually having dinner with Marcus in an hour," I said, cringing at the tone of happiness I knew Becky was bound to notice. "He asked me to meet him at Della's at seven."

"I'm so happy for you, Kat," she said. "He's a great guy. I'm glad that you have him in your life. It makes me feel better about leaving you alone. Now go and have a great time. I forbid you to worry about me. I'm just fine."

"I'll make an effort," I said. "Becky, may I tell Marcus of your test results. I know he'll guard your secret with the utmost discretion."

"Oh yes, Kathy, do," she replied. "Marcus must know, as we may need his help in the near future. Besides, he'll be someone for you to turn to when you're feeling sad."

"I love you, Becky," I said, my emotions tightening my throat. "You'll always be my best friend."

"Till the end?" she asked.

"Till the end," I replied, before hanging up.

An hour later, I pulled into the parking lot of Della's. Not seeing Marcus's red Mustang, I was glad that I was early. It gave me a few minutes to collect myself. Finding a booth, I checked my makeup and waited for him to arrive. When the bell above the door sounded a moment later, I looked up just in time to see him step through the door. I felt my heart skip a beat as he stood glancing around the diner, looking for me. He was indeed a very handsome man. I now took to carrying my singing sea stone in my purse. Silly, I know. But I wanted it with me each time I was with Marcus, for he was my proof that the magic of my stone was real.

This evening, he was wearing a dark-gray sports jacket over a crisp white dress shirt. He'd replaced his usual dark dress slacks with a pair of worn blue jeans with slightly flared legs. I smiled, when I saw the snakeskin cowboy boots on his feet. *Sexy.* Spotting me, he smiled and made his way over to my table. My heart melted within me.

"Hello, Kathy," he said, sliding in across from me. "Red is your color."

"Thank you, Marcus," I said, returning his smile. I genuinely needed his good humor this evening.

"Albert has informed me that you accompanied Becky to Portland for the results of her tests on

Tuesday," he said, reaching over to cup my hand. "I hope they revealed nothing serious." When I failed to answer him right away, he squeezed my hand. "Am I to assume the news is not good?"

"Oh, Marcus," I said, trying to hold back my tears. Knowing that I had Becky's permission to tell him of the diagnosis, I decided to tell him everything. "She…has stage 4 pancreatic cancer. She's so strong, Marcus. She's taking it better than I am, actually."

"Cancer!" he said, shaking his head. "It's a very ominous and greedy opponent, indeed. I've lost many a friend to its ravenous appetite. Where is she now?"

"She's at home, above the shop," I replied. "She has to make a decision whether she will take a stand and fight or simply walk boldly into the sunset."

"What is the prognosis?" he asked.

"Dr. Sheffield says the cancer has spread to her other organs," I replied. "And that the treatments, though bravely attempted, would only fill her remaining time with horrible side effects."

"How long does the doctor say she has?" he asked.

"He's given her perhaps a month," I replied. "That isn't much time when you're faced with your own death. She's already showing outward signs of her illness. I thought I'd stop over later and take her a bowl of Della's clam chowder. It's her favorite."

"Well, perhaps we can do that now," he suggested. "I'll wager she's not eaten. That kind of news has a tendency to weaken one's appetite."

"She's already skipping meals, which is not like her," I said. "I talked her into accepting a cheeseburger this afternoon and I'll bet she hasn't eaten it."

"Well, we'll soon fix that," he said, waving the waitress over. "We'll order dinner and take it to her."

Taking our orders to go, we walked the short distance to the flower shop. Marcus, sensing my sadness, reached over and enclosed my hand within his own. It felt warm, and I found comfort in this simple gesture. Reaching the rear of flower shop, we climbed the backstairs and knocked on Becky's door. When she answered, she was genuinely glad to see us.

"Pardon the intrusion, Rebecca," said Marcus, giving her a slight bow. "We thought that perhaps you could use a friendly visit. We came bearing Della's clam chowder," he added, holding the container up for her to see.

"Oh, it's my favorite!" she exclaimed, stepping back to give us room to enter.

As we stepped in, she switched on the small overhead fixture in the middle of the kitchen ceiling, filling the room with soft light. The small apartment hadn't changed since the first time I visited it, fifty-five years earlier. Its small teak-paneled kitchen still retained its warm coastal charm. I could see her mother's yellow-print dishes displayed behind the etched glass in the faded white kitchen cupboards. The small wooden table dominating the center of the room held a burning scented candle, and I caught a whiff of sandalwood in the air. Glancing through the small arched doorway into the living room, I was not surprised to see two new hanging gardens in front of the large bay window. Knowing her fate, I knew Becky would surround herself with living things. Several new rugs covered the worn but familiar hardwood floors.

"Please sit," said Becky, pulling out a chair from the table. "I'll get us each a glass of sparkling water. I'm afraid that's all I have."

"Sparkling water would do nicely, indeed," said Marcus, placing the food on the table. "Seafood demands a nice house white to enhance its flavor."

"Then I am the perfect host," said Becky. She amazed me at times with her ability to look past the tragic and see only the blessing. That was why I loved this woman. She reminded me of my Grandpa Jake, with her fortitude for navigating through painful situations. She was indeed the wind beneath my wings. How was I ever going to survive her imminent death?

As we sipped our water, her condition seemed to hover in the small room like a circus elephant. I made small talk, allowing her to bring it up when she was ready.

"So have you purchased your book on *The Art of Engineering in Ancient Egypt*?" I asked Marcus.

"I have," he replied. "It's even more interesting to read now that I am not forced to write a dissertation on it afterward."

"I thought you were in publishing?" asked Becky. "Did you study engineering as well?"

"I did," replied Marcus. "My first year of college, I majored in engineering. However, that all changed after reading a friend's manuscript. I enjoyed it so much that I encouraged him to get it published. What happened next changed the direction of my life."

"How so?" I asked.

"When I saw the cruel and feckless way the world of well-known publishers handled Daniel's work, I was outraged," replied Marcus. "They were willing to ignore a young man's hard work for the most ridiculous of reasons. One refused to read the manuscript solely because Daniel had typed it on the wrong kind of paper. Another thought his character was too dull and could Daniel possibly gift him with a superpower. They obviously had no clue as to the seriousness of either the book or its ability to draw the reader into the world of the story."

"What was the subject of his story?" asked Becky, intrigued.

"It was his father's memoirs," replied Marcus. "At a young age, Daniel's father, Gerard, finds himself stranded in war-torn London after the blitzkrieg. That is not light reading, and it certainly does not demand any superpowers!"

Seeing Marcus's obvious distress over his friend's rejection, I thought it best to lighten the moment. "Well, Marcus, a superpower could have helped his situation immensely," I said.

"She's right," said Becky, picking up on my cue. "He could have escaped the enemy by leaping over the tower of London in a single bound."

"Or he could have used his X-ray vision to find his way through the rubble." On a more serious note, I added, "Did your friend ever get his work published?"

"He did, indeed," replied Marcus, relaxing with a smile. "I'm pleased to report, they published Daniel's manuscript in 1969. He was a very grateful soul. You may have heard of his book, *Terror on the Thames: London's Blitzkrieg* by Daniel Osgood Rathbone."

We both shook our heads. "Sorry," I said. "In 1969, we were rocking at Woodstock, being amazed by the guitar playing of Jimi Hendrix and cheering on America's efforts to put the first man on the moon."

"You forgot to mention the war in Vietnam," said Marcus, quietly. "Too many of our youth were dying in the jungles of Southeast Asia without having lived first."

Becky, seeing this as a perfect opportunity to bring up her cancer, dove right in. "Well, I have lived a good life," she said, smiling. "And I have no regrets over anything. Did Kathy tell you the results of my tests?"

"She did," said Marcus, softly. "She said that you have cancer. Please, Becky, if you'd rather not talk about it, I would understand completely."

"Nonsense," said Becky, taking a sip of her water before continuing. "I want you to know what I'm dealing with, Marcus. I have stage 4 pancreatic cancer, and I've been given mere weeks to live."

"What are your options?" asked Marcus.

"For me, there are no options," replied Becky. "I am unwilling to spend what little time I have remaining, fighting a battle with no possible victory.

Therefore, I'm not going to take the chemo drugs or the radiation treatments. There is no cure for my cancer, so I'm going to take the doctor's advice and spend my last days doing the things I love."

"It's early yet, Becky," I told her, not surprised at her decision. "There still may be a way to—"

"Not for me," she said. "Don't be sad, Kathy. I'm not. Well, perhaps a little. I'm not going to be able to run my 5K this year. It was to be my last race. I wish I could borrow a body for just one day. Then I'd be able to run my final race for all those kids out there who suffer with juvenile diabetes. My heart was set on running."

Borrow a body, I thought. What a silly thing to ask for. Then her meaning touched my numbed senses and an idea struck me.

"You can borrow my body, Becky," I said, with conviction. "I'll run your race for you. Winning is off the table, of course, and I'm bound to finish somewhere down near the bottom of the list. However, I'll run the race for you."

"You'd do that for me?" she asked, looking genuinely shocked. "You hate any kind of exercise."

"That's true," I said, grinning at her. "However, it's for a good cause, remember? Of course, you'll have to help me get ready for it. We haven't much time, you know."

"Don't remind me," said Becky, replenishing our glasses with sparkling water. "I have just become a connoisseur of time. Let's raise our glasses to Kathy, my body double. Together, we're going to run for all those kids out there with juvenile diabetes."

"Perhaps we'll just call it 'walking kind of fast' for juvenile diabetes," I said, tapping my glass to hers and Marcus's. "I'm not sure how fast I'm going to run. But I'm going to give it my best shot."

"That's my girl," said Marcus, giving me a smile that melted my heart and made me blush clear to my toes. Glancing over at Becky, I smiled at her knowing wink.

"But first, you'll have to go see Doc Ferguson," she insisted, looking at me over her eyeglasses. "We wouldn't want you to start anything strenuous without his approval."

"Good idea," added Marcus. "Your health and well-being, Kathy, are very important to us."

"I agree," stated Becky. "So we'll leave the final decision up to the doc, okay?"

"Okay," I said, once again tapping my glass to hers. "Now let us dive into this food with gusto!"

"Gusto?" questioned Becky. "Perhaps we'll just call it 'wading in with good intentions.'"

After eating, we left Becky to finish writing her letters. Marcus and I, hand in hand, walked back to Della's to retrieve our cars. It was still early so we decided to take a walk on the beach below the boardwalk before heading home. The night was warm with a cool breeze blowing off the ocean. Removing our shoes, we rolled up our pant legs and walked in the surf. When a chill swept over me, I felt my body shiver. Sensing my distress, Marcus encircled me with his arm, bringing to me a warmth I'd never felt before. Knowing his sincerity, I leaned into his embrace.

"Oh, before I forget," he said, pulling a scrap of paper from his shirt pocket, "here's my new telephone number. Call it anytime, Kathleen."

"What changed your mind about a telephone?" I asked him.

"I now have someone I wish to call," he mused.

"Marcus, you said earlier that you had something to tell me," I reminded him.

"Oh yes," said Marcus, stopping to look at me, "I'd almost forgotten. I have a bit of good news to share. Albert has asked me to accompany him to Ireland."

"Ireland!" I exclaimed. "Why would Albert want you to take him to Ireland?"

"He's made the decision to return his wife's ashes to her family," he replied. "He wants to entomb them in her family crypt."

"Oh yes, he must do that," I said, thinking back to my birthday when Albert voiced his regret over not having returned his Kathleen to her family. "I only recently learned of his regret that she died so far away from her home and family. Have you agreed to take him?"

"I have," he replied. "The whole idea came to light one afternoon as we sat discussing a rare book. In conversation, he spoke to me of his desire to take his wife's ashes home and of his inability to make the trip alone. I understood his dilemma and offered to accompany him. We were planning to go the end of August, but family business calls me home to England as soon as possible. Two birds with one stone, as they say. Of course, while I'm in the UK, I'm going to visit my childhood home in England."

"You're homesick?" I asked, feeling a panic seize me. Losing Becky, I knew, was going to take me back into that dark place of mourning. Losing Marcus, however, could very well destroy me. My soul, I was sure, would not survive the loss of both. I turned and looked out to sea for my comfort. Tonight, she had none to offer.

"Kathy, are you okay?" asked Marcus, with a look of true concern.

I turned to face him. "Marcus, are you thinking of leaving Cutter's Cove?" I asked, knowing that my life depended on his answer. "Are you thinking of returning to England to live?"

"Oh heaven's no, my dearest Kathy," he said, pulling me into his embrace. "I simply have a bit of family business to attend to. My uncle Hamish has passed and he's left me an inheritance. I simply need to return home and meet with his solicitor about settling his estate." I nearly collapsed in his arms as relief swept over me like a warm blanket.

"You have my condolences," I said.

"Thank you," he said into my hair. "Cutter's Cove is my home now, Kathy. I plan on staying here till death do us part."

"I'm so happy to hear you say that, Marcus," I said, throwing caution to the wind. "I am about to lose my best friend in this world, and I'll need to lean on your wisdom and strength. I need you, Marcus."

"And I'm here, Kathy," he said. Placing his right index finger beneath my chin, he gently lifted my face. I waited, as if standing on the edge of a precipice, for him to touch his lips to mine. When he did, I felt my body slip over the edge and tumble into the sweet fire of passion. I knew at that moment that I was falling in love with Marcus Stone. Was he feeling the same? Now was when I needed the magic of my sea stone more than the very breath in my body. He had to love me in return for my life to continue. He simply had to!

That night, as I crawled into bed, I reached for the worn copy of *Romeo and Juliet*. Even though I'd found the story line difficult to follow with its medieval dialect, I did find the characters interesting. And when Juliet finally met her Romeo, I could, at last, relate to her feelings of sheer joy as she fell hopelessly in love with him. How sad that her first love turned out to be the son of her family's mortal enemy, Lord Montague. My heart went out to her as I read her words of anguish.

"O Romeo, Romeo!" she cried from her lonely balcony. "Wherefore art thou Romeo? Deny thy father and refuse thy name! Or, if thou wilt not, be but sworn my love, and I'll no longer be a Capulet." How she must have anguished over having to choose between her family and her heart. Closing the book, I switched off the light and lay in the darkness. How blessed I was in the knowledge that falling in love with Marcus would not violate some ancient family code. I drifted off to sleep with Marcus's image in my mind and the sound of the sea whispering to my heart, "love is but the beginning".

I was awake early the next morning, despite it being Sunday. Wandering over to my bedroom window, I looked at the sea below. The sky was clear, giving the promise of a pleasant day. As I walked into the kitchen, I caught the far-off sound of a church bell calling the faithful to worship. I was just setting my teapot to boil when my new telephone began to jingle on the wall. It was nice to, at last, be connected to the outside world.

"Hello," I said.

"Good morning, Kat," greeted Becky, sounding upbeat. "I'd like to ask you for a huge favor. Prepare yourself."

"Ask me anything, my friend," I replied, glad that she was sounding better.

"Will you go to church with me this morning?" she asked, hesitantly.

I was shocked at her request, for she hadn't set foot in the place in years. For that matter, neither had I. "I'll understand if you decline," she added.

"Nonsense!" I exclaimed, shoving my beef with the Almighty aside for Becky's sake. "If attending church is your desire on this beautiful Sunday morning, then we shall go."

"Thanks, Kat," she said, sounding genuinely relieved. "I know how difficult returning to the church will be for you. However, I simply don't have the courage to go alone."

"Then we must go together," I said, swallowing hard. I had my own reasons for staying away. But if Becky needed me to go with her, then I would do so. "Count me in."

"Wonderful," she said. "How about the two of us old wounded souls go and face God together? Come to the shop, we'll walk over together."

"I'll see you at nine," I said.

My surprise at Becky's request to attend church was genuine. Her desire to return to the church of her childhood, was for her, a definite change of heart. I knew she still blamed God for the death of her parents and baby brother on that dark and icy road so many years ago. After their deaths, her grandfather Earnest, fearing for her soul, forced young Becky to attend church with him despite her loud objections. Before bed, each night, her grandfather would force her read the Bible aloud to him and grill her on its interpretation. If Becky didn't know the answers to his questions, he berated her, accusing her of being the devil's child. She would have rebelled if not for the gentle urgings from her Grandma Eileen, who, despite having her own beef with God over the death of her precious little Hannah, wished to keep peace in the house.

When Becky was fourteen, she lost her only ally when Grandma Eileen died suddenly. After cooking Thanksgiving dinner for her family, Eileen suffered a massive stroke and died within the week. Becky's world turned dark as her grandfather pulled in her reins even tighter. She spoke to me often of running away to the big city, but I managed to talk her out of it. Knowing that a young girl from a small town could disappear in a strange environment, I urged her to stay in Cutter's Cove. Thankfully, she'd listened. However, life was hard for her without her grandmother's encouragement. When her grandfather died, two years later, Becky expressed no sadness at his passing. After his funeral, the townsfolk wondered what was to become of the flower shop now that the founders were dead. Becky soon put an end to their questions. Having grown up in the shop, she knew everything there was to know about its day to day operations. Therefore, despite being only sixteen, she engaged the help of a local banker and, with his help, kept the shop going.

On her own and free of her grandfather's demanding ways and harsh Bible teachings, Becky turned her back on his church, vowing never to return. Now, here she was, willing to put aside her differences with the Almighty and return to the very place that had caused her such grief as a child. How could I refuse her? She was going to need more than just my support to see her through her illness. Was she, at last, ready to face the God she had turned her back on so many years ago? Acquiescing, I pasted on a happy face and joined her on the worn front steps of the old church. Was I, myself, ready to face God after all these years? I was about to find out.

Chapter 7

The Cutter's Cove Church of God was an icon from my past. As a child, I had faithfully attended its weekly services with my Grandpa Jake. After his death, I, too, felt a separation from the loving God of my childhood, as I placed the death of the one person who had given my young life warmth and love squarely on His shoulders. After my grandfather's funeral, I vowed never to step through its doors again. Now here we both stood, two hurt and damaged souls willing to meet God halfway. Looking up at the church, it seemed much smaller then when I was a child. Erected in 1897, its builders had constructed its rough stone exterior from stones lovingly gathered from the rugged coastline. Darkened now from years of Northern winters, it had proved its divine protection by withstanding several violent nor'easters, that in years past, had damaged some of the newer buildings.

Glancing over at Becky, she appeared apprehensive yet determined. "Are you sure you're ready for this?" I asked, reaching over to squeeze her hand.

"I'm sure, Kat," she said, softly. "I've been waiting for a very long time to confront God on His own turf. Now, that I'm facing eternity, the time has come for me to face Him and tell Him how the loss of my family has made me distrust Him. Not to mention what my grandfather did to me in His name. You, too, have your own demons to purge, girlfriend. I'll understand if you don't want to face them at this moment."

"If not now, when?" I asked her. "No, you and I have faced many a trial together, Becky, and triumphed. We'll face this one together as well."

"Then shall we gird ourselves and face Him together?" she said, linking her arm with mine.

"Forward," I said.

"Forward," repeated Becky, as we stepped over the threshold to face a God whom we both secretly hoped did not hold a grudge.

Since childhood, I had in my mind this image of what I thought God surely looked like. When I was six, Grandpa Jake introduced me to a God in flowing white robes, long silver hair and beard, and the kind of face that spoke of a heart of love. To further my spiritual upbringing, he took me to Sunday service every week and read to me from his Bible. Together, we prayed that God would melt my father's heart and allow his baby girl to love him. Our prayers went unanswered, and after Grandpa Jake's death, I stopped praying. Left to care for a man who hated me, my image of God took on a sinister persona. I began to picture Him as a vengeful old man who looked at me the same way my father did. I harbored no hope that this image would ever change. That is, until now.

As we made our way into a back pew, we did so hoping to go unnoticed. Around fifty people were already seated and waiting for the service to begin. As soft music filled the sanctuary, others were slowly making their way in through the doors. Becky sat quietly beside me, deep in thought as she picked at a loose thread on the small brown purse in her lap. Glancing around, I saw Nicholas Patterson chatting with Carl Wyndom from the ice cream store. As the music played, I closed my eyes and allowed the soft cords of "Rock of Ages" to take me back to another Sunday, long ago, when I sat here with my Grandpa Jake. He knew every hymn by heart and seldom used a hymnal. With gentle patience, he'd direct me to the correct page and help me to follow along to the words. I now hummed softly to the well-loved tune.

"This was my Grandma Eileen's favorite hymn," whispered Becky. "I miss her so much. Perhaps, I'll see her soon. I hope she recognizes me, for I've aged a few years."

Her words brought tears to my eyes, and I wished I could say something to make this easier on her. Instead, I reached over and squeezed her hand, reassuring her, as always, that I was here for her. It's all that I knew to do.

When the music faded out, a very handsome man stepped into the pulpit. He looked to be in his early forties and was unlike any preacher I ever remembered. His dark hair hung slightly over his ears, and he'd replaced the black suit and tie from my youth with an open-necked white dress shirt and blue jeans. I knew from the bulletin that his name was Pastor Kevin Diamond, and his appearance made me painfully aware that I had been out of church for too long.

"Well, I'm thrilled to see a fresh face in the pulpit," whispered Becky. "The previous pastor, I heard, was eighty when he finally retired. He kept losing his train of thought, and the subject of his sermons was anyone's guess."

"This one is too young to be a pastor," I commented. "What can he possibly know about delivering a sermon? Wisdom comes with age, in my opinion." The young pastor was soon to make me eat those words.

Pastor Kevin, as he preferred, was amazing. He obviously loved his vocation as he spoke from his heart. His words were like a glass of cool water to a man dying of thirst. I heard nothing of the harsh words and fiery rhetoric preached in my youth. There were no loud declarations of what God would do to the unsuspecting sinner if He had the chance. This man spoke of God as if He were a close friend who lived next door. He shared that God loved all of His children and that we could trust Him for our every need.

"No need is too small for our God," he said, holding up his Bible. "He states that right here in His word. 'Come unto me all that labor and are heavy laden, and I will give you rest.' Rely on His promises, folks. Many of you are carrying around great burdens. Perhaps you're suffering financial worries. Give them to God. Perhaps it's a great burden for a lost family member. Give that loved one to God. Perhaps you—" Suddenly, Pastor Kevin stopped talking and his eyes slowly panned the sanctuary. "I sense a great need in this room. Someone here among us, is carrying a burden so heavy that it has brought them here, to God's house, after a very long absence. Give it to God, my child. His shoulders are strong enough to bear even the heaviest of trials."

Beside me, I heard Becky moan slightly. Glancing over at her, I saw the tears coursing unchecked down her face. My heart went out to her. How was I to help her through this? What could I possibly do? It was at that moment that I heard God speak to me for the first time in many years. "Pray for her," He said. "I'll do the rest." Not thinking, I slid off the pew and onto my knees. My body began to tingle, and a great warmth rushed over me.

Becky, sensing the change in me, slid to the floor beside me. "I heard Him too," she whispered, taking my hand. Bowing our heads, we did as He bid.

"Father, I'm so sorry for blaming you for all my pain," I said, softly. "Help me to remember all that my Grandpa Jake taught me about You when I was a little girl. Please lift me out of this darkness so that I can help Becky through her illness."

Beside me, Becky continued softly. "Please, God, forgive my foolish pride. I'm not afraid to die, Father, I only fear the unknown. Please help me fall upon You when I'm afraid. Prepare me for what lies ahead."

"Amen," said a soft male voice. Startled, we both looked up. Pastor Kevin stood above us, his eyes filled with love and compassion. Glancing around the room, I saw every head turned our way.

"You have come to the right place, Becky Porter," he said. "Here you will find guidance through whatever you are facing." Taking our right hands, he helped us to our feet.

Swiftly, everyone gathered around us, welcoming us back into the fold. I felt the weight of nearly five decades of anguish and resentment toward God, melt away like snow on a summer's day.

Becky fell into the arms of the pastor, as her own demons fled back into the darkness. "I'm dying," she said, softly. "I have cancer, and there's no hope for me."

"There's always hope, my child," said a small gray-haired woman beside her. Laying her wrinkled and boney hand on Becky's arm, she leaned in. "My name is Hilda Grant, and I just turned ninety-seven. I, too, will leave this world soon. Here, you'll learn how to look forward to heaven."

"Thank you, Mrs. Grant," said Becky tearfully, as she glanced around at the sea of smiling faces surrounding her. "I'm going to be okay."

"We both will be okay," I told her, pulling her into an embrace. "We gave God His day in court, and He pardoned us. How cool is that?"

After the service, we walked arm in arm back to Becky's apartment. My soul felt as light as a feather. Suddenly, I knew how to help Becky through her ordeal.

"Becky, I want you to come and live with me," I said, stopping to look at her. "I want to take care of you. I know that it's early yet. But when the time comes, I want you know that you have a place to go."

"Oh, Kat, thank you," she said, tears welling up in her eyes. "I'm going to take you up on your offer. I can't think of a better place to…die…than beside the sea, in the care of a friend."

"Then it's settled," I said. "When you're ready, just give the word."

"I will," she promised. "And, don't forget to call the doctor."

The following morning before work, I walked the beach with a lighter step. Gone were the ghosts that haunted me, demanding from me their pound of flesh. As I looked out to sea, I welcomed the day Becky would come to live at Sea Breeze Cottage. Bittersweet was the knowledge that it would be short-lived. How do you say good-bye to a lifelong friend?

With My help, that voice deep within me whispered.

"Thank you, God," I whispered in return. "I'll need You near." As I watched Mussolini play among a flock of sandpipers, I hummed the melody to the song "I Need Thee Every Hour."

Arriving at the bookshop, I unlocked the front door and switched on the OPEN sign. After a rush of customers, I finally got the chance at nine thirty to make the call to Dr. Ferguson's office. When the receptionist answered, I recognized her voice.

"Hello, Pamela," I said, thinking of the small petite blond-haired woman on the other end of the line. I recalled her recent wedding, held in a small white gazebo on the town square. Becky had asked me to assist her with the decorations. I was all too happy to help as I liked Pamela and the young man she'd married. "How was the honeymoon?" I asked.

"It was fabulous!" she exclaimed. "The Smokey Mountains are just coming alive in the spring. You really must make a trip to see them."

"I'll do that," I promised. "I'm calling this morning because I need to see Doc Ferguson about…a project that I'm about to start. When do you have an opening?" I held my breath, praying silently that the earliest appointment would be for sometime next week.

"This is your lucky day, Kathy," said Pamela. "I just happen to have a cancellation for two thirty this afternoon. Can I pencil you in?"

"That soon, huh?" I said, with waning enthusiasm. "Yes, I'll take it. Thank you, Pamela."

After hanging up, I wondered just what old Doc Ferguson was going to think when I informed him that I was about to start jogging. At my age, I'd better be prepared for him to drop to the floor and roll around in a fit of laughter. Then again, was I prepared to have him deem me too old to take on something so dangerous? I hoped this was not the case. I just couldn't let Becky down after giving her my word. Then another thought struck me. Was I prepared to have Marcus think of me as too old for any strenuous activities?

"I am not that old!" I muttered to myself. *Age is only a state of mind, and I can do anything I put my mind to doing. Well, perhaps sky diving was a bit of a stretch,* I thought, smiling to myself. Glancing at the shop calendar, I noted the date. Monday, June 20. Oh my, was it really the third week of June already? The third Monday of each month, I did my monthly balancing of the shop's financial books. How fast the days had flown by just since my birthday. As I pulled out the shop's faded green ledger, I thought about all that had happened since I turned sixty. My finding the singing sea stone had turned out to be that proverbial rock that started an avalanche. Meeting

Marcus soon after, as well as the memory of our first date, still left me breathless. I was amazed at how quickly my life had gone from lonely to living in such a short span of time. Then, there was Becky's illness.

The sound of Albert letting himself in the back door scattered my thoughts, and I rose to go and meet him. Stepping into the back room, I leaned against the doorframe.

"Good morning, Albert," I said. When he handed me a small paper sack and a large coffee, I gave him a surprised look. "You went to the Crab Cake Deli, this morning? That's wonderful, Albert." This was surprising, as I was always the one to make the daily run.

"I did," he said, settling behind his desk. "I'm celebrating. I have wonderful news to tell you, Kathy. I'll be making a trip to Ireland soon. I will, at last, return my dear Kathleen to the bosom of her family."

Not wishing to spoil his surprise by admitting I already knew, I smiled and opened my sack, pulling out my usual fare of a bagel and cream cheese.

"That is good news, Albert," I said. "I know how much you've dreamt of this. I, too, have a bit of good news. Becky and I went to church yesterday."

I was delighted when a broad smile split his ancient face. "Halleluiah!" he said, clasping his gnarled hands in front of him. "Am I to assume that you've finally forgiven God for taking your grandfather from you?"

Albert's words brought me up short. How was it that he knew of my beef with God? I didn't recall ever voicing my feelings to him on that subject.

"Albert, how did you…"

"Not much is missed by these old eyes, Kathy," he said, softly tapping his right temple with his index finger. "I have known you for many years. People are much like books, you know. The more you are around them, the more you're able to read their faces. How is Becky doing?"

"She is on a journey that doesn't include me, Albert," I said, sadly. "I will, however, see her on her way. She has agreed to come and live with me when the time comes."

"I am glad to hear this," said Albert. "She will leave this world in the care of a friend."

"Until then, I am only a phone call away," I added.

"Excellent. I worry about you living so far out of town," he admitted, raising an eyebrow.

"No worries, Albert," I said, sipping my coffee. "I have a guard dog, remember? Now today is the day I balance the books, so I'll be in the front should you need me. Oh, and Albert? Thank you for breakfast."

At noon, I received a most welcome surprise when Becky walked into the bookstore. As this was only Monday, I wasn't expecting her.

"Hello, Becky," I said, just finishing the task of wrapping an old book for shipment to a customer. "You're a day early."

"I've decided that from now on, every day will be a Tuesday," she said. "We have much to discuss, you know."

Touched by her words, I heartily agreed. Grabbing my purse, I followed her out the door. As we slid into our booth at Della's, I wondered how many more "Tuesdays" we would have together. Becky seemed her old self today, but I could see the dark shadows around her eyes and a grayish hollowness to her cheekbones. After Patty brought our iced teas and took our orders, we sat back to chat.

"The word is out that I have cancer," she said. "I've had three people, just this morning, offer me their help should I need it. I'm very touched."

"The people of this town think highly of you, Becky," I said. "You proved your worth, when you took over the flower shop after your grandparents died. Most young girls, in your shoes, would have simply sold it and pocketed the money."

"I was groomed to operate that shop from the time I was in diapers," she remarked. "Besides, who else was there to take care of me but me? After I met Michael, he supported me in running the shop, allowing me to keep my family business alive. He wanted me to be able to care for myself should anything happen to him."

"He was a wise man," I commented, thankful now for his wisdom to see to Becky's future. His death at age fifty-seven took us all by surprise.

"Did you call the doctor this morning?" asked Becky, breaking into my thoughts.

"I did," I replied, tearing open a third packet of sugar. "I have an appointment for this afternoon at two thirty."

"Excellent," said Becky, frowning as I reached for another packet of sugar. "As soon as he gives you the go-ahead to begin your training, we'll get started. Are you worried?"

"Not at all," I said, with a reassuring smile. "I'm in great health for my age. I'll live to be a hundred." I regretted my thoughtless words as soon as they left my mouth. "I'm sorry, Becky. That was very insensitive of me."

"Don't apologize, Kat," she said, with a slight wave of her hand. "I'm glad that you're in good health. I'm going to be leaning on you a lot over the next few weeks. Now, please let me know as soon as Doc Ferguson gives you the green light to begin your training."

"I'll call you as soon as I leave his office," I promised her.

"Good," she said. "I think we should begin your training as soon as possible. We've not much time to take you from couch potato to marathon runner."

"Couch potato?" I asked, peering at her over the top of my eyeglasses.

"It's just an expression used by runners, Kat," said Becky. "It's what you call someone who suddenly decides they want to be a runner."

"Well, you're partly correct," I admitted, smiling. "I'm more of a couch potato chip, though. I work a full-time job. Now where are we going to do this training?"

"Where you're most comfortable," she replied. "We'll do it on the beach below Sea Breeze Cottage."

"That sounds proper," I said. "What kind of equipment will I need?"

"You'll need a good pair of running shoes," she replied. "After your appointment, we'll run out to the sports shop at the mall and you can purchase a pair."

"I haven't bought anything but flats in years," I said. "How will I know what to buy?"

"You just leave it all to me," she replied. "I'll set you up. To the 5K run for juvenile diabetes!" she added, lifting her iced tea glass.

"To the 5K run!" I said, tapping my glass to hers. "As well as sore calves, blisters, and Bengay," I added, with a grimace.

At 2:15 p.m., I left the bookshop and walked the three blocks to the Cutter's Cove Medical Clinic. The small white brick building comfortably housed the town's three doctors. Each, in his or her own right, was considered a great asset to the community. Dr. Jennifer Fisk was the town's pediatrician and much loved by all. Her gentle manner was quick to put even the fussiest child at ease. Dr. Samuel Bird was our local dentist. In his seventies, I was sure he harbored high hopes for our young lawn-care enthusiast, Ricky Taylor. I was ashamed to admit that I hadn't been to see a dentist in well over a year, so I made a mental note to give him a call soon.

Stepping through the door marked "Dr. Wayne R. Ferguson, MD," I signed in at the window and found a seat next to a small table holding several magazines. Spying one with a beautiful young blond woman on the cover, I picked it up. The pretty cover girl was a twenty-one-year old Hollywood celebrity, the author identified as the sexiest girl in the world.

I was shocked at his choice. The young girl in question was rail thin with little or no curves. Her flawless skin and perfect blonde locks made her appear plastic. *So this is what the world considers sexy*, I thought. *Pathetic.*

"Well, enjoy it while it lasts, honey," I muttered to myself, flipping the page. "Old age is heading your way at ninety miles an hour." The title of the next article brought my attention up short. "Can A Woman Find Lasting Love After Fifty?" *Well, now this is more like it*, I thought. The female doctor, who'd written the article, claimed that a woman over fifty was better equipped mentally and emotionally for love than her younger counterparts.

"The older woman is more in control of her feelings and therefore knows more of what she wants and needs in a man," she wrote. "With age comes confidence. Having this, she no longer carries the fear of rejection and finds herself able to relax and enjoy the experience of falling in love. If the man is the same age as her, he will find her…"

"Kathleen Jennings," said a woman's voice, startling me. I looked up to see a tall, thin nurse, dressed in Betty Boop–themed scrubs, waiting for me at the door leading back to the examination rooms. I guessed her age at somewhere in her mid to late thirties and marveled at the way her short bobbed hair, colored a bright shade of pink, caught the light. "The doctor will see you now, Miss Jennings"

Darn it, I thought, closing the magazine and tossing it back onto the table. *Now I'll never know what a man over fifty wants in a woman my age. Curious minds want to know!*

As I followed Betty Boop back the hallway, I found myself beginning to feel anxious. The last time I walked this hallway, I was told that I was over-weight and was given a diet plan to follow. That was a year ago. I ignored that plan, so I already knew what the doctor was going to tell me. After settling into a room, Betty Boop took my blood pressure, listened to my heart and lungs, and checked my weight. *Here we go*, I thought. *I'm doomed.*

"Please be seated on the examining table," she said, closing her laptop. "The doctor will be in to see you as soon as he looks at your chart."

A few minutes later, Dr. Doom stepped into the room, his expression unreadable as he glanced down at my medical chart. He'd changed very little since I'd last seen him. Looking closer, I did notice that his dark hair now held a tinge of gray at the temples. His broad shoulders and narrow hips were a sign that he still spent time working out at the local gym. Good for him. Most men in their fifties were already fighting a large belly.

"Well, Kathleen," he said, still not looking at me. "I am surprised by what I'm seeing here in your chart today."

"Look, Doc, I can explain," I began, trying to keep the whining tone out of my voice. "I've been really busy lately and—"

"Well, it's paid off," he said, looking up at me. I'd almost forgotten his vivid green eyes. "Your blood pressure is way down and so is your weight."

"What?" I asked, leaning over to read the name on the chart. He had obviously picked up someone else's records.

"Last year I advised you to lose some weight, and you've wisely lost fifteen pounds. Your heart and lungs sound good as well. Was it the diet plan I gave you?"

"Not really," I admitted. I knew my clothes were a bit looser on me lately, but I had no idea I had lost as much as fifteen pounds. "I must admit that it wasn't because of any diet. Caring for my father kept me cooped up indoors every evening, cooking for him and seeing to his needs. After he died, I found myself with hours of free time, and I spent those hours walking on the beach. I don't own a bathroom scale, so I was unaware that I'd lost weight."

"Well, I'm giving you a good report," he said, closing my chart. "Now I recommend you engage in some form of exercise that goes beyond simply walking. I want you to get your heart rate up to between 90 and 130 and keep it there for at least twenty minutes. Perhaps some light aerobics would do the trick."

"How about training for a 5K run?" I asked him. Here it was—that final verdict that would make or break my running career.

"Well, I don't see why not," he said, hesitantly. "When is the race planned for?"

"July 23," I said. "It's the main event for the Founder's Day picnic."

"Who will your trainer be, if I may ask?"

"Becky Porter," I replied. "She's unable to run this year, so I agreed to take her place."

"Becky Porter is a seasoned runner," he said, nodding slowly. "She knows what she's doing. I suppose it wouldn't hurt for you to train for the race, if you do it sensibly. Eat a good balance diet and cut out the sweets. I want you to pace yourself and rest when you're winded. And, follow a sensible training plan for your age group. I don't want you trying to compete with the thirty-somethings in the two-hundred-dollar Nikes. Speaking of shoes, purchase a good pair of running shoes. Don't go for the bargain, go for the support. Got that?"

"Yes, sir," I said, relieved. "Thank you, Doc. You've just made Becky's day."

"Well, make sure you're careful," he warned. "If you have any questions, call me."

Leaving the doctor's office, I made my way back to the bookshop. After my good report, I did so with a new spring in my step. When I walked in, Albert was busy with a customer, so I retreated to my desk to call Becky.

"It's a go," I told her the moment she picked up. "Doc Ferguson gave me a great report. He said I could train with you if I didn't overexert myself."

"Kat, overexert is my middle name," she said, jokingly.

"That's what I was afraid of," I muttered before hanging up.

At five, I met Becky in the parking lot of Sam's Sports Shop, located inside the Sand Dollar Mall. She knew just what I needed, so the task of finding a good pair of running shoes took only a few minutes. I also purchased a water bottle, a stopwatch, and a pedometer. I was now ready for anything that Becky threw at me. I hoped. However, just in case, I slipped into Drug World and purchased a tube of muscle liniment, a large bottle of aspirin, and an ice pack. One can never be too prepared.

Arriving home, I quickly changed into a pair of shorts, an old tee shirt, and my new one-hundred-fifty-dollar running shoes. For that kind of money, I had better not end up with blisters. Thirty minutes later, Becky met me on the beach below the cottage, clipboard in hand. The shorts and tank top she wore only accentuated her recent weight loss. Despite my own weight loss, I felt fat standing next to her.

"Are you ready?" she asked, giving me an encouraging smile.

"As ready as I'll ever be," I replied, wondering what I'd gotten myself into this time.

Chapter 8

Becky's training plan was a simple one. I was to begin with a slow pace of running for sixty seconds and walking for ninety between the cottage and the old pier, which lay roughly a mile up the beach. After a few warm-up stretches, I was ready to go. The plan didn't sound too bad until I was thirty seconds into my first sprint. This is when the muscles in my calves began to develop a nasty cramp and my lungs caught fire. Oh, and did I mention the painful stitch I developed just below my right ribcage? Glancing down at my stopwatch, I saw that I still had thirty seconds to go. At that moment, it sounded like an eternity! Finally, the stopwatch said I could walk. Releasing a large breath, I slowed my pace and savored every step. My calves soon eased their cramping, and my breathing slowed. I was shocked at how fast the ninety seconds had sped past. Steeling myself, once again, I began another sixty-second sprint. Again, my calves began to cramp up and my lungs burned. Even though I'd lost the fifteen extra pounds, my body still felt like I was carrying a boulder in my pocket.

With one eye on the stopwatch and the other on my path, I finally reached the old pier. My lungs were screaming by now, and my legs felt like two water soaked logs. Leaning against a support beam, I nearly cried with frustration. What was I doing out here? I was sixty years old, for Pete's sake. After a long day on my job, I should be sitting in front of my fireplace, wearing a pair of cozy slippers and reading my newspaper. I had to be out of my mind training for a three-mile run I wasn't prepared for! What if Doc Ferguson missed something and, like my Grandpa Jake, I suffered a heart attack? Oh, why am I torturing myself like this? Why?

The small voice within me screamed, "Because you told Becky that you would do this!" The voice was right. I had volunteered to do this for Becky. I suddenly felt ashamed for I knew in my heart that Becky would be running this race herself, if she wasn't battling cancer. Who was I to complain about a little pain in my calves? Becky, I was sure, was enduring much more than this. Turning toward home, I took a deep breath and reset my stopwatch.

"You're running for Becky," I said aloud, breaking into my sixty-second sprint. "Now buck up, sister, and let's do this!"

My new resolve did wonders for me as I alternated between running and walking on the return trip. Pure determination helped me to endure the discomfort. However, despite my pep talk, the moment I reached Becky, I collapsed on my back at her feet. Looking down at me, the expression on her face was a cross between concern and amusement.

"Are you okay, Kat?" she asked, attempting to hide her smile.

"Never better," I croaked, dragging the words from my tortured lungs.

"Good," she said, helping me to my feet. "We do it all over again tomorrow. Now, go home and soak in a warm bath with some Epsom salts. That will help with the stiffness and cramping."

"No worries," I said, dusting the sand off my backside and legs. The last thing I wanted was for Becky to think I wasn't capable of running in her place. "I'm feeling none of those things."

"Wonderful," she said, dropping her clipboard onto the rocks. "Now let's run you through some stretches, and then I'll head for home."

The stretches were just what I needed to ease my cramped muscles. In no time, I felt my body begin to relax and my breathing slowed. *This isn't so bad*, I thought. *I can do this.*

"Same time tomorrow, girlfriend?" she asked, cocking her head to one side.

"Same time tomorrow," I replied, leading the way to the sea path.

After Becky left for town, I ran a bath, poured in a cup of Epsom salts, and lowered myself into the hot water. It felt like heaven on my stiff and sore muscles. After an hour-long soak, I toweled off, slipped into my pajamas, and made myself a bowl of canned soup. Looking for a comfortable place in which to moan, I snuggled down in my father's chair to drink a hot chocolate and look out to sea. This was now my favorite spot. *Like father, like daughter*, I mused. When the telephone rang, I forced my aching body to walk to the kitchen to answer it. On the way, I made myself a mental note to purchase a cordless telephone.

"Hello," I said, wincing at the pain in my voice.

"Hello, Kathy," said a low sultry voice. "How was your first training session?"

"Hello, Marcus," I said, feeling a warmth rush over my aching body. "It was good. I'm still alive, anyway. I'm a bit sore, but that's to be expected, is it not?"

"It is," he replied. "I thought of stopping by, but I knew you would be snuggled in your chair with a hot toddy. What is your beverage of choice tonight?"

"Cocoa," I replied, smiling.

"That'll work," he said. "I stopped in at the flower shop to check up on Rebecca today. She told me you were to start your training this afternoon. She looked tired."

"Yes, her illness is progressing," I said. "I'm bringing her out to live with me at Sea Breeze Cottage when she's ready."

"That's a wonderful idea," he said.

"What have you been up to today?" I asked him, curious as to what he did in his spare time.

"I've been working around the house today," he replied. "I have a few errands to run tomorrow. I have to run into Portland in the morning and purchase two airline tickets for Albert and myself. I wish there was an easier way, as I loathe the highway traffic."

"There is an easier way, Marcus," I said. "Come by the bookshop tomorrow, and we'll purchase them online."

"You can do that?" he asked, his voice showing surprise.

"Yes," I replied. "Drop by about nine, and I'll walk you through it. Oh, and bring your credit card."

"Excellent," he said. "That is a relief. I'll only keep you a moment, my sweet. I'm taking a break from a dreaded task."

"What task is that, Marcus?" I asked.

"I'm attempting to cut the grass with an ancient mowing machine I found in the shed," he replied. "I believe at one time it was self-propelled. However, with that feature no longer functioning, it's like trying to push a Volkswagen across my yard. I'm inclined to believe that a couple of goats would be a better choice. However, they're so temperamental."

"Well, I think I can save you from having to hire a goat with a bad attitude," I said, feeling sorry for him. "The solution is a lawn-care service. I recommend it, as I use one. Would you consider helping out a young man on his way to dental school?"

"I would indeed," declared Marcus. "If this means that I don't have to push this behemoth around my yard, then it'll be worth every penny."

"Wonderful," I said, amused at his dilemma. "Remind me to give you Ricky Taylor's number in the morning."

"You have saved my sanity, Kathy," he said. "Tomorrow is but a few hours away, yet an eternity will pass till the new day has dawned."

"Oh, Marcus, I just love the way you make a simple sentence sound like Shakespeare."

"Oh, so thou art familiar with the poet now, are you?" he asked, amused.

"I am," I said, giggling. "My ears have not yet drunk a hundred words, yet I'm already enamored with their story."

"Well done, Kathy," he exclaimed. "Parting is such sweet sorrow. Until the morrow?"

"Until the morrow," I repeated, feeling my heart fill with laughter. "Good night, Marcus."

"Good night, Kathleen," he said, his voice once again low and sultry.

After he hung up, I was amazed at how much better I felt after his call. By nine, I was ready for bed. As I slid down beneath the covers, I reached for my worn copy of Romeo and Juliet. Opening it to my bookmark, I picked up where I'd left off a few nights earlier. However, I barely read a sentence or two before my eyes grew heavy and the words begin to swim off the page.

"Sorry, Juliet," I muttered, closing the book and switching off the lamp. "But, tonight I must rest my weary mind and body in sleep's sweet embrace."

Hey, I'm getting good at this Shakespeare stuff, I mused, just before sleep claimed me.

The following morning, every muscle in my body felt like I'd been dashed against the rocks by an angry sea. Sliding my legs slowly over the side of the bed, I dreaded making contact with the floor. When the telephone in the kitchen set off an alarm in my head, I dragged myself out of bed and headed in that direction. As I stepped into the kitchen, my foot kicked over Mussolini's food dish, sending kibbles flying across the floor.

"Darn it!" I exclaimed. Walking through the mess in my bare feet, I could feel the kibbles sticking between my toes, and I cringed. "This had better be the Prize Patrol from Publishers Clearing House!"

Even the act of reaching for the telephone called on muscles that rebelled with every move. "Hello," I said with just a hint of impatience. Reaching down, I flicked the offending dog food off the bottom of my right foot. Mussolini, seeing his breakfast spread over the entire floor, left the room in a huff.

"Hello, Kat. How are you feeling this morning?" Becky asked, with more enthusiasm than I could bear to muster. "Now I know you're feeling a bit stiff and sore. Despair not. I want you to lay the phone down and repeat the stretching exercises that I gave you yesterday. Come on. You can do it!" Placing the phone's receiver on the counter, I did as she asked. I could hear her tinny voice giving me instructions.

"Stretch out those leg muscles," she urged over the wire. "Bend over and touch those toes. Come on, girl. Lift those arms high above your head. Feel the stretch and lean into it."

As I went through the movements, I was amazed at how quickly the stiffness eased up. I actually felt the strength return to my body. Dropping forward, I allowed my body to hang, and my tense back muscles began to relax. *Oooh, this feels good*, I thought, as I felt the blood rush to my face.

"Kat, are you there?" I heard Becky ask. "Kat?"

Reaching up for the telephone, I pulled it down to my ear. "I'm still here," I said, as I stared at my feet. "I was just feeling the stretch."

"Whew! I thought perhaps I overexerted you and you left me," she said, laughing. "How do you feel now?"

"Much better," I admitted, standing up. "I can at least move. Will every morning feel this way?"

"No," she replied. "Each morning will get easier. Now up and at 'em. It's a beautiful summer's day out there. I'll meet you at Della's at noon. Ta ta."

After she hung up, I dragged myself into the bathroom and into the shower. As the hot water washed over my sore muscles, I brightened when I remembered that I was seeing Marcus this morning. Suddenly, the day looked remarkably better, and by the time I was dressed for work, I was whistling a merry tune. Mussolini, watching me from the doorway, was not amused. Apparently, he was still thinking of his scattered kibbles. Before leaving my bedroom, I stepped in front of my full-length mirror. The doctor was right. I had lost weight. My brown dress slacks now bagged a little in the hips and legs, and the buttons on the white blouse I was wearing no longer strained at the threads.

"Eat your heart out, Oprah. I am lookin' good," I muttered, admiring my new curves. Giving my hair a last-minute flip with my fingers, I hurried off to work.

At nine on the dot, Marcus walked into the bookshop. The man was punctual, I'll give him that. He was casually dressed in a pair of crisp blue jeans and his usual white dress shirt. The smell of British Sterling aftershave drifted in ahead of him.

"Good morning, Marcus," I said, giving him my best smile.

"You look surprisingly well for someone who has run her first mile," he said, returning my smile. "How do you feel?"

"Remarkable," I replied. "However, I'm to repeat yesterday's training session this afternoon, so who knows how I'll feel in the morning."

"Each day will get easier," he said, glancing around the shop. "Is Albert not in yet?"

"He ran to the post office," I replied. "For the past fifteen years, that task was left up to me. Now, suddenly, he wants to do it. It's almost as if he's regained the strength and vitality of his sixties. I don't know what's come over him?"

"I do," said Marcus. "He's finally getting the chance to fulfill the promise he made to his late wife. That is what gives him back his youth. I, for one, am happy to be a part of that fulfillment. Now shall we fire up your magic machine and allow it to whisk us off to another world, where we may hire a magic carpet to Never Never Land?"

"You do have a way with words, Marcus," I said, with a smile. "Now what airlines will you be using?"

An hour later, Marcus, having purchased two round-trip tickets to the UK, strolled from the shop singing with gusto, a song I'd never heard before. "Rule Britannia! Britannia rule the waves!" he sang, merrily. "Britons never, never, never shall be slaves!"

At noon, I met Becky at Della's. Although she was wearing a smile, it failed to reach her eyes. She appeared more yellowish today, and the shadows had deepened around her eyes and cheekbones. I grew concerned and told her so.

"Becky, you look tired," I said. "Perhaps it's time to close the shop for a while until you're feeling stronger." With this suggestion, I was taken aback by her response. It broke my heart!

"Oh, Kat, how can I?" she said, sighing heavily. "You heard Dr. Sheffield say I needed to put my house in order. Unfortunately, I owe too much to close the shop, even temporarily."

"If I may ask, Becky, how much is 'too much'?"

"An enormous amount," she said, lowering her eyes. "I'm still carrying the debt from last spring when the cooler failed, and I lost an entire shipment of flowers. The cost of replacing both, cost me a bundle. And I owe for the flowers that I just had shipped in from several states. I've been keeping the shop open, but people just don't think of flowers anymore when they're on vacation. And the majority of our young people are heading to the big cities now instead of marrying local and settling in Cutter's Cove."

"How much is an enormous amount?" I asked, trying not to sound as if I was prying into her personal business. Okay, I was prying into her personal business.

"At least ten thousand dollars," she said, softly. "I haven't the liquid assets to pay such an amount. Oh, Kat, am I to die a debtor?"

"Of course not, Becky," I exclaimed. "We'll think of something. We always do."

"Thank you, Kat," she said, through her tears. "But this is my debt. Therefore, it's my responsibility to find a way out from under it."

"Nonsense," I said, patting her on the hand. It felt cold. "I'm your best friend, and I forbid you to fret over this. You have enough to worry about at the moment."

"I'll see you on your beach after work," she said, changing the subject. "Day 2 will be much easier, I promise."

"I'll be there," I said. "Now where is our lunch?"

Returning to the shop, I thought about Becky's problem. Ten thousand dollars wasn't much in the world of debt, but it was a mountain to someone with little time to earn it. I needed to come up with a way to raise some money fast. My own meager bank account wouldn't do it. My father hadn't left me in debt, but he hadn't left me an inheritance, either. Although his paintings sold for a tidy sum, his constant care and expenses over the last few years had consumed the lion's share of his income. And it was still a mystery as to what became of his earlier paintings of my mother. Those had all disappeared when I was a child, leaving me with no memory of my mother's face. I had a vague memory of her long brown hair and the way it drifted about her face in the ocean's breeze. However, her features were a blur, forever lost to my memory.

At five, Becky and I made our way to the beach below the cottage. The way the sunshine touched her face, she appeared almost normal until I got closer. Then I could see the obvious signs of her illness. Despite her fatigue, she was raring to go.

"Okay, Kat, fall into position," she said, holding up her clipboard. "Let's get you warmed up. Today, we repeat what we did yesterday. Wait. How sore are you?"

"Well…I am…" I began.

"Truthfully," she urged, looking at me over her glasses.

"Okay. My muscles feel like overcooked spaghetti," I replied. "Charlie has attached himself to my calves and thighs, and my lungs feel like they've turned to stone."

"Now don't hold back, Kat," she said, hiding her smile. "How do you really feel?"

Not wishing to ruin her joke, I just smiled. I was serious! "Like a runner," I replied. "Now let's get this torture session under way."

Seeing my obvious distress and feeling just a bit sorry for me, Becky toned down the routine. Today, I was to alternate running for thirty seconds and walking for sixty. Now, this I could handle. And, by the time I returned to the rocks, I was feeling exhilarated though winded. I found Becky perched on my father's rock.

"How did it go today?" she asked, getting to her feet.

"It went much better," I admitted. "Cutting the time in half was easier on me. Perhaps tomorrow I'll try running for forty-five seconds."

"No, you won't," she said, writing something on her clipboard. "You've earned a day of rest. No running, tomorrow."

"Really?" I asked, hopefully. "You're not just saying that to make me beg?"

"You're silly," she said. "Come. Let's do our cool down stretches."

Later, as I showered, I again thought about Becky's problem. How were we going to raise ten thousand dollars in a month? Perhaps, I had something of value that I could sell. That idea didn't hold water for long. All I had was some old furniture and a few knick-knacks. I promised Becky that I would come up with a solution, and at the moment, I had precious little to offer her. Pulling on a pair of jeans and an old T-shirt, I called to Mussolini, who came bounding from beneath the kitchen table.

"Come on, boy," I said, opening the kitchen door. "How about we return to the beach? Only this time, we're walking not running. Got that?" His reply was to fly past me, nearly knocking me off my feet.

As we strolled along the surf, I thought of my Grandpa Jake. He died just eight weeks after turning sixty six. In my mind's eye, I could see him walking his dogs along the surf and myself running after them, picking up seashells. *Has it really been forty-five years since his death?* I thought. Missing him, I could almost smell his cigar smoke on the breeze. Even after all these years, his face still remained strong in my mind. He was always my rock when I was a child. I depended on his strong will and no-nonsense way of seeing the world. Of course, there was that story he told me about the black creature in the attic. This still remained a quandary, after all these years. My child's mind still saw the attic as a dangerous place, whereas the adult in me wondered at his intention to frighten me the way he did. I was a good ways down the beach when I heard a male voice calling my name from somewhere far off.

"Kathleen!" the voice called. "Ahoy, Kathy!"

Glancing down the beach toward home, I was surprised to see Marcus just stepping off the sea path. Waving in his direction, I turned and made my way toward him. For a moment, I allowed my wish to be with him, override my common sense, and I nearly broke into a run. Catching myself, I forced my legs to walk the distance. It wouldn't do to portray myself as too anxious. It seemed like an eternity before I finally joined him at the rocks. Mussolini, always my protector, was already there checking him out.

"Marcus, what a pleasant surprise," I said, slightly winded. I noticed that he'd shed his shoes and socks and had rolled up his trouser legs. "What brings you out this way?"

"Oh, I guess I just wanted to see where you hung out in your spare time," he said, leaning over to plant a small kiss on my lips. His gesture touched me.

"I come here when I need to think," I said. The evening was clear and warm, and the twilight sky was just coming alive with stars. "And tonight, I have much to think about. I have to come up with a solution to a very dire problem."

"Perhaps, I can be of help," he said. "I have been around the block a few times, as they say. I've traveled the world and have learned much. What troubles you, Kathy?"

Taking his words as an opportunity to share my thoughts, I motioned him toward the rocks, and we sat down. *Do I tell him what really weighs on my mind? If I mention Becky's problem, will I be betraying a friend's confidence?* Then again, perhaps Marcus could provide an idea for solving the dilemma. I decided to take him into my confidence.

"I'm concerned about Becky," I began. "And I'm not just speaking of her illness. Becky is worried that she'll die in debt. She's in need of at least ten thousand dollars to settle her estate. I have taken it upon myself to figure out a way to do this without making her feel as though she's taking charity. She's a very loving and generous soul, and making sure that she keeps her dignity throughout her ordeal is of the utmost importance to me. Anything you can add will be much appreciated."

"Well, perhaps we can hold a benefit auction for her," Marcus suggested. "I have learned, in my few short months of living here, the folks of Cutter's Cove are very loyal to their residents. If we were to hold such an event, I'm sure we could raise that amount easily. Becky, I've come to discover, is much loved and respected by her friends and neighbors. In my thinking, they only need to know that one of their own is in trouble to get them to open their hearts and wallets. And when they find out that Becky is ill, they will rally around her. Mark my words."

"Oh, Marcus, that's a wonderful idea," I exclaimed. "How does one go about planning such an event?"

"Well, first things first," he said. "We'll discuss the idea with Becky and get her approval. Then we print up a few flyers and distribute them around town. The rest will unfold like magic."

"Thank you, Marcus," I said, leaning into him. "I knew you would have a solution. Will you help me?"

"I will, indeed, madam," he said, looking deep into my eyes. When his kiss came, I was ready for it. I knew at that moment that I could trust him with my heart. Relief flooded my soul as I put my hopes and dreams into Marcus's loving hands. When the kiss ended, he pulled me back against him, and we sat watching the stars above us twinkle into existence.

"I am at peace," I heard him softly say, against my hair. "We shall together sail this ship safely into shore."

I feel the same, I thought, as I relaxed against his beating heart.

The next day was Thursday, and I had a lot to accomplish before end of day. Just before lunch, Marcus met me in front of the Posey Pot flower shop, and we steeled ourselves for our conversation with Becky. As luck would have it, the shop was empty. We found Becky arranging a bouquet of deep purple calla lilies at her table near the back. Their dark trumpet-like blooms stood out in stark contrast to her pale complexion. Seeing us, she dropped what she was doing and came over to greet us.

"Marcus, Kathy, how nice of you to drop in," she said, genuinely happy to see us. Her face looked flushed, and her hands shook slightly. "Am I late for lunch?"

"No, no," I replied. "We just wanted to have a word with you before we head for Della's."

"We aren't disturbing you, are we?" asked Marcus.

"No, not at all," she replied, wiping her hands on a towel. "Please, come over and have a seat in my consultation area."

She directed us over to a small sitting area where she met with her perspective customers. Four black wrought-iron chairs surrounded a large matching glass topped patio table. In its center, a bouquet of fresh cut roses in a soft shade of pink, filled a clear glass vase. Once seated, I started the ball rolling.

"Becky, Marcus and I have something we'd like to discuss with you," I said, choosing my words carefully. "I told him about your debt problem, and he's agreed to help us come up with the funds to pay it off."

"What?" she asked, looking at me in shock. "No! I'll not allow you to do this. I won't take money from either of you!"

Marcus, thankfully, came to my rescue. "Becky, may I speak?" he asked. With a nod from her, he continued. "Please understand, Kathy confided in me with only your best interest at heart. Her concern for you is about more than just your well-being. We are not talking about paying off the debt for you. We are merely suggesting that we hold a fund-raiser, thus allowing your friends and neighbors to help you in your hour of need."

"I have no intention of asking my neighbors for money!" exclaimed Becky, jumping to her feet. "What will they think of me? My grandfather was a very proud man who never once asked for help when times got tough. His hard work and sacrifice kept this flower shop going through two wars. How can I do anything less?"

"Becky, the people in this town love you," I said, hurrying to her side. "Your family has been a part of Cutter's Cove for nearly ninety years. When your family died in that car accident, did the people of this town not chip in and buy them a headstone? They watched over you after your grandparents died knowing that a young teenage girl would need guidance in running a business. They stood by you when Michael died, giving their support when you needed them most. Now, once again, I know they will be willing to step up and help you. And, Becky, you have the church now. Remember? They will gather around you and bathe you in prayers and God's love. You need them, Becky. You've no family to fall back on now. You are the last."

I could tell that my words were finally getting through to her when she leaned her head against me. After a long moment she spoke.

"What must I do?" she asked, in a childlike voice. "I've never planned a fund-raiser before. I've always used my running to benefit my causes."

"You leave it all up to Marcus and me," I said, leading her back to her chair. "We know just what to do."

"Please, Rebecca, let me know if there is anything I can do to help," said Marcus, cupping her hand.

"I will," she promised. "Thank you to both of you. In my situation, I have no recourse but to place myself in your capable hands and to trust in your judgment. You have my blessing." Then looking at me, she smiled. "And as for you, girlfriend, tomorrow is training day on the beach, so enjoy your day off."

For the next two days, my training progressed with ease. I was back to running for sixty seconds and walking for ninety. My legs continued to cramp, and my lungs still screamed in horror, but their cry was gradually weakening to a dull roar. On Sunday, Becky and I took a break and attended church. This time, we were welcomed at the door and invited to sit with Mr. and Mrs. Wilmot, who owned the video shop at the mall. The church ladies, knowing of Becky's illness, offered their assistance where needed. Becky felt truly touched by their kindness. Everyone promised to pray for her and hugged her for encouragement. After the service, I suggested we have a picnic on the beach. We walked and talked over old times of when we were in school. I tried not to think of how little time we had left together.

On Monday, I awoke a little stiff, but after a quick warm up, I was ready to face the day. Albert arrived early in his usual pleasant mood, and I caught him humming a soft tune as he leafed through a copy of Beatrix Potter's famous children's tales. As the morning passed, the temperatures outside grew warmer, and I heard the old air-conditioner in the back kick on. Since Becky had a consultation for wedding flowers, I ordered in and ate at my desk. When I'd finished, Albert summoned me to his office.

"Is everything all right, Albert?" I asked, taking a chair inside the door.

"No worries," he replied, taking his seat at his desk. "I simply have something to discuss with you."

"You're smiling, so it must not be dire," I said, relaxing. "What's on your mind?"

"How long have you worked for me, Kathleen?" he asked.

"Well, it was nineteen years in April," I replied. "Are you thinking of hiring someone younger, Albert?"

"Not at all," he replied. "Today's youth have no interest in books. They're all about electronics. No, I'm thinking of giving you a raise."

"You're giving me a raise?" I asked, touched by his generosity. "What brought this on?"

"Well, I am still paying you the same hourly wage as I did seven years ago. And, since you're taking on many of the tasks I used to do, I think you're due for a raise in pay."

"Thank you, Albert," I said. "That's very generous of you."

"And, I want you to know how much I appreciate your loyalty," he added. "You will, after all, be in charge of the shop while I'm in Ireland. I can't think of anyone better qualified."

"I appreciate the vote of confidence, Albert," I said.

"I'm thinking of adding a dollar to your hourly wage," he said. "Would that be sufficient?"

"It would indeed," I said, thinking of what I could do with a bit of extra money. The fact that Sea Breeze Cottage was in need of a facelift was top on my list.

"Well, I'm going out for a while," he said, rising. "I have to purchase some luggage for my trip overseas. My old suitcase, I'm afraid, will never make the trip in one piece."

"The sports shop at the mall will have what you need, Albert," I offered. "And don't forget to buy a couple of name tags."

"Why would I need name tags?" he asked. "I will surely know my own luggage."

"True," I said, smiling at his naiveté. "However, when the airport loses it, they'll need to know how to find you."

"Good thinking," he replied. "See, you're earning your raise already."

After work, I met Becky on the beach below the cottage for my daily run. I was still running sixty seconds and walking ninety, and my legs were getting stronger each day I trained. However, I was still crawling out of bed every morning like a corpse escaping his coffin. With four weeks until Founder's Day, I had little time to complain, especially to Becky and her wicked clipboard.

"I'm very proud of you, Kat," she said, as I finished my run on Wednesday afternoon. "Soon we'll be shortening your walking time and you'll be running longer."

"I'm feeling better about my training, Becky," I said, stretching my legs to ward off any cramps. "I hate to take any time off. I don't want to lose what I've gained."

"I'm glad," said Becky. "Tomorrow I'm speeding you up a notch."

In the morning, when I walked into the bookshop, Marcus met me at the door.

"Good morning, Kathy," he said, winking at me. "Albert and I have been finalizing the plans for our trip to the UK. We leave on the morning of July 6. We should return fairly early on the sixteenth."

"That does sound like fun," I said, dropping my purse into the drawer of my desk. Retrieving a sheet of paper from my top drawer, I handed it to him. "By the way, I've done a rough draft of the flyer for Becky's benefit auction. I propose that we ask for a donation of items and perhaps have a food stand. What do you think?"

Reading it, he nodded his head in approval. "This will work nicely," he said. "Now all we have to do is pick a date and collect the items. We could hold it on July 16, the Saturday before Founder's Day. Our plane arrives in Portland in the early hours, so we should be back in town by 9:00 a.m."

"That'll work," I said, penciling in the day on the flyer. "Once the word is out, all I have to do is see to the venue and collect the donated items."

"I loathe the fact that I'll be leaving the lion's share of the work to you, Kathy," he said, looking regretful. "However, circumstances demand that I return to England at this time. If it weren't so dire, I would have waited—"

"Please, Marcus, don't fret," I said, easing his worry. "I'll be just fine. You see to your uncle's estate and get Albert safely to Ireland, and I'll have everything ready to go when you get back."

"I still feel wretched," he said, leaning over to plant a soft kiss on my cheek. "The sixteenth will do then?"

"Yes. That leaves a full two weeks for folks to gather up their auction items. I'll finalize this draft and get it to the printers right away."

"I suppose everyone will have something they'll wish to donate," said Marcus. "Perhaps, I'll look around my place. Do you suppose anyone would want a lazy self-propelled lawn mower?"

"I'm planning on donating a few items myself," I added. "Marcus, would you like to join Becky and me for lunch? We can fill her in on the benefit plans."

"I would love to have lunch with you," he said, heading toward the door. "I'll see you at Della's. 12:00 sharp."

After he left, I waited on customers and swept the shop. My life was moving so fast since finding my sea stone. Marcus and I were no longer two strangers leery of each other's intentions. Our relationship had grown into a warm, easy friendship where the occasional kiss felt natural and welcomed. When Albert announced that he was going to the post office, I looked up at the clock. It was 12:15! I was supposed to meet Marcus and Becky fifteen minutes ago. Grabbing my purse, I took a moment to freshen up in my compact. After locking up the shop, I hurried to Della's.

Arriving at the diner, I was pleased to see Marcus and Becky already enjoying iced tea in our booth. Becky's paler was more obvious today, and her skin still held that hint of a yellowish tinge.

"Well, it's about time," she said, jovially looking at her watch. "Did you lose track of time or forget?"

"I lost track of time," I confessed, sliding in next to Marcus.

"Well, we're glad you're here," he said, handing me a menu. "We were just about to order."

"I could eat a horse!" Becky declared, as Patty started our way.

Becky's horse turned out to be more of a miniature pony. She barely touched her small chicken salad croissant. Marcus and I, however, devoured our fish sandwiches and bowls of hot clam chowder. When we finished, I pulled out the draft of the flyer announcing Becky's benefit auction.

"This will go to print only with your approval," I stated, handing her the flyer.

She looked it over and read it aloud. "Announcing a benefit auction to be held on Saturday, July 16, in the Cutter's Cove square. The fun will begin at 1:00 p.m. and go until all items are sold. All proceeds will go to help Becky Porter with expenses. For more information, contact Kathy Jennings at Bristol's Antique and Rare Book Store on Main Street."

"Well, what do you think?" I asked.

"I like it," said Becky. "Do you think folks will donate?"

"Our cup will runneth over," said Marcus, patting her on the hand. "I've made arrangements with the mayor to have the donations for the auction dropped off at the recreation center."

"Good thinking," said Becky.

"I, too, may have a few old family heirlooms to donate," I said, stirring sugar into my iced tea.

"Really?" asked Becky. "You'd be willing to part with your family's belongings?"

"The furniture in my living room is outrageously outdated," I pointed out. "The sofa alone dates back to the 1940s."

"That, my dear Kathleen, makes them antiques," said Marcus, holding up his right index finger to make his point. "Never refer to your furniture as outdated. People will pay good money for an antique that's in excellent condition."

"Well, the living room suit has sat unused since the Kennedy years," I said. "I've dusted and kept it immaculate for reasons that escape me at the moment."

"What about your attic?" asked Becky, raising an eyebrow. She, of all people, knew of my fear of the attic. "What's up there, that you could part with? Well?"

"I have no idea what's in my attic," I said, hesitantly.

"How long has it been since you've been up there?" asked Marcus. I shrugged my shoulders and hoped they would drop the subject. "Well, you must make the sojourn. Attics are a treasure trove of items from a bygone era."

"I'm afraid our Kathy has no idea what her attic holds," stated Becky. "She never goes up there."

"Oh my," said Marcus, surprised. "Why? Is it full of bats?"

"Something lives in the attic, all right," said Becky, winking at me. "However, it isn't a bat."

"I've just been too busy to think about the attic," I said, begging her with my eyes to let it go.

"Really?" asked Marcus. "Why, attics are the best place to store extras if you live in a cottage. Exactly how long has it been since you've been up there?"

He patiently awaited my answer. "Years," I said, softly. "I really can't remember."

"What? Is this true?" Marcus asked. "You've lived in the house all your life and you don't recall the last time you've been to the attic?"

"You make it sound so dramatic," I said, looking around for the server. "Where's Patty? I need more ice."

"I'll tell you why she doesn't recall the last time she's been to the attic, Marcus," said Becky. "When she was a child, her grandfather told her that the boogeyman lived there. He made her swear to never again set foot in the attic."

"Remarkable," said Marcus. "I couldn't guess why your grandfather would burden you with such a dark tale. Did he not think it would frighten you?"

"It's strange, I know," I said.

"Here is what I want to know, Kat?" asked Becky. "You told me about the creature when we were eight. You're now sixty. You should have seen through your grandfather's ruse years ago. Why are you still clinging to it? Surely, you know by now that the boogeyman isn't real."

"Why would he tell you such a tale?" asked Marcus, shaking his head in disbelief.

"To tell you the truth, Marcus, I've no clue why my grandfather would want to frighten me so," I confessed. "I've wrestled with that question for years."

"Interesting," said Marcus, rubbing his bearded chin. "Aren't you the least bit curious as why he would forbid you to go into the attic?"

"Not really," I said, shrugging. "Well, perhaps a little."

"I've got an idea," said Becky, brightening. "Why don't the three of us go together and face the evil that lurks among the rafters?"

"That sounds like a good plan," said Marcus, glancing over at me. "What do you say, Kathy? Will you make the sojourn into the beast's lair if we accompany you?"

"Come on, Kat," urged Becky. "You've been avoiding that attic for years. Isn't it high time you find out what you're so afraid of?"

"Oh why not?" I declared. "Let's do this. I'm tired of imagining I hear heavy breathing every time I walk past the attic door."

"Shall we storm the castle wall this afternoon?" asked Marcus, glancing from Becky to me. "I'm free."

"As luck would have it, my calendar's open as well," added Becky.

"Excellent," said Marcus. "I'll get the check and see you both at the cottage at four thirty."

Chapter 9

At a quarter past four, I sat on the front steps of Sea Breeze Cottage, awaiting Becky and Marcus's arrival. Mussolini lay at my feet, oblivious as to what was about to happen. I was as anxious as anyone, to exorcize the black entity that, for most of my life, had occupied my home and dreams. I needed to know the reasoning behind my Grandpa Jake's wish to keep me from the attic. As I sat on the porch, basking in the afternoon sun, I leaned against the post and allowed my mind to drift back to that fateful day, so long ago, when he issued his dire warning.

I was eight the day I overheard my father and Grandpa Jake arguing in the kitchen. They were so engrossed in their heated exchange, they failed to hear the big yellow school bus drop me off in front of our cottage. Hearing their angry voices, I hesitated on the porch, for I'd never before heard them argue.

"You have an obligation to the child, Ellery," stated my Grandpa Jake. "She has a right to know who she is. After all, she is your daughter."

"What I possess has nothing to offer her but heartache, Jacob," my father warned. "She is better off not knowing. Now I've asked you to perform a task for me. If you cannot accomplish it, then I will find someone who will."

"I'll do as you ask, Ellery." Grandpa Jake warned, lowering his voice, "However, I will not be the one to tell Kathleen what we have done this day. That burden will lie squarely on your shoulders. And mark my words, Ellery Jennings, she will hate you for this."

"So be it," replied my father. "She'll be better off. Now get it done."

The next afternoon, Grandpa Jake and I took the dogs to the beach. It wasn't long before my child's intuition sensed that something was bothering him. Instead of walking with me, he sat on the rocks, gazing out to sea and smoking his cigar in silence. As I stood watching him, he motioned me near.

"Grandpa, is something wrong?" I asked him.

"Yes, Button, I'm afraid there is," he replied, knocking the fire from his cigar. "I've something important to tell you, and you must listen to me with great attention."

"Are you going away?" I asked, voicing my concern. My greatest fear was that he would leave me as my mother had.

"No, no, I'm not leaving you," he replied. "However, I have a strange story to tell you. I'm afraid that it's a dark and frightening tale, and you must heed my warnings."

"What kind of warnings, Grandpa?" I asked, filled with fear. He sat looking at me for several moments before he finally spoke the words that have haunted me for over half a century.

"A dire warning, Button," he said, turning me to face him. "I need you to promise me that you will never again go up into the attic."

Looking now at our cottage, I failed to understand his warning. The attic held no danger for me. Becky and I often played up there on rainy days. I had a small table and chairs tucked in beneath the eaves, where we enjoyed tea and biscuits with our dollies. The small table and chairs, holding the rose-colored tea set, were his birthday gift to me a year earlier. Miss Emma, my beloved dolly, was at that very moment sitting in her small chair awaiting our next rainy day tea party. A Christmas gift from my mother when I was five, I treasured Miss Emma more than anything in the world. She was beautiful, with long curly locks of golden hair and blue eyes that opened and closed when you moved her. Barely a foot high, she was dressed in a red velvet coat, trimmed in dark fur, and held a matching fur muffler. Sitting next to Miss Emma was Becky's doll, Fiona. She was Becky's pride and joy, with her red curls and pink frilly dress. *What of their fate,* I wondered. What could possibly be in the attic that would send my grandpa into such a panic?

"What's wrong with the attic?" I asked him, confused.

"Listen closely, Button," he said. I could tell that what he had to say was costing him greatly. "I was up there just last night and…I saw the most hideous sight. It was a huge black creature full of hate and evil thoughts. I sensed that it was something very wicked and dangerous. You must promise me, Button, that you will never again go up there. If it should ever get its huge claws into you, it will surely be the end of you." With that said, he turned away to hide his tears.

How could something so vile live in the attic alongside our dollies and my tea set? How was it, that until now, I had failed to sense its presence? Knowing that my Grandpa Jake would never lie to me, I felt a sense of dread sweep over me like a suffocating fog.

As I stood looking up at the two small round attic windows, their friendly little faces suddenly took on a sinister stare that chilled me to the bone.

"I promise, Grandpa," I whispered, leaning into the safety of his arms. "Where can I go, now, where the monster cannot find me?"

"The black creature is bound to the darkness of the attic and cannot pass into the rooms below," said Grandpa Jake, holding me to him. "You're safe as long as you never go into the attic. Do you understand? And one other thing. We must never mention this to your pappa. It will be our secret."

"Yes, Grandpa," I said, my eyes again wandering to the little windows under the eaves. My heart sank within me, at the sudden realization that my dear Miss Emma was now all alone in the attic with a foul and sinister beast. The mere thought of never seeing her again, brought me to tears.

"Now, don't cry, Button," said Grandpa, wiping my tears on his white handkerchief. "It's for your own good that you heed my warnings. Look at me, little one. I promise to always be here, to protect you from all the monsters in this wicked old world. Of that, you can be sure." And, he had kept that promise until two weeks after my fifteenth birthday when his sudden death rocked my world. On that fateful day,

I grew concerned when his dogs, Hector and Percy, returned from the beach without him. Fearing the worst, I ran down to the beach and went in search of him. At first, I didn't see him and hope soared. Then I spotted a yellow object lying on the sand up near the old pier. I found myself praying as I ran as fast as my legs would carry me.

"Please, God," I begged. "Don't let it be Grandpa. Please!" As I neared the old pier, the details began to emerge, and I recognized my Grandpa's old yellow slicker.

When I finally reached him, I found him lying on his side, facing away from me. Several seagulls surrounded his still form as if waiting for him to rise up and feed them.

"Grandpa!" I cried out. Fearing that he was hurt, I knelt down beside him. Perhaps he'd fallen and was unable to get up on his own.

"I'm here, Grandpa," I said, placing my hand on his shoulder. "Are you ill?"

Not getting a response, I steeled myself against the inevitable and rolled him over. The moment I saw his face, I knew that he was gone. His mouth hung slightly ajar, and he looked out through eyes empty and lifeless. Encircling him in my arms, I felt the tears come. No longer would he be my protector against the monster that dwelled in the attic. I was, once again, on my own with an angry and distant father.

The very day we laid Grandpa Jake to rest, Becky and I shoved my old bedroom dresser into place in front of the attic door. Without my grandpa to watch my back, I was taking measures into my own hands. That was forty-five years ago! Becky was right. It was high time I faced my old nemesis and banished it from my life. I hated to admit that I simply didn't have the heart to deal with the problem beyond the attic door. The fact that I was sixty was only a testament as to how well my grandfather's ruse had worked. Mussolini came over to sit beside me on the porch step, assuring me that he was in charge of security and I had nothing to fear.

"Prepare yourself, my old friend," I said, petting his ears. "We are about to invade the enemy's stronghold."

The sight of a yellow Volkswagen Beetle pulling into my driveway interrupted my thoughts. A moment later, a sporty red Mustang filled the space behind it. Mussolini announced in a wave of friendly barking that the cavalry had arrived.

"Well, are we ready?" asked Becky, as she approached the cottage. Her bright, oversized pink

T-shirt and baggy jeans shorts were in sharp contrast to her yellow-tinged skin.

"It's a go!" I said, giving her a high five.

"Then let's do this!" she exclaimed, as she walked past me. "We each have a dolly that has been held captive in your attic for far too long." I was surprised that she still remembered Fiona after all these years.

"Is that so?" asked Marcus, giving me a quick hug and a peck on the cheek. I saw Becky's grin of approval. "What do you say we liberate them by storming the dungeon?"

"Charge!" I exclaimed, leading the way into the cottage. Mussolini, following close on our heels, was on high alert. As we made our way through the kitchen and down the hallway, my apprehension increased, and I could feel the sweat in my palms.

"Here we are," I said. Turning to my right, I faced my old dresser and the door it had guarded for most of my life.

"Well, I say we do this before Kathy loses her nerve," remarked Becky, giving me a playful nudge.

"I'm not going to lose my nerve," I stated, cringing at the weakness in my voice.

"Fear not, my fair maiden," Marcus whispered in my ear. "This time, a knight accompanies you into the dragon's lair."

As the three of us slid the old dresser aside, I gave out a loud moan at what it revealed. Several decades of dust and cobwebs now draped the door like a funeral shroud. Becky started to laugh aloud, and I turned to stare at her.

"What's so funny?" I asked. The situation was embarrassing enough for me without her making light of it. I shuddered to think of what Marcus was thinking about my lack of housekeeping skills.

"Sorry, Kat," she said, stifling another laugh. "With cobwebs like these, there has to be at least one skeleton buried behind that door. Relax, you'll find worse than this in the basement of my flower shop. I haven't ventured down there in years. Spiders.

"Well, for your information, this was a trap," I said, in an attempt to save face. "You'll notice that the cobwebs have not been disturbed. That can only mean that the creature has made no attempts to escape. Wise choice, as I've always kept an arsenal to defend myself should he ever try."

"Such as?" Marcus asked, raising an eyebrow.

Reaching behind my bedroom door, I retrieved an item that had long awaited a time, such as this, when a champion would step forward to wield it. Long and lean, it was just what was required at this moment.

"What is this?" asked Marcus.

"It's a sword I made from an old Erector set," I replied, handing it to him. "You'll need it." Looking at it now, I felt embarrassed with its flimsiness. "Of course, I was ten when I made it," I added.

My "monster slayer" was made from three short sections of an Erector set's steel rods, fastened together with several small nuts and bolts. A shorter section of steel rod made up the hilt. I had covered it in aluminum foil and construction paper gems.

"Remarkable ingenuity," commented Marcus, holding it up to examine it.

"Somehow, it looked more lethal when I was a kid," I said, shrugging my shoulders.

"I shall wield it with honor, madam," stated Marcus, with a look of serious banter.

"Oh, and if that doesn't do the trick, I have this," I said, handing him my old twirling baton. The glittery pink pompoms protruding from the ends, were now gnarled and kinked from years of sitting behind my door.

"This will work even better," said Marcus, trying to hide his amusement. "At our age, blunt force must suffice when speed is no longer a factor. By the way, how fast is your running speed?"

"Fair," I replied, trying to hide my grin. "Remember, I'm only in training. But then again, I only have to be slightly faster than either of you, right?"

"Point well taken," muttered Marcus, handing me back the Erector set sword. "I think I'll go with blunt force in this case."

Becky chuckled.

"I agree," I said, stepping back.

"Shall we open the gate, ladies?" asked Marcus, reaching for the doorknob.

As the door swung outward, I glanced up into the darkness. Thick cobwebs hung along the walls of the stairwell like torn fishing nets. Now that I was literally looking down the throat of the beast, I, once again, thought of my Grandpa Jake's long ago warning and shuddered.

Fighting my childhood fear, I allowed my rational mind to weigh out the situation. Monsters are not real! Marcus, sensing my hesitation, thankfully, took charge.

"I'll go first, Kathy," he said, stepping in front of me. "After all, I'm the one wielding the…twir-lee thing."

As he reached into the ropes of dust and flipped on the ancient light switch, relief flooded over me when the bulb at the top of the steps sprang to life.

"Well, that is a feather in Thomas Edison's cap," muttered Marcus, pulling a flashlight from his back pocket. "However, I'm still partial to a good torch."

The three of us made our way slowly up the steps, our shoes leaving footprints in the thick dust. Marcus was the first to step out into the large room at the top. When nothing jumped out at him, Becky and I bravely joined him. I winced at the sight of the evening sun, as it struggled to penetrate the layers of dust clinging to the glass of the two small dormer windows in front of me.

"It's surprising cool up here," said Marcus, looking around.

As my eyes adjusted to the low light, familiar objects began to jump out at me, and I felt my throat tighten with emotion. I was unprepared for the flood of memories that hit me. To my left, I saw my grandfather's old cane bottom chair. The hole in its seat was the exact size of a seven-year-old's bare foot. I smiled at the memory of the day I'd put it there while attempting to reach the cookie jar atop the refrigerator. I recognized an old lamp made from a buoy, its shade now cracked with age. When I spotted my rocking horse, Misty, I nearly squealed with delight. Still vivid in my mind were the many rides we enjoyed and the magical places we visited.

Surrounding my faithful steed were several dusty brown boxes, littering the floor and filling the corners. Dust and cobwebs draped them like soiled lace doilies. I spotted the cradle, I knew, held the books and toys of my childhood beneath its dust-covered shroud. Oh, how I longed to touch them again. Just beyond stood my mother's sewing mannequin, an unfinished red-and-white striped dress, still pinned to its shapely form. Beside it, a cracked oval mirror hung on its wooden stand, shattering my reflection in a Picasso-style image. A memory flooded back to the day my grandfather carried it up here.

"This mirror belonged to your Grandma Sarah," he'd told me on that day long ago. "Percy knocked it over. Clumsy brute. I wonder if dogs can suffer seven years of bad luck? Someday, I'll replace the broken mirror, and it will be yours, Button. It's an heirloom, you know, for it originally belonged to your maternal great-grandmother, Aubrey Hennesy." *Memories.*

"My dolly!" exclaimed Becky, shattering my thoughts like the shards of the old oval mirror. Brushing past me, she hurried across the room. Here the dirt on the small dormer windows blocked out the view of the ocean below. I smiled as she lifted her dolly out of the miniature rocking chair and hugged it tightly to her chest. Marcus looked at me and smiled. I was happy to see Becky reunited, once again, with the beautiful doll with the red curls and frilly pink dress.

"Oh, Kat, look," she said. "It's my beautiful Fiona!"

I was amazed at the way her voice suddenly took on a childlike softness as she spoke. Stepping nearer to the window, my eyes found my little wooden table and chairs tucked in beneath the attic's eave and my heart wept. The tiny rose-colored tea set, now draped in a thick layer of dust, still graced the table in readiness for my next rainy-day tea party. Then, I saw her. She was still sitting in the chair where I'd left her, all those years earlier. Dust and time had dimmed her locks of golden hair and fur-trimmed red velvet dress, but she was still quite beautiful.

"Miss Emma," I whispered, as the room faded away. My throat tightened with unshed tears, as I leaned over and gently picked up my own precious dolly. As I held her against me, I felt the years fall away like shattered glass. "Oh, how I've dreamed about you, my darling. I'm so sorry I'm late for tea. Will you ever forgive me?" I felt Becky's arm slip around me, and I smiled at her.

"We've waited a long time for this moment," she said, softly. "May I take Fiona home with me?"

"Of course, Becky," I exclaimed. "We both have a lot of lost years to make up." Leaning against me, Becky nodded in agreement.

"Look at this," exclaimed Marcus, pulling our attention elsewhere. "Now this is a worthy find, I'm sure." He was standing in front of an old bicycle, a dusty sheet dangling from his hand.

"It's just an old bicycle," I said, dodging several boxes to reach him.

"This, my dear, is no ordinary bicycle," he said, grinning from ear to ear. "This is a 1928 Shelby Lindy bicycle. My grandfather had one of these on his farm in England. I used to ride it every summer when we took the lorry up to visit him. It'll soar like the wind."

"It belonged to my Grandpa Jake," I said. "He tried to give it to me, but it was too much for me to handle. So, he bought me a pink bike with a banana seat. It had high handle bars with pink and white streamers dangling from the grips."

"Please stop," said Marcus, feigning a look of absolute horror. "Such talk won't do in the presence of a classic such as this."

"I, too, had a cool bike," said Becky, joining in the fun. "Mine was green. It had a banana seat covered in pink and yellow daisies, and beads on the spokes. Remember, Kat? I named it Betsy. What was the name of your bike, again?"

"Chloe," I replied, watching a pained expression cross Marcus's face. "I even had a license plate with my name on it, attached to the back fender."

"I did too!" exclaimed Becky. "We got them from a special offer on the back of our box of Lucky Charms."

"Have the two of you finished?" asked Marcus, giving us a look of feigned disgust. "Forget your pink poodle bikes and your fancy handlebars. This, ladies, is the holy grail of bicycles. The Lindy was the first to include chrome in its construction and the first to promote a national icon. That icon was, of course, Charles Lindbergh's *Spirit of St. Louis*. Behold the miniature model of his famous airplane mounted on the front fender."

"To me, it's just an old bike," I said, nudging Becky. "What are your thoughts, Becky?"

"Yep," she replied, turning away. "If it wasn't pink, it wasn't popular."

"This baby takes me back to my time spent with my grandfather," said Marcus, ignoring our friendly jabs. Gently, his hand caressed the curve of the chrome handle bar, slid down the wide crossbar, across the leather seat, ending at the back fender. His voice took on an almost reverent tone as he spoke. "My father died when I was a lad. My Grandpa Quimby, then a widower himself, moved in with my mother and me and taught me how to be a boy. We'd fish together, and I'd help him tend the sheep in the meadows. He taught me to ride on one of these. He was my greatest hero."

"Hey, aren't we forgetting something?" asked Becky, glancing around. "What about the vile, evil creature that lives up here? Shouldn't he have eaten us by now?"

"She's right," I said, glancing over my right shoulder. "Don't tell me that I've been dreading this attic for nothing?"

"Sorry, girlfriend," said Becky, shaking her head, "but you've been dreading this attic for nothing."

"Here's what I believe," said Marcus, dropping the sheet back over the old bicycle. "I believe that your grandfather told you that tale to keep you out of this attic for a reason. Now, you must ask yourself, what *is* that reason?"

"Good point, Marcus," said Becky, glancing around. "Shall we seek to find an answer?"

For the next three hours, we combed through box after box, finding nothing but children's clothes and a stack of old records dating back to the days of the crank phonographs. I found a stack of *Life* magazines from the early Kennedy years that Albert might deem worthy of keeping. However, after a thorough search, we found nothing that would warrant my grandfather banishing me from the attic.

"Well, I'm confused, Kat," said Becky, wiping her dirty face on the hem of her T-shirt. "Why would your grandpa lie to you just to keep you from finding some old records and a box of old magazines? It just doesn't make sense."

"I would like to have a friend of mine take a look at this, if you don't mind," said Marcus, handing me an old gilded clock.

I was sure that I'd never seen it before. Ten inches high, its domed glass front covered a light-blue porcelain face, representing a sky filled with white fluffy clouds. Two childlike angels, each clutching a rose, graced its golden front. The base, itself in the shape of a cloud, held two tiny birds in flight. The clock's twelve numerals were what caught my eye. Tiny red jewels outlined each number in stark contrast to the blue face. The clock's two silver hands, still from years of sitting idle, resembled tiny outstretched arms.

"It's beautiful, Marcus," I said, handing it back to him. "I don't recall seeing it before. However, my Grandpa Jake stored several of his own belongings up here when he came to live with us. Perhaps it belonged to him."

"Well, I have a friend in New York who deals in old clocks," said Marcus. "I'll give him a call."

"I'm exhausted!" exclaimed Becky. "Can you believe it's nearly seven thirty? Oh, Kat, you missed your training."

"Relax, Becky," I said. "I can do my own training this evening. I have my stopwatch."

"Are you sure?" she asked, looking relieved. "I could stay if you like."

"No, I got this," I offered, shooing her toward the steps. "I don't know about the two of you, but I need a shower."

"I'll second that idea," said Marcus. "I'll lead the way back to civilization."

As we made our way down the steep steps and into the hallway below, I thought of my Grandpa Jake and his boogeyman.

"I can't believe my grandfather lied to me for no reason," I said. "However, I'm relieved to find no creature living up there."

"Well, I for one, am glad that our trip into the unknown was uneventful," said Marcus, flipping off the light switch and closing the door. "With good reason, as I was to be the creature's first meal in decades."

We all laughed at his statement as we made our way to the kitchen. Becky and I, happy to be reunited with our childhood dollies, clutched them to our chest. Marcus, dirt smudged on his face, held the little golden clock. *We have each found a treasure*, I thought. Stepping over to the refrigerator, I handed each treasure hunter a cold bottle of soda.

"This just hits the spot," said Marcus, after downing nearly half the bottle. "Thank you for the trip down memory lane, Kathy. I will probably never see another Shelby Lindy bicycle in my lifetime. Not one in as good a shape as yours, that is."

"Well, I'm off," said Becky, stepping over to the front door. "I've been reunited with my Fiona, and I'm taking her home. We'll both get a thorough cleaning, and then I'll catch her up on what's been happening since she was taken hostage by the Jennings family."

"I plan on doing the same," I said, giving Becky a hug. After she left, I turned to Marcus. "Do you think my little clock could be worth something?"

"Well, I'm not sure," he said, handing me the empty soda bottle. "It's really too bad that it's missing its key. Perhaps, I can find one at an antique shop."

"Let's take a look in my grandfather's jewelry box," I said. "I recall seeing a funny-looking key in there. The box is in my bedroom closet."

"Splendid," said Marcus. Placing his little clock on the kitchen table, he followed me into my bedroom.

Reaching into my closet, I pulled out a small oak box with the initials JEW etched into its wooden lid. I knew the initials stood for Jacob Evan Windsor and that he'd made the box when he was a teenager. As I rummaged through my grandfather's cufflinks and old watches, Marcus wandered over to the window overlooking the sea.

"You have a wonderful view of the ocean, Kathy," he said. "I know why you chose this room."

When I saw his gaze drop to the windowsill holding my sea stone collection, I froze. How was I going to explain what they were without divulging too much? *Perhaps, he won't notice them*, I thought. I was wrong.

"Kathy, why do you have stones littering your windowsill?" he asked. "Are they to frighten off pesky suitors below your window?"

"Not exactly," I said. *How much should I tell him at this point in our relationship?* I wondered. *If Marcus was going to be in my life, and I hoped he was, then he needed to know what things were important to me.* "That, Marcus, is my sea stone collection."

"Sea stones?" he asked. "Why do you call them sea stones?"

"Well, because they came from the sea," I replied, walking over to join him at the window. "What you see here is nearly fifty years of searching the beach. They're magic, you know."

"Magic?" he asked, looking at me. "How so?"

Oh boy, now what was I going to say to him? Then I thought of my Grandpa Jake, and I knew the answer.

"Let me explain it the way my grandfather explained it to me," I said, picking up a darkish stone and holding it in the palm of my hand. "This particular stone holds a mystery as old as time itself, as it could very well be millions of years old. It could be a piece of a faraway continent, sent adrift by a powerful earthquake or the shifting of the continents. After millions of years of being pushed along on the bottom of the ocean by the currents, it somehow ended up here, washed ashore on my beach."

"Is that the magic?" asked Marcus, gently transferring the stone into his own palm.

"No," I replied. "The magic of the sea stone is in finding it. Not every stone on the beach is special, mind you. The special ones beckon you to stop and pick them up. You must learn to listen for their invitation."

"How did you start such a collection?"

"My grandfather found my first sea stone and gave it over into my keeping. After that, I found another and another and so on. Once you find your first stone, you're hooked. I have twelve of them now."

"Is that it?" he asked, sensing I was still holding something back.

"No," I replied, unsure of how to proceed. Turning, I looked out at the sea. "There is one very special stone that only the very blessed find. It's known as the singing sea stone."

"The singing sea stone?" he asked. Leaning back against the window frame, he looked into my face. "How is it magic?"

"Well, its invitation is pretty much like all the others," I said, feeling his closeness. "It beckons to you to pick it up, and you do. However, the moment you enclose it within your hand, your very being breaks into the song of the ages. The music emanates from deep within your heart, letting you know that true love is about to find you and sweep you off your feet. You're blessed indeed if you find a singing sea stone within your lifetime. Some find their stone when they're young and have a lifetime to enjoy its rewards. Some find theirs near the end of their life and can only savor the magic for a short time. However, some never find it and, therefore, have to be content with whomever their destiny sends them."

"And when did you find your singing sea stone, Kathleen?" he asked, leaning in close to my face. Knowing he was expecting my honesty, I looked him in the eye and answered his question.

"I found it on my sixtieth birthday," I replied. "I found it just fifteen days before you walked into my life, Marcus Stone."

When I'd finished, I waited for his reaction. Would he scoff at my silliness or take me serious? I couldn't bear the thought of him laughing at me or thinking me eccentric. After a moment, he turned away from me and returned the stone to the windowsill. At that moment, I felt my heart sink. I couldn't face him, so I looked away. Silence fell over the room leaving only the sound of the sea below. Then he spoke.

"So, you think our chance meeting was the result of you finding this singing sea stone?" he asked, softly. "Am I to believe that you think some rock brought us together and I'm now supposed to fall madly in love with you? Is that it?"

As he awaited my answer, I felt as if the world had stopped turning and I was about to tumble over the edge into blackness. Then he spoke the words that pulled me back from the edge.

"Well, Miss Kathleen Jennings," he said, pulling me into his arms. "I'm here to tell you that the magic of your sea stone is real. I have indeed, fallen in love with you. Now, does that magic work both ways? You weren't clear on that point." His words cascaded over me like a shower of fresh rain. He loved me!

"Yes, the magic works both ways," I said, imagining I could hear the stone's song burst forth from within my heart as it filled with love for this man. "I love you too, Marcus."

As he pulled me into his arms, I melted into his embrace. Marcus loved me! When his lips found mine, I felt the love we had just confessed to each other course through my body. *This must be that special kind of enduring love, that Becky mentioned,* I thought. When we parted, he leaned me back to look at my face.

"May I see our special sea stone?" he asked, smiling. "I'll bet it's as beautiful as your hazel eyes and sprinkled with those same flecks of gold."

His words made me laugh aloud. Reaching into my collection, I chose the stone with the mottled shades of grey and the small uneven pockmarks. Turning it in my fingers, I saw the fine spidery lines. Smiling, I handed it to him. His face took on a confused expression, and he looked to me for an explanation.

"I have come to believe, Marcus, that it's not the appearance of the stone that makes it special but the beautiful love you create from its magic."

Nodding his head in agreement, he carefully replaced our sea stone back among the others on the windowsill and stepped back.

"Here's to our sea stone," he whispered, planting an affectionate kiss on the end of my nose. "Together, we'll make our own magic."

"That we will, Marcus," I said. "It's a funny thing, though. It was on my eleventh birthday that Grandpa Jake gifted me with my very first sea stone."

"So it's a birthday thing?" he asked.

"I don't believe so," I replied. Then I remembered the reason we had come into the room. "By the way, I found the key."

"To my heart?" he said, pulling me against him.

"No, silly. The key to the little clock," I said, holding up the brass key. "At least, I think it is."

"Well, let's go see if it fits," said Marcus, leading me back to the kitchen.

"It fits!" I exclaimed, as Marcus slid the key into the hole in the clock's face. "Shall we wind it up?"

"I don't think I will," he said. "The clock has been sitting for who knows how many years, in an unstable environment. Wallace, my clock expert from New York, will clean and oil it good before winding it."

"Well, you know best," I said.

"Now, I'm going home and make a few phone calls," said Marcus. "Keep your sword handy now that we've freed your beast from the attic."

"I will," I replied,

"I will depart your company, my sweet, and return to my own stronghold," he said, pecking me on the lips. "However, my heart will remain behind to guard you in my absence. Treat it well."

After Marcus drove away, I put on my running shoes and headed for the beach with Mussolini leading the way. Even though it was late, I needed to sort out all that had happened to me today, and the sea was a good listener. After warming up, I set my stopwatch and began my run. Becky had bumped me up to running for ninety seconds and walking sixty. My body, surprisingly, didn't seem to mind the change. However, as I ran, I was having trouble keeping track of my time. Slowing to a walk, my mind tried desperately to sort out all that had happened to me over the last couple of days. Between falling in love with Marcus and Becky's illness, my emotions were so torn. How was I going to find that delicate balance between my happiness with Marcus and my sadness over losing Becky? Was it even possible? How was I going to conceal the joy I felt knowing that Marcus was in love with me and I with him?

Looking down at my stopwatch, I realized that I'd been walking for a full three minutes. Yikes! Looking down the beach, I could see that I was about a minute and a half from the rocks, so I kicked it into high gear, and by the time I reach the sea path, I was breathing hard. Flopping down on the warm sand, I lay back and looked up at the sun-tinged clouds. As my breathing slowed, I could feel my heart beating within my chest. "I'm in love, I'm in love, I'm in love," it seemed to say. When my old friend Charlie began to attack my right calf, I stood up and began my stretching exercises. *I'm feeling pretty good for a sixty-year-old woman*, I thought. Of course, being in love did wonders for my well-being.

After a hot shower, I carried my bottle of cold water and a plate holding a ham and cheese sandwich into the sitting room. Mussolini, stretched out on the rug, lay snoring contently. Curling up in my father's chair, I watched the sea darken with the coming night. As I nibbled at my sandwich, the white elephant in the room was still the question of why Grandpa Jake would lie to me when his faith made him the most honest of men. What reason did he have to keep me out of the attic? I was only a child. What harm could I have possibly done to a collection of old magazines and a stack of dusty old boxes? Then an epiphany struck me. What if his fear was not in my damaging something in the attic but rather in my discovery of something hidden there? What was in the attic that Grandpa Jake was trying to conceal?

"Good question!" I exclaimed, aloud.

Mussolini rolled over and looked at me as if to say, "Do you mind? I'm sleeping here!"

"I'm going back to the attic, Pup," I said, looking down at him. "You're welcome to come with me if you think I need a champion." He groaned loudly and eyed up the remainder of my ham sandwich. Some watchdog!

Taking a flashlight from a kitchen drawer, I approached the attic door. Right on cue, the old fear rose in me, and I hesitated. Suddenly, a new strength filled me, and I felt that fear vanish like smoke.

"Not this time!" I said, pulling the door open. "Ready or not, Mr. Monster, here I come!" Flipping on the light switch, inside the door, I climbed the steps with a renewed purpose.

Chapter 10

The light at the top of the stairs gave little illumination in the darkened attic, so I turned on my flashlight and swept the room with its beam. When the light hit my rocking horse, Misty, I walked over to check her out. With a gentle push of my hand, I set her in motion. She still looked the same as I remembered. Her huge brown glass eyes sparkled in the light, and I smiled at the memories she invoked. Beside her sat my cradle full of toys and books. I thought of removing the sheet and having a peek inside, but I decided against the impulse. Toys and books, I knew, were not the reason for my banishment. No, there had to be something else up here. Something I was not supposed to find until I was older.

The boxes we'd sorted through earlier now littered the floor and I carefully made my way among them. Suddenly, the beam of my flashlight shattered,

KATHLEEN MARTIN

sending light fragments bouncing around the room. I was momentarily frozen with fear until I spied what had caused the light to dance. Aiming my flashlight beam at the broken shards of the oval mirror, I relaxed as the fractured light danced on the walls. Laughing at myself, I stepped closer to the mirror. Recalling that the mirror had belonged to my grandmother, I examined it closer. The frame was in surprisingly good shape for being over a century old. With a new mirror and a good polishing, I could bring it back to life. Wondering what it would take to replace the mirror, I carefully flipped the mirror over to examine the backing. As I did, I disturbed a stack of old quilts hiding behind it.

As the blankets fell to the floor, the light from my flashlight fell onto an old dusty trunk hidden beneath. *This is new*, I thought. *How did we miss this?* I was sure we had looked at everything this afternoon. Sliding the mirror aside, I tugged the old trunk out of its dark hiding place and positioned it under the light. I had no memory of the trunk before this moment. But then again, as a child, I'd only played near the windows, where the light was good. Dusting off the cobwebs with my hand, I guessed its dimensions as roughly 2 ½ feet long, 1 ½ feet deep and 2 feet tall, including its humpback lid that revealed its

262

age. Black in color, it was in very good shape for its years. The brass straps and handle were a different story, however, as they were now nearly as dark at the trunk itself. Unadorned, I saw no identification as to whom it once belonged. As I lifted the lid, I wondered if this was my grandfather's secret.

Aiming my flashlight beam into its interior, I felt my excitement quickly dissipate. Inside, I found only another quilt. This one, however, had obviously belonged to a child. Made of yellow and white squares, the creator had delicately embroidered each with childlike puppies and kittens in various forms of play. It needed only a good washing to bring it back to life. Was I only to find more old blankets? What was it that I had expected to find? I was just about to close the lid when I spotted an envelope, yellowed now with age, tucked beneath the edge of the quilt. Lifting it out, I was shocked to see my name written across its front. Holding it closer to the beam of the flashlight, I recognized my grandfather's handwriting. Excitement, once again, quickened my heart as I quickly tore the end from the envelope and slid the letter free. Will my grandfather's letter hold my answers?

September 22, 1958

My dearest Kathleen,

If you are reading this letter, then you have finally overcome your extreme fear of the monster in the attic. I am so very sorry for what I have done to you, but as you will discover, I had no choice in the matter. It broke your old grandpa's heart to have to frighten you from going into the attic again, but I did so with good intentions. It was hard for me to look you in the eye, knowing that I was the villain ruining the tiny tea parties that you and little Becky Fraser enjoyed with your dollies. I am hoping that you are now old enough to understand my reasons and are able to someday forgive your father and me for what we've done. Read on and I will attempt to explain myself.

This past week, your father received a letter from his father, your grandfather, Howard Jennings, who lives in Southeastern British Columbia, Canada. The Jennings family, as you may not be aware, owns Kavaloy Farms just outside of Kimberley in the Purcell Mountains. The lush mountain farm is a 5,000-acre estate that has been in their family for three generations. The early death of Robert Jennings, your father's only brother, meant that your father is now the sole heir to the family's vast holdings. However, his refusal to return to Canada and take his rightful place within the family has prompted your grandfather to do the unthinkable. His recent letter, addressed to your father, states simply that the name of Ellery Baines Jennings is hereby stricken from his last will and testament and

that your father is now banished
from the family. This is a dire
development, Kathleen, as the
farm will now fall into the hands
of the in-laws. Your great uncle
Marwood Brannon, brother
to your grandmother Gerta
Jennings, cares nothing of raising
prime beef cows and will most
assuredly inherit the farm and sell
off the vast Kavaloy holdings for
his own gain.

Upon hearing of his ban-
ishment, your father, in his rage,
vowed to destroy all that he possessed of his Canadian family.
When he found that he lacked
the courage to do so, he engaged
me to perform the dastardly
deed. As you will discover, I was
unwilling to follow through with
his demands. You have a right to
know of your Canadian ances-
tors and their history. In addition, he bid me to destroy all that
reminded him of your beautiful

mother and how much her death has hurt him. I simply could not allow this to happen, either. I knew I had to keep these items safely within the house, so I hid them away.

I chose the attic because I knew your father, who suffers from extreme claustrophobia, would never venture there. You, however, were a different matter. I knew of your fondness for playing there with your dollies. My greatest fear was that during your play, you would discover this trunk and its contents and alert your father to its existence. Once he'd discovered my act of deceit, he would have taken matters into his own hands, and all would have disappeared. Therefore, I placed my soul in eternal jeopardy by inventing the vile and frightening monster in hopes its presence would keep you out of the attic. Since you have now discovered the trunk, I am confident that you are now old enough to debunk my lie. If you inform your father of your discovery, fight him for possession, Kathleen. These treasures are your legacy, and he will destroy them if he gets his hands on them. Your children and your children's children will thank you for your steadfastness on this matter. You remain always in my heart.

Your loving Grandpa Jake

P.S. Your mother made this pretty yellow-and-white quilt for your birth and homecoming. Perhaps you will use it, someday, to swaddle your own babes.

My hands shook as I returned my Grandpa Jake's letter to its envelope. At last, I had the answer to the decades-old mystery of the attic. How could I have allowed my fear to live within me for so long?

If I had to be honest with myself, my childhood fear was only part of the reason I avoided the attic. What was the other? By the time I was in my twenties, logic dictates that I should have put all childish fears behind me. Shame washed over me as I realized that pure stubbornness was what kept me from marching up these stairs, years ago, and discovering my grandfather's secret. I knew now that his deception was simply a ruse to hide something very precious from my father. Of course, he never expected it to take me over five decades to discover what that something was. And I suspect that even Grandpa Jake, wouldn't have guessed that my father would live well into his eighties.

"Okay, Grandpa Jake," I said, aloud. "Show me what you've hidden away."

As I lifted the quilt from the trunk, my heart leapt into my throat at the sight of what lay beneath. It was an 11x14 portrait of a young woman bearing a strange resemblance to myself at that age. The skilled hand of the artist had captured her perfectly, and I knew in my heart that I was looking into the face of my mother. Tears spilled over as I stared into hazel eyes that matched my own. Her dark hair, cut to shoulder length, framed her heart-shaped face and graceful neck. The face of my long-lost mother, now revealed to me at last, filled me with wonder. Lifting it carefully into the light, I was not surprised to see the name of Ellery Jennings etched into the lower right-hand corner. A feeling of pure love for my Grandpa Jake now washed over me for his thoughtfulness. Propping the portrait in the lid of the trunk, I turned my attention to what else this trunk of wonders held for me.

My flashlight revealed three tarnished 8x10 metal frames and their black and white photographs. Carefully, I lifted the top frame into the light. In the picture, a middle-aged couple and two small, dark-haired boys, stood on the front steps of a large white clapboard farmhouse. I guessed, by their manner of dress, that the picture was taken sometime around the 1930s. The boys wore white shirts and short, dark pants, reminiscent of that era. The tall, thin man, standing behind them, was a younger image of my father.

At his side, stood a small plump woman, encircled within his right arm. She looked every bit the typical farmer's wife, in her long cotton dress, protected by an apron. The visor of her flower print bonnet, hid her face in shadow. *My father's family*, I thought.

Turning the picture over, someone had penciled in the details on the back. *Howard, Gerta, and boys. Taken in 1929, on the farm in Kimberley.*

Howard and Gerta were the grandparents I had never met. Turning the picture back over, I looked closer at the two boys.

The smaller of the two, appeared to be around the age of six. *My father*, I thought, recognizing the same long, thin face and dark hair as that of the man I knew as Pappa. The older boy, I knew was my uncle Robert, who was older by two years. I knew, from Grandpa Jake, that Robert had died suddenly from a fall in the barn at age 22.

Lifting the next picture into the light, I felt a rush of emotion sweep over me. As I gazed at the picture of my *own* family, the years seemed to fall away, and I was once more little Kathy Jennings. This picture was of a young couple in their early twenties, obviously my parents in their early years. Standing directly in front of them, a small dark-haired girl, dressed in a white spring dress and matching bonnet, smiled happily into the camera. In her hands, she clutched the handle of an Easter basket. My father wore a black suit and tie, and my mother, a beautiful white mid length dress. She wore her dark hair swept up in an attractive hairstyle from the fifties. By the way their arms encircled each other's waist, it was obvious that they were very much in love.

Behind my parents stood Sea Breeze Cottage, with the sea gleaming in the background. I marveled at the way our cottage looked in its early years compared to how it appeared today, a half a century later. The freshly coated white clapboard siding was now faded and covered in peeling paint. The fancy white porch railing of my childhood, today, was missing a couple of rungs and had a noticeable sag on its northern corner. How could we have allowed our beloved home to fall into such disrepair? What would it take to return it to its original condition? How the years had changed the scenery as well. The two massive trees that now shaded the cottage were, in the photograph, spindly saplings just beginning to show their spring buds. And there was a porch swing. A sudden memory swept through my mind of an early summer's day long, long ago, when a small girl sat swinging on the front porch swing with her grandpa beside her. *What became of the swing?* I wondered.

Turning the picture over, I read the details aloud, "Ellery, Paula, and Kathleen. Easter 1955." I didn't remember the day, but it must have been very special, for my smile spoke of my happiness.

The third framed photograph was of a youthful Jacob Windsor and his young bride, Sarah Hennesy Windsor. I'd never met my grandmother as she had died long before I was born. What a beauty she was, with her fashionable bob of soft dark curls. Sprigs of baby's breath framed her oval face in place of a veil. I now could see where my mother got her good looks. The picture was taken in front of an old stone church I didn't recognize. The couple's clothes spoke of the bygone era in which they'd lived. They were old fashioned yet very chic. Grandma Sarah looked stunning in her white wedding dress. Sleeveless for early June, it fit her small thin frame beautifully as it fell gracefully to her ankles. Grandpa Jake, dressed in a dark three-piece suit and tie, held a black fedora in his right hand. His left hand held tightly to that of his bride. Both were smiling happily for the camera. Turning the picture over, I read, *"Jacob and Sarah on their wedding day, June 2, 1923, Lisbon Falls, Maine."*

How precious these pictures are to me, I thought. They were indeed my legacy, and I felt grateful they had not come to light while my father was still alive. In his frame of mind, he would have surely found a way to deprive me of them.

Beneath the framed pictures, was a folded black and white checkered table cloth. In its center, lay a faded blue book. Plain and unadorned, the cover gave no hint to its contents. Laying it aside, I decided to take it downstairs to view later. As I pulled the tablecloth away, my breath caught in my throat, and I stared at yet another painting of my mother. In this larger painting, she stood barefoot at the water's edge, smiling down at the small dark-haired child playing in the water at her feet. The little girl, obviously me, was dressed in a tiny pink bathing suit with a ruffled bottom. My mother wore a beautiful white sundress, and in her hand, she held a white floppy beach hat. In this painting, the artist's brush had caught the light perfectly as it touched her sun-kissed cheeks. This was, to my knowledge, the only painting of my mother and me in existence. My legacy, my grandfather had called it. How true.

Digging deeper, I pulled out three old books. Working for Albert, I knew that old books were a toss-up when it came to their value. Most were simply just that—old books. I laid them aside. Reaching in, I pulled out a flat box covered in aged wallpaper. In its prime, the paper had displayed a splash of delicate pink roses against a background of off white. Now, however, the cream had faded to a gray and the pink roses to an off shade of brown. It must hold something precious to have survived for so long, I guessed. Curious, I raised the lid and peered inside.

The box contained my mother's mementoes from the past. Lying on top was my birth certificate and a tiny pink plastic bracelet with the name *"Baby Girl Jennings"* written on it. Beneath the certificate, I found two old black-and-white photographs of people that I was now able to identify from the earlier framed pictures. Lifting the top photograph from the stack, I turned it over and read aloud, the caption on the back.

"Sarah, Paula and I. Christmas 1936." The photograph was of Grandpa Jake and Grandma Sarah as a young couple. They were standing in front of an old fashioned Christmas tree, heavily laden with glass ornaments and silver tinsel. Between them, a small dark-haired girl in a pale ruffled dress stood clutching a dolly tightly in her arms. The child, I knew, was my mother at the age of three. Beneath the tree, I counted only three small wrapped packages, a telltale sign that times were tough. Grandpa Jake had told me of the lean years suffered by the country following the crash of 1929. Their smiles, however, painted a different picture. Lean years or not, they were obviously very happy.

In the second photo, a younger version of my father, stood leaning against the hood of a large dark Chevy automobile. My guess was that it was taken on the family farm in Canada. In his right hand, he dangled a set of car keys. Turning it over, I read the caption, *Ellery and his first car. 1942*. Again, his youthful smile filled his face. I was amazed at the transformation it lent him. In my memories, he'd always worn a scowl on his face. *What a shame*, I thought, placing the photographs back into the box. He was quite a handsome man when he smiled.

In the bottom of the trunk lay a small bouquet of faded pink silk flowers encircled by a red ribbon. Time had dulled their once vivid colors. Beneath the bouquet lay what appeared to be a large white lace tablecloth. When I lifted it out of the trunk, I received the surprise of my life. It was a wedding dress! Unfolding it, I was careful not to let it touch the dirty attic floor. It was very delicate, and I knew from the 1940s style that it had belonged to my mother. It was a sleeveless, floor length silk gown, covered in beaded Venice lace and fine mesh tulle. Above the bodice, was a sweetheart neckline covered in tiny pearl buttons. Folded within the dress, was a short white lace jacket, to be worn over the dress. I was speechless. Never in a million years did I expect to discover my mother's wedding dress tucked away in a dusty old trunk in the attic. I couldn't wait for Becky to see the treasures I'd found.

For a long moment, I sat quietly holding my mother's wedding dress, feeling her presence for the first time in many years. The pictures that lay around me proved that I was once a part of a very loving family. Before tonight, I had only stories as the sole content of my family history. To me, they were merely impersonal names without faces.

Now, after finding the trunk, I felt as though I'd attended a sort of ghostly family reunion. I now had a sense of belonging to something bigger then myself—my family.

It took me two trips to transfer the contents of the attic trunk down to the kitchen table. After taking another hot shower, I made a cup of oolong tea and stood gazing at my treasures. Now examining the old books, I was elated as I ran through their titles. I had a copy of Bram Stoker's *Dracula*, Ernest Hemmingway's *The Old Man and the Sea*, and J. R. R. Tolkien's *The Hobbit*, all signed by the authors. They were all in excellent condition for having spent the last five decades in the bottom of an old trunk. Albert, I was sure, would know their value.

As I sipped my tea, I felt my emotions begin to slip. So much had happened this day that I was having trouble putting it all into perspective. Just since this afternoon, I'd faced down an imaginary monster, found out the man of my dreams was in love with me, and discovered a treasure trove of memories in an old attic trunk. What could possibly top this day? Thinking of my father and his wish to destroy all that lay before me, my anger surfaced.

"I've found Grandpa Jake's secret, Pappa!" I exclaimed, aloud. "And I will no longer allow you to banish our family to the darkness. Do you hear me?"

Carrying my mother's portrait into the sitting room, I glanced around for a place to display it. When my eyes fell on my father's unfinished seascape, I removed it from the easel and gently replaced it with my mother's image. "Welcome home, Momma," I said, stepping back to admire her. "You've been gone too long. I've missed you terribly."

Suddenly, I felt the overwhelming presence of my father in the room. A chill swept over me, and I sensed that he was not happy.

"I don't care what you think, Pappa?" I shouted to the room. "My mother has finally returned to Sea Breeze Cottage, and you no longer have any say in the matter!"

Returning to the kitchen, I fetched the stack of framed photographs and placed them around the sitting room. Both sets of grandparents now smiled at me from the end tables. I placed the painting of my mother and me on the mantelpiece and stood back with a determined look of triumph on my face.

"There, Pappa!" I shouted, tears stinging my eyes. "Now everyone has returned, including your parents, whom you kept from me all these years. This is my house now, and it will no longer be a place of darkness and regret. From now on, it'll be filled with light and love."

A good psychologist would deem this a substantial breakthrough, I thought, smiling through my tears.

After finishing my tea, I turned my attention to my mother's wedding dress, draped over the back of a kitchen chair. Placing it on a hanger, I hung it from the broken hall tree in the sitting room where I could enjoy it. It was quite becoming with an old-fashioned flare. All it required was a thorough cleaning to return it to its glory. Sizing up the narrow waist, I toyed with the idea that with just a few alterations, I might wear it someday. *And why shouldn't I wear it?* I asked myself. My mother would have wanted me to have it. Of this, I was sure.

Satisfied with my progress, I brewed myself a fresh cup of oolong tea and retrieved the blue cloth-bound book from the kitchen table. Returning to the sitting room, I curled up in my father's chair. The moon, illuminating the clouds gathering on the horizon, held the promise of rain in their billowing heights.

Turning my attention to the book, I turned to the first page. My excitement grew as I read the words, *Paula's Journal,* in an easy sweeping style. I had never seen my mother's handwriting before, and it instantly drew me closer to her. The date of the first entry, I noticed, was a few weeks before she died.

> July 1, 1957.
>
> This week I received the devastating news that I have lung cancer. The cough that I've been enduring for the past few weeks was obviously not a summer cold. I've been told there's nothing that can be done for me. We don't have the funds to go to one of the better clinics in Portland, so I am under the care of our own Dr. Sheldon. He's doing his best, but he's just a simple country doctor. They tell me I have mere weeks to live. Ellery is angry that with so little money, he cannot do more for me. My father is devastated and fears for my well-being. He has sold his car to pay for my care.

July 16, 1957.

What do I tell my darling Kathy? How do I tell her that her momma is going to die? I simply cannot do it! My father has agreed to tell her when the time comes. In the meantime, I continue to care for her as if nothing is amiss. However, my little stories and lullabies have become more meaningful, as one day, soon, they will be my last. Her little prayers now include me, and it breaks my heart. Oh, how can I leave my baby? Ellery has pledged to me that after I'm gone, he'll care for her and see that she is raised in a loving home. He has given me his word, and for that, I am grateful. I wish my mother were alive.

August 15, 1957.

My time is getting short. The pain is unbearable. The powders, given to me by the doctor, cause me to sleep a lot. My darling Kathy sits with me every day and comforts me. She is only six and cannot comprehend what is happening to me. The cancer has taken my voice so she has become the storyteller. At bedtime, she sits with me and sings her favorite lullabies. Tonight she sang, "Jesus Loves Me," and I cried. I listen to her little prayers, and she always asks God to make me better. What will she think when He fails to do so? I embrace every moment with her, as I have but a few days left on this earthly plane. Ellery has now abandoned our bedroom and seldom comes to see me. He prefers, instead, to spend his days sitting with his easel, on the beach. How can he paint at a time like this? I am concerned that he will not honor our agreement where our child is concerned. My father has vowed to care for my precious Kathy if Ellery should fail her.

August 30, 1957.

The good Reverend Peterson has given me last rites this afternoon, as we both know the end is near. I haven't seen Ellery in days. My father sits with me now and comforts me with stories of my mother and of when I was a little girl. I can feel God's presence very near, so I will now devote the pages of this journal to my baby girl.

August 31, 1957.

My Darling Kathy, you are my precious child. My cancer will take my body but not my love. That, you will always possess. Do not grieve for me when I am gone for I am with Jesus in Heaven. Though you will no longer see me, I will never truly leave you. I will be there with you at bedtime when you say your little prayers and watch over you as you sleep. Be strong, my child. Your Pappa has vowed to love and care for you as I have. He will need you now more than ever.

September 1, 1957.

Today, I dreamed of your Grandma Sarah, my mother. She awaits me at the gates of Heaven. I'll always remember your precious smile, Kathy, for I am taking with me your grin with its missing tooth, your pink baby cheeks, and the way you always giggle over bubbles. As you lay down to sleep, listen for my gentle lullaby in the sounds of the ocean below your room. I am sad that I will miss you growing into a young woman and starting your own family. When you hold your own precious babies in your arms, Kathy, tell them that their grandmother watches over them from Heaven. Plant a tiny whispered kiss upon their brow and tell them it's from me.

September 3, 1957.

My darling, Kathy, I will leave you soon. But take heart, for we will not be apart forever. One day, many, many years from now, you too will be as I am. When that moment arrives, my child, I will be there waiting for you with open arms, at the gates of Heaven."

This was her last entry.

By the time I finished and closed the book, I was sobbing. My mother died just three days later while I was away at school. *Why can't I remember sitting with her as she lay dying? Why have I blocked out something so precious to me as my mother's last moments?* Looking now at her portrait, I strongly felt her presence in the room. She died thinking that my father was going to love and care for me as she had. Thinking back on the way he treated me, anger again threatened to overwhelm my emotions. He'd failed to keep the promises he'd made to my mother. How many other promises had he failed to keep? The chiming of the mantel clock broke into my thoughts. It was 11:00 p.m. I turned out the light and went to bed knowing that sleep would be difficult. Sliding my mother's journal beneath my pillow, I asked God to let me dream of her.

The next morning, I awoke feeling groggy. As I listened to the day's weather forecast, it reminded that it was the first day of July. As the sun warmed the beach, I made my run with Mussolini. I was awake until after 2:00 a.m. so my feet felt as though they were trudging through molasses. I gave up after a few minutes and returned to the cottage to get ready for work.

When I walked into the bookshop at 8:00 a.m., Albert was busy at his desk. It looked like a good time to have him assess my grandfather's old books pulled from the attic trunk. Approaching him, I quietly placed them on his desk in front of him and took a seat. In silence, his expert hands carefully examined each one. His love of old books was obvious by the way he caressed each one as if it were a priceless crystal vase. After a few moments, he looked up at me with a look of pure joy.

"Where, may I ask, did you come by these books, Kathleen?" he asked, his voice barely containing his pleasure. "Do you know what you have here?"

"Surprise, Albert," I said. "I found them in my attic. I was hoping that you could shed some light on their value. You're the book expert. I just dust them."

"Can you give me a couple of days to do some research?" he said, picking up the copy of *Dracula*. "I'll need to make a few phone calls. If I am any book dealer, I'd say that this book, alone, could fetch you a very nice price from a collector. It's actually signed by Bram Stoker. Extraordinary!"

"Take all the time you need, Albert," I said. "The books belonged to my Grandpa Jake, but I'm sure he wouldn't mind if I sold them. Do you agree?"

"I do indeed," Albert replied, leafing through the pages of J. R. R. Tolkien's epic tale of dragons, elves, and little folk. "Your grandfather, however, may not have known what he had. In his day, these were simply books to read and enjoy. Each could be purchased for less than a dollar at any mercantile. During the years before and after the Depression, books were a means of entertainment for those who couldn't afford a radio. Now, however, it is rare to find the original copies in such excellent condition. As the world stepped into the age of television, most books were discarded or left to rot in damp basements and, yes, attics. I feel it an honor just to handle the works of these masters."

"Well, I'll leave you and Bilbo Baggins alone," I said, getting to my feet. Checking the time, I went to open the shop.

As I threw myself into the morning's routine, my thoughts turned to the business of selling books. At nine, faced with an empty shop, I set my sights on the dust bunnies skipping across the worn hardwood floors. Retrieving the dust mop from the back room, I set to work. I was dealing with a few stubborn ones beneath my desk when I was suddenly struck with a premonition that disaster was about to strike. Now I have always been one to believe in woman's intuition. The day before my father died, a sense of doom had followed me around like a stray pup. I learned to listen to that sixth sense over the years and to heed its warnings. Keeping myself attuned to that wee small voice within is what alerted me, at 10:17 a.m., that Becky was in trouble.

As the image of her popped into my head, I could feel her distress. Unsure if the feeling was real or my imagination, I hesitated for a moment to see if it would reoccur. When it happened again, a moment later, I knew in my soul that Becky needed me. Abandoning my dust mop against the wall, I hurried to grab my purse from my desk drawer.

"Albert, I have to go out," I shouted as I hurried out the door. "I'll explain later."

The street in front of the bookshop was busy with tourists despite the heat of the morning.

Glancing across the street, I wasn't surprised to see the ice cream shop doing a brisk business. With no time to think, I broke into a sprint in the direction of the Posey Pot flower shop. As I ran down the sidewalk, a few of the vacationers stopped to stare at me but all stepped aside.

As I neared Becky's corner, I slowed down to a brisk walk. If the dire alarm were all in my head, I'd have to explain to her why I felt the need to burst into her flower shop, disrupting her customers on what, a whim? However, as I reached the shop's front door, I was dismayed to see the CLOSED sign still displayed in the front window. At that moment, I knew the urgency was not a figment of my imagination. A rather portly man, who appeared as if he were poured into his tank top and terrycloth shorts, stood shading his eyes with his hand as he peered into the interior.

"What kind of a flower shop is still closed at twenty past ten in the morning?" he asked, gruffly. "Today is my wife's birthday, and I was hoping to get her a bouquet of roses. I'll be in the doghouse, for sure, if this place doesn't open soon."

"It's closed for the day!" I shouted as I ran around the side of the building. "Take her out to dinner!"

Hurrying up the back steps to Becky's apartment, I rapped several times on the screen door and waited for her to answer. Glancing behind me, I noticed the shop's delivery van, and Becky's yellow Volkswagen Beetle, were parked in their usual spaces next to the alley. She was home, so why was the shop still closed? When I failed to hear any sounds from inside, I opened the screen door and peered through the window glass into the interior of the kitchen. Through the yellow ruffled curtains, I observed the neat little kitchen table and the spotless counters. Then, as my eyes swept beyond the kitchen to her small living room, my heart stopped. She was lying on the floor beside the sofa, curled up into a fetal position, still wearing her favorite pink silk pajamas.

"Becky!" I shouted, rattling the door handle. Locked! Knowing the seriousness of the situation, I did the unthinkable. Holding my purse up like a battering ram, I shoved it through the glass window of the door. *Just let them make fun of my large purse now!* The sound of shattering glass broke the quiet morning, and I hoped the neighbors weren't dialing the police. Reaching into the ragged hole of the window, I slid the bolt open and stepped inside.

"I'm coming, Becky!" I exclaimed, as I hurried in to her. I found her motionless on her side, facing away from me. At that moment, a cascade of memories pulled me back to the day when I found my grandfather's still form lying in the sand. Would I now roll Becky over and discover that I was too late for her as well? Oh, I couldn't stand the thought of finding Becky dead.

"Please, God!" I prayed, just as I had for my Grandpa Jake. "Don't let it happen this way!" Then I heard a soft moan, and I knew she was still with me. Gently, I rolled her over toward me and peered into her face. Her cheeks were ashen, and her lips held a tinge of blue. When she opened her eyes, I saw the look of terror in them.

"Help me, Kat," she croaked out between parched lips. "Pain." Then she fainted.

"I'll get help, Becky!" I assured her. Jumping to my feet, I retraced my steps to the kitchen. Reaching for the wall phone, I quickly dialed the three magic numbers everyone hopes they never have to dial. After only two rings, a woman's voice answered.

"Nine-one-one," she chirped, in a brisk tone. "What's your emergency?"

"This is Kathy Jennings," I stated, quickly. "I'm in the apartment above the Posey Pot flower shop. Becky Porter is in terrible pain and needs help."

"Relax, ma'am," the woman urged. "Breathe deeply. You'll be no good to your friend if you panic. Now give me the location of the shop and stay calm. She needs you to be in charge right now."

After giving her the street address, I hung up and hurried in to Becky. Sliding to the floor, I cradled her unconscious body against me. It felt as though I was holding a bag of clothes hangers. Why did I not pay more attention to her extreme weight loss? Now I knew why she wore loose clothing.

"Where is that ambulance?" I exclaimed, as Becky's body began to shiver uncontrollably. When I finally heard its shrill siren in the distance, I breathed a huge sigh of relief.

As the ambulance pulled into the ally below, I could hear the tires sliding to a halt in the gravel through the broken window. A moment later, a paramedic pounded up the steps and entered the kitchen, his boots crunching in the broken glass inside the door.

"We'll take it from here, ma'am," said the kindly man of about forty. His pressed white shirt accentuated his shock of blond hair and tanned complexion, and he put me in mind of more a surfer than an EMT. Yielding to him, I stepped out of his way.

On his heels were two more similarly clad men, carrying a gurney. They went right to work on Becky, taking her vitals and inserting an IV into her arm. A moment later, they strapped Becky on to the gurney and wheeled her down the steps to the waiting ambulance. When the siren began to wail its mournful cry, I just stood there in shock as it faded into the distance.

"Wake up, Kathleen!" my inner voice demanded. "Becky needs you!" I could feel the tears coursing down my cheeks. Wiping my face, I closed the apartment the best I could and hurried back to the bookshop. After giving Albert a quick assessment of the situation, I headed for Portland.

Arriving at the Portland Hospital forty minutes later, I immediately went in search of Becky. Stepping into the large emergency room bustling with activity, I pinpointed a single window at the far side of the room marked ADMISSIONS, and headed in that direction.

"Excuse me, I'm looking for Rebecca Porter," I asked the portly blond woman at the admitting window. Upon hearing Becky's name, an ER nurse holding a clipboard hurried out to me.

"Are you Kathleen Jennings?" she asked me, rather abruptly.

"Yes, yes I am," I stammered.

"It's about time you arrived," she said, thrusting the clipboard at me. "Mrs. Porter said that you are her next of kin and to direct all of her paperwork to you. We'll need permission to do immediate surgery. Sign here, please."

"But I'm only her—" I began before she cut me off.

"Hurry up now," she said, handing me a pen. "Mrs. Porter's life depends on her having emergency surgery." With no further protest, I signed the papers, and she was gone.

Emergency surgery, I thought, shaking my head in confusion. What was wrong with Becky that she required an operation? It couldn't be her appendix, as I knew she'd had them removed in the eighth grade. Dazed and sick with worry, I went in search of a pay phone to call Marcus. Grateful that I didn't have to deal with the crisis on my own, I silently thanked God for bringing him into my life. *Oh yes, and kudos to my magical singing sea stone*, I added for good measure.

Thankfully, I was able to find a small unoccupied waiting room and I slipped in to await news of Becky's condition. The muted television, mounted on the wall, showed a young and very pretty blonde news reporter standing in front of a massive train derailment. In the background, several rescue workers were busy pulling victims from the crushed and burning rail cars. Flashing lights and smoke gave seriousness to the death and destruction. I nearly laughed aloud at the absurdity of it all. *Surely, they could have found a man to do the story*, I thought. Dressed in a bright yellow sundress, this angelic being looked as though she would be better suited reporting the outcome of a beach volleyball game instead of the bloody aftermath unfolding behind her.

The angle of the shadows outside the room's single window told me it was past the noon hour. When I'd phoned Marcus, he'd given me the same advice as the 911 operator. "Don't panic, Kathy," he'd told me. "I'll be there as soon as I possibly can."

Knowing that Marcus was on his way eased my anxious thoughts. Knowing that Becky was now in God's hands eased my panic.

The coffee I'd bought earlier, from the vending machine in the hallway, had the same taste and consistency of hot motor oil. Cold, it was even worse. Dropping the nearly full cup into a nearby trash can, I dug into my purse for another dollar. Stepping out into the hallway, I eyed up the machine's selections. I was just trying to decide if I wanted another cup of motor oil or the hot chocolate when I heard a familiar male voice behind me.

"That stuff is bad for you, my love," he said, putting his arms around me from behind. "If I were you in this situation, I'd skip the caffeine."

"Marcus!" I exclaimed, spinning around and throwing myself into his waiting arms. "I'm so glad you're here. The waiting has been excruciating."

"What do they say?" he asked.

"The nurse will only tell me that Becky is still in surgery," I said, against his neck. "Oh, Marcus, what has happened to her?"

"Whatever it is, the doctors will fix it," he replied. "Come, we'll wait on the news together."

Two hours later, Dr. Sheffield walked into the waiting room. Still dressed in his surgical scrubs, he looked exhausted. We both anxiously got to our feet.

"Becky is awake and in recovery," he said, removing his surgical cap. "She's asking for you, Kathy."

"What happened?" I asked, relieved that she was going to be ok. "Why was she in so much pain? She actually passed out."

"Becky had a blocked bile duct," he explained. "The pain from an obstruction of this type can be very extreme."

"I'm Marcus Stone," said Marcus, offering the doctor his hand. "What caused the obstruction?"

"I'm Becky's oncologist, Dr. Andrew Sheffield," the doctor replied, returning his handshake. With a loud sigh, he turned and sank into the nearest chair. "Please sit, both of you."

Returning to our chairs, we awaited his explanation.

"In answer to your question, it's part of her illness" he said. "Allow me to explain in layman's terms.

The bile duct carries bile fluid from the liver, which is then stored in the gallbladder. After a big meal, your gallbladder releases this mixture of cholesterol and bile salts into the small intestine, which helps your body break down your food. Becky's bile duct was obstructed so we simply went in and inserted a small stent to reopen it."

"But I thought her cancer was in her pancreas," I pointed out.

"It is," he replied. "However, I'm afraid it has spread to her liver. In Becky's case, a small tumor formed in the duct and blocked it from releasing fluid. This caused the buildup of bilirubin in her system, giving her the jaundiced or yellowish skin. She's very lucky that you found her in time."

"Will she be all right?" asked Marcus, reaching for my hand.

"She will for now," replied Dr. Sheffield. "We've inserted a small drainage tube into the liver to allow the fluid to drain properly. I'm going to keep her a day or so just to monitor her bilirubin levels as well as her enzymes. She only has a small incision, which should heal quickly. Now I'll take you to see her."

"Thank you, Dr. Sheffield," I said. Getting to our feet, we followed the good doctor into his realm of machines and miracles.

Chapter 11

As Marcus and I approached the ICU, my palms begin to sweat. I still felt that all was not settled. My woman's intuition was on full alert. Stepping into the dimly lit room, I allowed my eyes to adjust to the low light as I approached Becky's bed. Marcus, sensing our need for privacy, held back. *Deja vu*, I thought, thinking back to her previous hospital stay a mere three weeks earlier. However, this time, Becky's thin frame barely raised the sheets. In the low light, her skin was the color of creamed coffee. Reaching for her hand, I gently squeezed it.

"I'm here, Becky," I whispered, softly.

When she opened her eyes, they appeared glassy and distant. "I knew you'd find me this morning," she said. "We have that kind of radar that only best friends possess. Did the doctor tell you the news?"

"What news is this?" I asked. Recalling the doctor's prognosis, I knew what she was about to tell me.

"I've less time than we previously believed," she said.

"What's this?" asked Marcus, stepping forward.

"The surgery revealed that the cancer has spread to my liver and my adrenal glands," she replied, tears filling her yellowed eyes. "I'm a goner now, for sure."

I felt my heart break at her shattered expression, and I knew that I now had to be strong for both of us. "Then we'll make the most of what time you have left," I told her, giving her hand a squeeze. "And for starters, I want you to come live with me. It's time."

"Why? Doc fixed my problem," she said.

"True. And what of the next problem that arises?" I asked her. "You know there will be a next time."

She was quiet for a moment. "I don't want to be a burden on you, Kat," she said. "Friends don't mooch off each other."

"Mooch!" I exclaimed. "Becky, you're the closest thing I have to a sister. And to ease your mind, I'll simply put the refrigerator off limits to you, and you'll be on strict hot-water rations."

"Why?" she asked, giving me a look of dismay.

"Simple," I said, with a wicked grin, "I detest moochers. Now get some rest, and I'll be back to take you home when the doctor releases you."

"Thanks, Kat," she said softly, giving me a weak smile. "I think I'll rest now."

Arriving at the cottage two hours later, Marcus saw me safely to my door before heading for home himself. As I watched him drive away, I felt as though someone had just swiped my security blanket.

After my run on the beach, I showered and retreated to the sitting room with my glass of iced tea. Assessing the layout of the room, I began making plans for Becky's homecoming. I decided to place her hospital bed facing the bay windows, where she would have a good view of the sea. Marcus was returning the next day to help me rearrange the room, so I made a quick sweep, banishing any dust bunnies that might be lurking behind the furniture. When my eyes fell on my mother's wedding dress hanging on the old hall tree, I moved it to my bedroom. I wasn't ready for Marcus to see it just yet.

I took my run early the next morning, and after my cool down, I sat on the rocks, watching the morning come alive. I was grateful that it was Saturday, as I had much to do to prepare for Becky's arrival. After breakfast, I called the hospital and checked on her progress. When they put me through to her room, I was pleased to find her in good spirits. I knew she was feeling better when she complained about the food.

"They're releasing me tomorrow morning, Kat," she informed me. "I'm glad as they have me on a tasteless liquid diet. You will be here to get me early, won't you?"

"Relax," I told her. "And yes, I'll be there early."

Marcus showed up just after lunch to help me clear the sitting room. When he noticed my mother's portrait perched on my father's easel, he walked over to examine it closer.

"What an exceptional work of art," he exclaimed. "How old were you when this was done?"

"That is actually my mother," I stated proudly, joining him in front of the easel.

"She's a beautiful woman," he said, looking into my face. "Like mother, like daughter."

After filling him in on my return search of the attic, I introduced him to my newly found family.

"Didn't I tell you that attics were a treasure trove?" he asked, pulling me into his arms. "Your search turned up a long-lost family and solved a mystery."

"It did," I said, leaning against him. "My grandfather's monster was actually guarding my family's legacy all these years. Who knew?"

"I'm glad you overcame your fears, Kathy," he said. "Now you can have closure."

"Closure, concerning my grandfather only," I pointed out. "The jury is still out on my father."

After enjoying an iced tea, we cleared a space in the sitting room for Becky by moving the sofa and coffee table into the unused living room. Finally, after decades of sitting idle, the living room was being called into service as storage. Using the information given to me by the hospital, I ordered a hospital bed for Becky. With an assurance that it would be delivered the next morning well before Becky's arrival, I finally allowed myself to relax.

"By the way," said Marcus, as I rejoined him in the sitting room, "when I left you last evening, I took the liberty of cleaning up and replacing the window glass in Becky's door."

"Thank you," I said. "With all that's happened, the fact that I broke it had completely slipped my mind."

"Our Becky will find peace here," stated Marcus, looking out of the bay window. "She'll be able to see the ocean. She is blessed to have you as a friend, Kathy."

"I believe that I'm the one who is blessed, Marcus," I said, coming to stand beside him. When his arms encircled my body, I leaned into them. "Becky and I share a friendship that has carried us through a childhood of pain and need. Later on, we depended on each other's strength when we lost that one person who held our heart within their own. For me, it was my grandfather. For Becky, it was her husband, Michael. Now I'm losing her to cancer, and I feel as though I'm balancing on one leg. We've been each other's rock for over five decades, Marcus. Whatever will I do without her?"

"You can always trade your rock for a Stone," he said, softly.

"A stone?" I asked, turning to face him. Suddenly his play on words became clear, and I buried my face in his chest. "I get it. Lean on a Stone. Clever, Marcus."

"I'm here for you, Kathy," he said, into my hair. "Together, we'll survive the heartaches ahead."

"Thank you," I whispered, turning my face up to accept his kiss. As we stood holding on to each other and watching the sea below us, the rumbling of my stomach suddenly interrupted the romantic moment. I was horrified!

"Oh, my," I said, looking embarrassed. "I must be hungry."

"As am I," said Marcus, stepping away from me. "What shall we do to remedy the situation?"

"If you'd like, come back about seven this evening," I said. "I'm taking you to the Sea Shanty for dinner. They serve up the best steamed crab on the east coast."

"Steamed crab it is," he said. "I'll be here at seven. Now, I must depart. I have several errands to run." Taking me by the hand, he led me back to the kitchen.

"So do I," I said. "Mussolini is out of kibbles. He's been pushing his bowl around all morning."

"I shall rejoice when we are reunited over shell-fish" said Marcus.

"As will I," I said, planting a light kiss on his lips.

As he drove away, I stood on the porch watching his car until it disappeared around the bend in the road. *I have a date*, I thought, smiling.

Glancing around for Mussolini, I found him busy digging a hole beneath the hydrangea bush. With a couple of hours before Marcus was due to return for dinner, I took my run on the beach to clear my head before my grocery run. This was day 12, and my new running time of ninety seconds and walking for thirty, was working out nicely. At Becky's suggestion, I tried making two round trips to the pier and back. *She would be proud of me*, I thought. Although, I was still struggling with the increased running time, I was recovering much quicker. I was enjoying it now that I was suffering less. I still had a long way to go, and I was determined to do this for Becky. Returning from the grocery store, I showered and dressed for my date with Marcus. As a last-minute thought, I draped a cloth over my mother's portrait and the painting on the mantelpiece of my mother and me. They would make a nice surprise for Becky.

"Do you realize I leave for the UK on Wednesday?" Marcus commented, as we enjoyed our meal on the open veranda of the Sea Shanty. Surrounded by the detritus of seafaring memorabilia, the quaint seafood restaurant gave its customers the feeling of dining in a grass hut on a tropical island.

"So soon?" I asked, not wishing to discuss his leaving me.

"By the way, these steamed crabs are incredible," he said, beforc breaking into a hard British accent. "Just like me mum used to make."

We laughed. It felt good.

"Your absence, if only for a few days, will be an eternity for me," I stated, dipping a succulent piece of crab into my butter. "I shall miss you terribly."

"You'll be much too busy to miss me, my sweet," he mused. "They'll deliver Becky's hospital bed in the morning, and by noon, you'll have her to care for."

"I'll still miss you," I insisted.

The following morning, promptly at 7:30, a huge delivery truck from Greer Medical Supply backed into my driveway and off-loaded a fully functional hospital bed. The two men delivering it took no more than an hour to set it up and run it through its paces.

"There you go, ma'am," said the burly man in charge, handing me his clipboard to sign. He reminded me of Mr. Clean with his baldhead and shiny earring piercing his right earlobe. "If you have any problems with the bed, call our office. The number is on the rental agreement."

"Thank you, gentlemen," I said, following them back out to their truck. "I'm sorry to bring you out here on a Sunday."

"That's not a problem, ma'am," replied Mr. Clean's assistant. "Greer Medical Supply works seven days a week to ensure our customers receive the medical supplies they require." He sounded like a radio ad.

"He's new," said Mr. Clean, nodding his head in the other man's direction. "Actually, you're our only customer today. I've plans to go parasailing on the ocean later this morning."

"Oh, that sounds dangerous," I said.

"No more dangerous than driving in traffic," he replied, climbing up into the cab of his delivery truck. "It's expensive, but the adrenalin rush is worth it."

After they left, I stood in the yard listening to the morning birds. The day was already heating up and promised to be a typical early July day. The bees, lured by the nectar in the flowers, were going about their business of collecting. Turning around, I stood looking at my cottage. *I love this place*, I thought. Giving it a critical eye, I had to admit that even though it was in need of a few repairs, it was still home. I hoped that my grandfather's books were worth at least enough to paint the peeling clapboard siding, replace the missing spindles in the front porch railing, and purchase a new porch swing. Despite the obvious blemishes, I couldn't imagine living any-where else.

By 9:00 a.m., I was on my way to Portland to retrieve Becky from the hospital. Traffic was light, so I made it in good time. When I walked into her room, she was dressed and sitting in a wheelchair. Although her color still appeared a little on the yellowish side, she smiled brightly when I walked in.

"Kat, thank God you've arrived," she said. "I'm anxious to get out of here."

"Don't be too hasty," I said, leaning down to give her a quick hug. "Once we leave the hospital, you'll be stuck eating my cooking. After a few days, you'll be dreaming about those delicious liquid meals you were complaining about. Now let's get you checked out of here, Cinderella."

On the drive home, Becky dozed in her seat. The traffic had picked up some, but we still arrived at the cottage in time for a late lunch. Helping Becky into the house, she was pleased to see the arrangements I'd made for her.

"I'm being given the ocean suite?" she asked. "I'm honored."

"It will only be the best for you, my friend," I said.

After settling her on the bed, I went to the kitchen to make a fresh pitcher of lemonade. When Mussolini announced that I had company, I stepped to the porch to see who it could be. My heart leapt when I saw the sleek red Mustang sitting in the driveway. Smiling, I stepped out to greet my visitor.

"Hello, Marcus," I said, leaning into the driver's window. "What brings you out this way?"

"Do I need a reason to drive out and see my favorite girl?" he asked.

"Am I your favorite girl?" I questioned him, enjoying the lighthearted banter.

"You'd better be," he said. "I've already sent a warning to all the guys in town to keep their distance."

"I'm flattered," I said, stepping back so he could exit the car.

"Madam, flattery is my specialty," he said, leaning in for a quick kiss. "I just wanted to make sure that Becky arrived home safe and sound. I hope I'm not intruding."

"Never," I said. "She's trying out her new digs. Come, I've made fresh lemonade."

As we entered the sitting room, we found Becky stretched out on her bed, resting.

"Hello, Marcus, what brings you out this way?" she asked, sitting up.

"It's July," he replied. "I'm in search of a cool place to sit and enjoy a cold glass of lemonade. A cottage by the sea sounded like the perfect spot."

"It is," replied Becky. "I'm not sure about the lemonade, but if I'm going to be incapacitated, I couldn't think of a grander place."

"I knew you would love this room, Becky," I said, fluffing up her pillow. "It was always my favorite room, despite—"

"Despite the fact that your father died in here?" finished Becky. "Come. I refuse to think about the negative today. I have fond memories of this room as a child. Remember the nights when I'd sleep over and the two of us would play cards with your grandfather? I want to remember only the happy times now. I haven't got the time to dwell on the sad and tearful."

Despite her words, her face took on a faraway look of sadness. My mind searched for something to say that would break her somber mood.

Marcus, sensing my dilemma, came to my rescue. "Becky, I've repaired the broken window in the door to your apartment," he said. "And, I've secured your door."

"Thank you, Marcus," she said. "You're a saint."

"I'll fetch the lemonade," I offered.

When I returned, Becky and Marcus were deep in conversation about the fate of the flowers in his yard due to his lack of a green thumb. As I handed out the tall glasses of lemonade, I was glad that Marcus had succeeded in getting Becky's mind off the reason she was here. When Mussolini suddenly leapt from his place at my feet and ran into the kitchen barking, I rose.

"My redneck doorbell is on the job, I see," I said, hurrying after him. *Now who could this be on a Sunday*, I wondered, as I shushed Mussolini and opened the door.

On my porch stood the tiniest of ladies. Barely five feet tall, she appeared to be in her late fifties. She was dressed for the heat and carried a black satchel. I immediately wondered just what she was trying to sell.

"Hello there," she said, smiling up at me. "I'm Ann Kelter, Becky's hospice nurse."

"Oh, yes," I said, stepping aside for her to enter. "I'm sorry. I'm afraid I didn't expect you so soon. Please come in."

"Everyone, this is Ann Kelter," I said, introducing her to Marcus and Becky. "She'll be Becky's… nurse." I thought it best not to emphasize that she was from hospice.

"I'm so glad to meet you, Mrs. Kelter," said Becky, leaning forward to greet her.

"I'm here for all your medical needs, Becky," Ann announced, with a reassuring smile. "And please call me Ann. I can help you with any pain you're experiencing as well as answer any questions you may have."

"Well, ladies, I'll leave you to your guest," said Marcus. "I've much to do before my trip overseas."

"I'll see you out," I told him, allowing Becky a chance to speak with Ann in private. I knew nothing of what Becky was facing, and Ann's presence was a godsend.

After Marcus left, I made myself a cup of tea and sipped it until Ann appeared at the kitchen doorway.

"I'll be going now," she said. "I've given Becky something to help with the pain. If you should need me, I left my card on her stand. If you have any questions, Kathy, I'm here for you as well."

"What am I to do?" I whispered to her, suddenly feeling overwhelmed by it all. "When my father was dying, he asked nothing of me. He simply slipped away without a word. However, Becky—"

"Inviting her to live with you was a great idea," replied Ann. "She'll need someone to lean on as she gets closer to the end. Allow her to do what she wants. She knows her limits. As her caregiver, I'll instruct you on how to administer any medications she may need. For now, she should be comfortable."

"Thank you, Ann," I said, "I'm afraid we'll both come to rely on you over the next few weeks."

"That's what I'm here for," she said, as she stepped out the door. After seeing Ann out, I returned to the sitting room and my new boarder.

"I've a surprise for you," I told Becky, stepping over to my father's easel.

"I hope it's a good surprise," she said. "I've had all the bad news I can take for one lifetime. What's your surprise?"

"My mother has finally returned to Sea Breeze Cottage," I announced, removing the cloth covering her portrait.

Becky's audible gasp told me of her delight. "Oh, Kat, she's beautiful!" she exclaimed. "I thought all paintings of her were lost. Where did you get it?"

"After you and Marcus left the other night, I returned to the attic to search for what it was my grandfather was hiding," I replied. "I just knew there had to be something else other than old magazines and toys. Behind my grandmother's oval mirror, I discovered an old trunk. Inside, I found my mother's portrait and several old photographs of relatives."

"Remarkable," said Becky, now noticing the framed pictures around the room. "And, this is why your grandfather invented the monster in the attic?"

"It is," I replied, handing her my Grandpa Jake's letter. "Read this. It'll explain everything." After she'd finished reading, she looked at me in wonder.

"All these years, your legacy has been hiding right under your very nose," she said. "I'll bet your grandfather didn't think it would take fifty years for you to find it."

"I'm not proud of that fact," I said, walking over to the fireplace. "He also left me this." Unveiling the portrait of my mother and me propped up on the mantelpiece, a feeling of pride swept over me. "I finally have my mother back in my life."

"How blessed you are, Kat," exclaimed Becky. Rising to her feet, she stepped over to have a better look. "To finally know your mother's face must bring you a sense of unspeakable joy."

"Yes, it does," I said. The look on Becky's face, as she gazed at the portrait of my mother and I, was one of longing. "I wish that you, too, could discover your own family legacy, Becky."

"I harbor no such hopes," she said, softly. "Besides, I'll soon be reunited with them all in a place where we will never, again, be parted."

"It does feel good to be surrounded by my family again," I said, glancing around at their pictures. "Having them here makes me feel less of an orphan."

"What of your father's family in Canada?" asked Becky, picking up the framed photograph of the early Jennings'. "Have you thought of how you're going to inform them that he's dead?"

"I'm at a loss there," I replied. "I know he came from British Columbia, but where in that vast province lay his roots, I have no clue. I never met my grandparents. Howard and Gerta are surely long dead, and I know of no other kin. When I'd ask my father about his parents, he simply refused to speak of them."

"Well, look at it this way, Kat," said Becky. "You can surround yourself with relatives without having to listen to them go on and on about boring family dramatics."

"True," I said. "However, I wouldn't mind hearing a few stories."

"That would be nice, Kat," said Becky. "I don't have any pictures of my family. Now I guess it doesn't matter. How sad that you, alone, are left to mourn your family. Just as I am."

Seeing her good mood dissolve, I quickly changed the subject. "I've decided to donate my antique living room furniture to your benefit auction," I said, "It'll give me a good excuse to buy something new. The Good Lord knows, this place could use a facelift. By the way, Albert gave me a dollar raise."

"That's great, Kat," she said, yawning. "You deserve it. I think I'll rest now. Moving into a new house is always stressful."

"So it is," I said.

After Becky's short nap, we received a surprise visit from the young and handsome, Pastor Kevin. His very presence did wonders to lift her sagging spirits.

Leaving the two of them alone, I took Mussolini to the beach for my run. And today, despite my jumbled thoughts, I made good time. I was settling in good with my run time of ninety seconds, and making progress. This pleased me as the day of the Founder's Day race was approaching fast. Tomorrow was already the Fourth of July.

Chapter 12

I ndependence Day dawned warm, with the promise of clear weather for the day's festivities. With
the bookshop closed for the day, I made Becky and
me breakfast, which we enjoyed in front of the bay
window. As we ate, we talked of the days ahead.
When she surprised me with a request to take a walk
on the beach, Mussolini was all for it.

"Are you sure?" I asked her, as she dressed in a
pair of gray slacks and a white pullover top sporting
an American flag. "You've only been out of the hospital one day." Her answer made my heart want to cry
out for all the injustice her illness had brought to her.

"I've been told that I have but a short time to
live," she said. "If not now, when? I'll get weaker and
weaker as the cancer progresses. I want to feel the
sand beneath my toes and reconnect with Mother
Earth. Shall we?"

"Lead the way," I replied.

As we stepped off the sea path and onto the sand, we kicked off our sandals, enjoying the feel of the hot sand beneath our bare feet. The hissing sound of the surf breaking on the shore, and the screech of the gulls overhead, could always invoke within me a sense of peace and a promise that all was well with the world. Not this day. As I stood looking at Becky's upturned face, I found myself begging God for a miracle. I needed him to restore her to that vibrant, happy woman I knew. What was I to do without her strong will and positive outlook on life?

"You know, despite my prognosis, I see my glass as half-full," she said, breaking into my thoughts. "I'll soon be with my beloved Michael, in a place where death will never again come between us."

"How far can you walk?" I asked her.

"Lead the way," she replied. "Today, I'm pleasing me."

"You're amazing, Becky," I said, looping my arm with hers.

"I've no time to be anything else," she said. "Oh, I meant to ask you, how is your training progressing?"

"Wonderful, actually," I replied. "I'll bump my run time up this afternoon to running for a full two minutes and walking for thirty seconds. I'm making two round trips to the pier now."

"That's great, Kat," she said. "I'm happy that you've stuck with it."

"I'm running for a good cause," I said, using her own words. "And I'm doing it for my best friend," I added.

When we returned to the cottage, the telephone was ringing in the kitchen, and I hurried to answer it.

"Marcus, how are you?" I asked, hearing his voice on the other end. "Becky and I just returned from a walk on the beach."

"Splendid," he said. "I was wondering if the two of you would like to accompany me to the fireworks display this evening. I hear you can see them from the boardwalk near the ice-cream shop."

"They are also visible from the beach below the cottage," I stated. "Perhaps you'd like to come here instead? We'll be away from the crowds."

"That's an even better idea," he said. "And it'll be much easier on Becky, I'm sure. I'll meet you down on the rocks this evening." After he hung up, I went to inform Becky of our plans.

After a late supper of steamed clams and pasta, we made our way to the beach to wait on Marcus. This evening, Becky wore a light cardigan to cover her arms. Her weight loss was now painfully apparent. As we walked along the surf, lost in our own thoughts, neither of us spoke. My own thoughts were now of Marcus and his upcoming trip to the UK. It frightened me to even imagine where Becky's thoughts were leading her. Suddenly, without notice, she stopped and stood staring down at her bare feet.

"Is a crab threatening to nip your toes?" I mused, coming up beside her.

"No, silly, I found a little stone," she replied, reaching down and scooping it into her hand. "I could have sworn that it beckoned me to pick it up."

"Oh, Becky, you've found your first sea stone!" I exclaimed. "That's incredible!"

Holding out her hand, she dumped the stone into mine. It was smooth on one side, and pocked with small indentations on the other. Tan in color, it was about the size of my thumb. Small flecks of quartz, on the surface, reflected the evening sun making it sparkle.

"So, this is the magic of the sea stone?" she asked, quietly amazed. I returned it to her hand, and she cupped it to her breast. "I shall cherish it. Does this mean that I can make a wish?"

"Absolutely," I replied, smiling at her child-like wonder. "What will you wish for?"

"My wish is simple," she replied. "When it is my time to leave this world, I want it to be my Michael who comes to lead me home."

When Mussolini's barking drew our attention back toward the rocks, I was delighted to see Marcus standing by the sea path. Waving to him, we started in his direction.

"There awaits the magic of your own sea stone, Kat," said Becky.

"I couldn't agree more," I said, looping my arm with hers.

Mussolini was the first to reach Marcus and immediately flopped over onto his back, exposing his belly for a quick rub. Marcus, dropping to one knee, quickly obliged. Observing the affectionate scene in front of me, my heart pounded with the sheer anticipation of being with Marcus again. *If this is love*, I thought, *I welcomed it.*

"Hello, ladies," said Marcus. Rising, he dusted the sand off the knee of his trousers and leaned in to kiss me on the cheek. "I see you are already enjoying the evening."

"Hello again, Marcus," said Becky.

"You are looking well rested this evening, Becky," said Marcus, giving her a quick hug.

"I'm…better," she replied.

"You mentioned that you can see the fireworks from your beach," stated Marcus, taking my hand.

"Yes," I replied. "See the lighthouse out on the point? They set them off from there. My Grandpa Jake and I would watch them from this very spot. We have about an hour yet. Can I run back to the cottage and get anyone something to drink? Iced tea perhaps?"

"I have provided the beverages for this evening's activities," replied Marcus, retrieving a picnic basket from beneath a bush near to the path. "I've iced tea and scones for all to enjoy."

"Scones?" asked Becky.

"He's British," I reminded her. "They're famous for tea and scones."

Opening his basket, Marcus spread a small tablecloth on the sand.

"Will you join me, ladies?" he inquired, motioning for us to sit.

Finding his idea of a beach picnic fun, Becky and I followed his lead. The sand, still warm from the day's heat, felt good now as evening approached. As I watched Marcus fussing with his preparations, I marveled at his spontaneity as he passed around a small plate of lightly browned biscuits and bid us to take one. Mussolini waited patiently for his, and I tossed him one. Next, Marcus passed around a jar of reddish colored jam and a butter knife. Smothering my scone in the jam, I took a bite and closed my eyes in pure bliss.

"Oh, Marcus, this is wonderful," I purred. "What is the jam?"

"Boysenberry," he replied, smiling at my pleasure. Breaking into his strong British accent, he added, "It's me mum's recipe. She got it from the Queen herself, she did!"

Becky and I laughed, as we enjoyed our first taste of scones and Mum Stone's royal boysenberry jam.

"Oh, Marcus, I have something for you," said Becky, reaching into the pocket of her cardigan.

"A gift?" he said, smiling. "What's the occasion?"

"You're a wonderful friend who deserves a bit of magic," she replied. "Open your hand." When he did so, she placed her sea stone in his palm.

"Is this what I think it is?" asked Marcus, examining it.

"Yes," said Becky. "I found my first sea stone just this afternoon. And, since I'm in no position to start a collection, I'm giving it to you. Is this how it's done, Kat?"

"It is," I said, touched by her generosity. "My grandfather gave me my first stone when I was eleven so I could start my own sea stone collection."

"Then I shall use it to start my own," stated Marcus. "I will treasure it, Becky."

"Kat, I have a question," said Becky. "What happens to one's sea stone collection when they die? Are the stones willed to another?"

"No. They must be returned to the ocean," I replied. "After my grandfather's death, I brought his collection here to the rocks and, one by one, threw them into the sea."

"So, they can, in time, be found by someone else," remarked Becky, in wonder. "Well, if this is the way you pass on the magic, I'm all for it."

"Becky has shared with you the magic of the stones, Marcus," I said, leaning against him. "Stay vigilant, for there will be others in your path."

As we ate, we chatted about the upcoming benefit auction. Marcus informed us that people were already leaving items at the recreation center.

"The Mayor tells me that we have collected some very nice items," he said. "To name a few, we have a new mountain bike, several gift certificates, a gently used outdoor grill, and a small sailboat. Oh yes, and someone donated a one-year-old black Labrador retriever."

"Someone actually donated a dog?" asked Becky, amazed.

"They did," replied Marcus. "And the mayor begged me to take immediate possession of him. Which, I did. The dog has made himself quite at home in my recliner. I've named him Merlin."

"Merlin?" I asked. "Why? Is he magical?"

"He is, indeed," replied Marcus, giving us a boyish grin. "When I demand that he get out of my chair, he does so immediately. However, he magically reappears there a moment later."

"How funny!" exclaimed Becky, laughing aloud. It sounded good to hear her laughter again. Very few, I'm sure, are able to enjoy humor in her situation.

"Marcus, are you packed for your trip?" I asked him.

"Actually, no," he replied. "I'll not need much, so it won't take long."

"Who will keep your Merlin while you're in the UK?" Becky asked him, tossing her last bite of scone into Mussolini's eager mouth.

"Young Douglas from the grocery store, has generously offered to board him while I'm gone," he replied. From a large thermos, he replenished our glasses of iced tea.

"Is that so?" asked Becky. "Well, your Merlin will surely eat his weight in junk food if Dougie has his way. The boy lives on tacos and pizza."

"He'll only have him for a few days," said Marcus. "I assured Douglas that I will return in time to retrieve him for the auction. Someone will get themselves an exceptionally fine dog."

"I'm sure," said Becky, with a knowing smile. "He'll be a fine fat dog if he eats what Dougie eats."

"I shall miss my Merlin," said Marcus.

"You sound as if you're already attached to him," remarked Becky. "Perhaps you should keep him yourself."

"The thought has entered my mind," said Marcus, leaning back with his glass of tea. "However, he's a donation, just like the gift certificates and the sailboat. He, too, must go on the auction block."

"Then you must bid on him for yourself," I suggested, scratching Mussolini's ears. "Having a dog around the house does wonders for easing the loneliness of living alone."

"I ease my loneliness with houseplants," remarked Becky. "They're easier to care for, and you don't have to walk them every couple of hours."

I looked down at Mussolini, stretched out on the sand beside me, and knew that a houseplant could never compare to the unconditional love one received from a beloved pet.

"Folks have been asking why the flower shop is closed, Becky," said Marcus, on a more serious note. "I hope you don't mind, but I took the liberty of putting a sign on the door that reads CLOSED UNTIL FURTHER NOTICE."

"Thank you, Marcus," said Becky. "I've already informed Mr. Preston that I'll no longer require his services. Of course, with the doors closed, the business isn't making any money."

"Forgive me for asking, Becky," said Marcus, hesitantly. "What is to become of the Posey Pot? If we need to find a buyer, we must do so, post haste."

"You're forgiven," replied Becky. "And I've already dealt with the flower shop."

"You have?" Marcus and I chorused.

"Yes," she said, turning to look me straight in the eye. "I'm leaving the Posey Pot to you, Kat. Lock, stock, and flower pot."

"Oh, Becky, are you sure?" I asked, feeling overwhelmed by her offer.

"I'm sure," she replied. "You can either sell it or reopen it. It's your decision. I've no one else to leave it to, Kat. My lawyer is drawing up all the necessary papers as well as power of attorney. He'll be in touch with you in a couple of days. All I ask in return is that you give me a small funeral and lay me to rest beside my Michael. Deal?"

"Deal," I replied, touched.

When the fireworks began, we were like three kids at heart. We oohed and aahed along with the rest of Cutter's Cove as the night sky came alive with brilliant colors and noise. When the display ended, Marcus saw Becky and I safely back to the cottage before bidding us good night.

"I've had a wonderful evening, Kathy" he whispered into my hair as we held each other beside his car. "However, I must start my packing, so I'll take my leave of you."

I was already feeling his absence as I clung to him. After a quick good-night kiss, he drove away into the gathering night. Feeling torn between love and longing, I made my way back indoors, where Becky was just setting the teapot to boil. I secretly hoped that Wednesday wouldn't arrive too soon.

Chapter 13

"I'll miss you so much, Marcus!" I declared, on Wednesday afternoon, as we said goodbye at the Portland International Jetport. I was grateful the crowd was light as we stood in the line at the security checkpoint leading to the boarding area. Albert stood nearby, looking fragile and excited. He was dressed in his usual dark-brown suit and carried his silver cane draped over his left forearm. On his head sat his worn bowler hat. Cradled within his right arm, he held the small silver urn I knew held the ashes of his beloved Kathleen. After my declaration that the airlines might lose his luggage, he was taking no chances with his precious cargo.

"Our flight leaves in twenty minutes," said Marcus, kissing me lightly on the lips. "I'll ring you when we get to Ireland and we're settled in our hotel. And don't worry. Our return flight is early morning on the sixteenth, so we'll be home in plenty of time for the auction."

"Have a safe trip, my love," I whispered into his ear. "And take care of Albert."

"I shall do both," Marcus replied. "Now we must go. I love you, Kathleen."

"And I love you, Marcus," I whispered, accepting his parting kiss. "Parting is such sweet sorrow."

"Farewell, Kathleen," said Albert, giving me a slight bow. "Watch over the bookshop for me. I'll see you in ten days."

A few minutes later, as I stood at the window watching their plane taxi onto the runway, I asked God to grant them traveling mercies. On the drive back to Cutter's Cove, I wondered just what the days ahead held for me. Becky's benefit auction was in ten days, and I had much to do to get ready for it.

On Thursday, I left Becky sleeping and went to work. The shop seemed empty without Albert shuffling about. Just before noon, Marcus's call came in, informing me that they were safely ensconced in a comfortable hotel room for the night. Over dinner, they'd finalized the plans to go in search of Kathleen's relatives and were leaving for Larne in the morning. Knowing the cost of an overseas telephone call, we kept it short. At noon, I stopped by Della's to pick up lunch for Becky. When I arrived home, I found her reading in my father's chair.

"I couldn't stay in bed any longer," she said. "I just felt the need to be up and about."

"I'm glad, Becky," I said, placing her food tray on the stand next to her chair. "I brought you a bowl of Della's clam chowder. Are you hungry?"

"Perhaps, I could eat something," she said. It was then I caught a glimpse of the book she was reading—*Heaven and What Awaits You*.

"I see you're doing a bit of light reading," I remarked.

"The book belongs to Pastor Kevin," she said. "He's quite knowledgeable about such things. He recommended I read it. In his words, no one embarks on a great journey without first mapping out the area and checking out the accommodations."

"He has a good point there," I remarked, smiling.

"I hope that heaven is my destination," I heard her softly mutter.

"Whatever do you mean?" I asked, leaning down to drape my arm around her thin shoulders. "Why wouldn't you go to heaven?"

"I've ignored God for years, Kat," she said, leaning into my arm. "I hate to admit it, but I can hold a grudge when I feel I've been wronged. And, blaming God for my awful childhood just seemed like the right thing to do at the time. Then losing Michael so suddenly…well, I'm afraid God bore the blame for that as well. I could hear Him calling to me, wanting to talk this out, but the years just seemed to fly by, and I never took the time. We both know that my illness is what finally brought me back to Him."

"Better late than never, Becky," I said. "It was still your choice to ask God for forgiveness."

"Why should He accept a procrastinator like me?" she asked, shrugging her shoulders. "Being tardy is my middle name, you know. Surely, you must remember when I was a young girl and the times I was late for supper because we'd played too long at the park. As punishment, my grandfather would make me eat my meal alone on the back steps of the flower shop."

The very thought of Becky deeming herself unworthy of heaven made me want to weep. How could I reassure her? Then I heard, once again, that still, soft voice within me. *"Tell her of My love,"* it whispered.

"Becky, God loves you," I said, feeling His gentle nod of approval. "We don't serve a God who punishes us for being late for supper. Both of us have chosen to return to His table and beg His forgiveness. He's a God of forgiveness."

"Yes, He is," she said, softly. "And I am looking forward to meeting Him when my journey's over."

"Well, don't start packing just yet," I chided her, sliding her food tray over in front of her. "You've much to accomplish yet. Do you need me to do anything? With Albert gone, I should get back to the bookshop."

"Go. I'll be fine," she replied. "A couple of the ladies from the church are going to stop by and visit with me."

"Sounds like a plan," I said. "Call me if you need me, Becky."

On the drive back to the bookshop, I thought about all that lay ahead for Becky. I couldn't even imagine being in her shoes. "Please God," I whispered, "you know what we're up against here. All I ask is that You give comfort where comfort is needed." Again, I felt His nod of approval.

On Friday morning, Marcus called me at work to inform me they'd located Kathleen's family and were entombing her ashes in the family crypt the following morning. Fergus MacNealy, a great nephew of Kathleen's, was in charge of the arrangements. I was grateful that all was going as planned for Albert. He was such a dear, and I knew what returning Kathleen's ashes to her family meant to him.

Marcus was correct in assuming that I'd be too busy to miss him. Handling things at the bookshop and caring for Becky left me little time to think about my own woes. I had no complaints, though. Becky was so much easier to care for than my father. She constantly told me how much she appreciated my efforts, and her grateful smile was proof. With my father, my only reward for a hard day's work was his stone-faced silence. Obligation drove me to endure his scorn each day. For Becky, it was our lifelong friendship and love that made me want to give her the best care possible. Every night, I fell into bed exhausted, filled with the knowledge that I was making a difference.

When I awoke Saturday morning, the day, though warm, was made bearable by the ocean breezes. I decided that it was a good day for a home project. Soft music played on my father's old radio, as Becky and I set to work scraping the years of paint from around the edges of the two crank-out windows flanking the bay window. Finally, after an hour's sweat, they swung free for the first time in my memory.

"Smell that fresh air!" I exclaimed, breathing deep. "I should have opened these windows years ago."

"Now we can enjoy the sea breezes indoors," Becky remarked, collapsing into my father's chair. "Whew! What a workout."

In minutes, she was asleep, the air from the open windows softly cooling her sweaty cheeks. Mussolini lay stretched out at her feet.

"Hey, Pup," I called, quietly. "Let's go for a run." He beat me to the door.

I now looked forward to my run each day. Now that I was so close to the end of my training, I resisted the urge to break, even for a day, for fear of losing my momentum. This morning, day 19, I decided to increase my running to two and a half minutes while continuing to walk for thirty seconds. Thankfully, I was no longer gasping for breath at the end of each sprint as my body was adjusting. The muscles of my legs were getting stronger now, and a good stretch at the end of the run prevented any cramps.

As I ran, my thoughts turned to Becky. Her pain was increasing now, and Ann was coming by on a regular basis. Late at night, I found myself checking on her more than once. Though her illness was progressing, her sunny and positive attitude remained intact, doing wonders to keep us both from falling apart.

On Sunday, Becky and I attended the morning service at the Church of God. Unsure of how many Sunday's she had left, I remained upbeat as we dressed for the morning's outing. Despite the July heat outside, she wore her shawl over her pale-yellow sundress. When we entered the church, many expressed their joy at seeing us again and no mention was made of Becky's illness. However, even my carefully applied makeup failed to hide the pallor of her cheeks and the dark circles beneath her eyes.

When Pastor Kevin came to the pulpit, he bid everyone to surround Becky as he prayed over her. His words of comfort no longer spoke of her healing in this world but of her glorious arrival in the next. His words were a balm to our souls. The knowledge that we could rely on these precious God-filled people in the days ahead, gave me hope. As my tears fell, I realized that they were not just for Becky. I felt immense regret over my walking away from this church when I lost my Grandpa Jake. As a result, I turned my mourning inward and allowed it to harden my heart against the very thing that could have helped me through the pain. Now, feeling God's love envelop me, I felt my anguish over the loss of my grandfather, vanish. At last, I knew in my heart that I was, indeed, forgiven. His assurance that He would be there for me when Becky passed, gave me that long sought-after "peace that passeth all understanding".

On the way home, Becky suggested a detour through the cemetery. "If we've time to spare, I'd like to check on Michael's grave," she said. "My time, I feel, is getting short and I want to have one last look at it before—"

"Sure thing, Becky," I replied, before finishing her sentence in my mind,—*I'm buried here.* "We've all afternoon."

The Shores of Heaven Cemetery, located on the east end of town, sat peacefully on a rise overlooking the sea. Its oldest section, nearest the remains of an old stone church, held several marble headstones dating back to the mid-1600s when pirates still roamed the seas. Every year, the VFW placed small American flags on the graves of several veterans from wars, ranging from the Revolutionary War down through the war in Afghanistan. Our most famous grave, however, was that of Captain Nathanial Kindig, a local sailing merchant who graciously turned his cargo ship into a floating hospital after the Battles of Lexington and Concord in 1775. Every citizen of Cutter's Cove had at least one relative buried within the cemetery's hallowed grounds. I was no exception, as my Grandpa Jake and my parents rested out near the seawall.

"My family is resting at the base of that huge elm tree," said Becky, breaking into my thoughts.

Spotting the large elm, I pulled my car over to the side of the narrow road and turned off the ignition. "I'll give you a few minutes alone, Becky," I offered.

"Thanks Kat," she replied, getting out of the car.

The warmth of the late morning had given way to the heat of early afternoon. However, the breeze off the ocean kept the air moving. Stepping out of the car, I decided to take a walk. Becky, crouched in front of Michael's stone, was busily dusting the dried grass away from its base.

Winding my way between the headstones, I gratefully sought refuge in the shade of the ancient stone mausoleum where Cutters as far back as the late 1600s were entombed. I knew from my history class that it was Percival Cutter who founded the town of Cutter's Cove in 1690. One of seven survivors aboard a doomed ship, beached on the rocks in a storm, Percival married the daughter of a local fisherman and built the town. Leaning against the cold stone, I read the name of the last Cutter laid to rest behind its massive stone door.

Isabella Rose Cutter, wife of Ezekiel Cutter.

Aged 23 yrs. 3 mos.
Born 1888, died 1911. Lost in
childbirth.
Here in lies my precious Rose.
With God, she sleeps in sweet
repose.

The last of the Cutters, I thought. I, too, suffered her fate, as I was the last of the Jennings. I thought of Becky and the loss of her precious babies, making her the last of her own bloodline. Stepping back into the sunshine, I made my way to where my own family lay buried.

As I stood before their headstones, I felt a sort of envy. How blessed the dead were to no longer be concerned with living. They'd paid their earthly dues of pain and regret and were now reaping their rewards. Jacob Evan Windsor, I was sure, had found peace. He was with his beloved wife, Sarah Hennesy Windsor, the grandmother I never knew. Next to their headstone was that of my parents, Paula Irene Jennings and Ellery Banes Jennings. The new grass atop my father's grave was coming in nicely where the soil had been disturbed the previous winter. Had my father finally found solace for his tortured soul? How sad that he'd found so little in this life. Despite the distance he'd put between us over the years, my hope was that he was at peace and not wandering the earth still in search of it.

"Your father is with your mother, Kat," said Becky, stepping up beside me. "I know he's at peace."

Becky and I could always tell what the other was thinking. Uncanny.

"How did you know that I was thinking that very thing?" I asked her, linking her arm with mine.

"The same way you sensed I was in trouble and needed an ambulance," she replied. "Our hearts are connected."

As the day of Becky's benefit grew closer, folks began dropping off their smaller, donated items, at the bookshop, as well. After a busy Tuesday morning, I left the shop at eleven and picked up two lunches from Della's and went home to check on Becky. I found her reading in my father's chair and she was genuinely delighted to see me. I found this so refreshing that I stayed with her for over an hour. Returning to the bookshop, I found Carl Wyndom waiting for me on the bench outside. He was stopping in to donate a gift card entitling the purchaser to a free ice cream cone every day until Labor Day. Before he left the shop, he asked about Becky.

"She's as good as can be expected," I said, adding his gift card to the stack of donated items. "She's living with me now. How are things coming along with the Founder's Day picnic?"

"Extremely well," he replied. "Now that I'm in charge, I've added a few new and fun things to the list of activities. We're having a bouncy house for the kids and a cornhole competition for the adults. The annual run for juvenile diabetes is to take off right after the flag presentation at the war memorial. We'll miss Becky this year. She was an inspiration to all the older folks."

"I'm sure she would be," I said. "The good news is that I'm taking her place."

"You!" he exclaimed, with obvious surprise. "I mean, that's great, Kathy. I had no idea that you were a runner."

"I wasn't until three weeks ago," I said, leaning on the counter. "I've agreed to run in her place."

"That's very generous of you," he said. "I'm sure Becky will appreciate your efforts."

After he'd gone, I spent the rest of the afternoon cataloging a box of books. At ten minutes until closing time, the bell above the door sounded, and I stepped out of the back room to attend to what I hoped was my last customer of the day. My shopper turned out to be very tall, thin man dressed in a stylish black suit. His short, neatly cropped hair was shot-through with gray. His hairline, having receded to three inches above his ears, left the top of his head as shiny as a new penny. In his left hand, he carried a black, rather heavy-looking briefcase.

"May I help you?" I asked, smiling. "If you're looking for a book, just give me the title, and I can see if we have it in stock. Albert carries a large selection of authors."

"Oh, I'm not a customer, Miss Jennings," he said, offering his hand. His voice was deep yet gentle. "I'm Calvin Dorset, Rebecca Porter's attorney. If you can spare a few minutes, I have some papers for you to sign."

"I've been expecting you," I replied, switching on the CLOSED sign in the window. "Becky mentioned that you would be in contact."

"Excellent," he said, opening his briefcase on the counter. "It is my understanding that you have agreed to be the executor of Rebecca's estate. And, as her only heir, she is leaving you all of her worldly possessions, including the business, the company van, and her personal automobile. Her last will and testament, filed on June 28, 2011, will state these facts. In return, she asks that you serve as her power of attorney, which will give you legal authority to deal with any business decisions for her. She has already seen to my fee. On a more immediate note, she is giving you medical power of attorney as well, so you are able to make any medical decisions in the event she is unable to do so. Do you have any questions before you sign the papers?"

"No, sir," I said, not hesitating. "I'll do anything she requires."

"Excellent," he said, again, opening a bundle of papers on the counter. "Just sign on the dotted line next to the *x*."

After placing my signature on three legal documents, I stood back and handed him back his pen. "Is that it?" I asked.

"It is," he stated, returning the documents to his briefcase and snapping it shut. "You will, of course, inform me when Rebecca has passed? That, Miss Jennings, is when I do my best work. I thank you for your time."

As I saw him out, I thought about what I just agreed to take on. "I got your back, Becky," I said, as I turned out the lights and let myself out, locking the door behind me.

When I returned to the cottage, I found Ann and Becky in front of the bay window watching a brewing storm move in. The breeze coming through the windows cooled the room comfortably.

"You have a wonderful view of the ocean," remarked Ann. "The breeze is fabulous."

"It is," I replied, stepping behind them. "How are you feeling, Becky?"

"A little tired," she said, pulling her coverlet over her legs. "Pastor Kevin stopped by while you were out. I've asked him to officiate over my funeral, and he said it would be his honor. I've also contacted Dawson's Funeral Home, and they will meet with me here tomorrow afternoon. You'll not have much fuss."

"I don't mind," I said. The thought of her making her own funeral arrangements told me that she had truly given up any hope of recovery.

"If you girls need me for anything, call me," said Ann, getting to her feet. "I have another patient to see."

"I'll walk you out," I offered. I had a few questions for her that I simply could not address in front of Becky.

When we reached her car, I laid out my concerns. "What can I expect, Ann?" I asked. "When I cared for my father, he asked for nothing. He was still able to do for himself, and in the end, he simply sat in his chair and willed himself to die. Becky is another matter. I love her and want to see her…die with dignity."

"Of course, you do," said Ann, retrieving a thin blue booklet from her bag. "This booklet will explain everything, better than I can."

"Thank you," I said.

"Your Becky is amazing," she added. "Her pain is much worse today, yet she puts on a brave face. Bless her heart." As she slid behind the wheel of her small blue compact car, a loud clap of thunder boomed overhead and lightening split the sky.

"Safe travels, Ann," I called back over my shoulder as I ran for the porch, dodging the raindrops.

"The storm is here," Becky announced, as I joined her in the sitting room. "I've closed the windows. I'm already missing the breeze."

"Well, so much for my evening run," I said, as the raindrops pounded the window. "I hate to take even one day off. However, I've been pushing myself pretty hard lately. What shall we do with our evening?"

"Let's chat," she said, moving to her bed. "Come and tell me about your day."

"Okay. Your attorney, Calvin Dorset, stopped in today," I informed her. "I signed all the necessary legal papers."

"Thank you, Kat," she said, with a great sigh. "That's one less worry, knowing that you legally have my back."

"That's what I'm here for," I said. "Now relax and let me handle everything."

"Gladly."

After a light supper, Becky napped. Her weight was dropping again despite my encouraging her to eat. Was it my cooking? I had warned her. Settling into my father's chair, I opened the booklet Ann had given me. Written by a hospice nurse, it was indeed very informative. It listed the many changes that occur in the body at the different stages of the dying process. It explained why Becky was so cold, despite it being July. Reading on, I learned that as the end nears, the dying will start sleeping more. And that their fear of unfinished business is often the decisive factor in how they meet death. Well, as Becky's friend, and now her power of attorney, it was my job to alleviate those worries.

Looking now at her small sleeping form cradled in the white sheets of her hospital bed, I mourned for the time she was losing. Cancer was robbing her of her golden years, and this time, there was nothing our friendship could do to make it better. What was it Pastor Kevin had told us in his sermon last Sunday?

In Joel 2:25, God promises to "restore to us, the years the locusts have eaten". I wondered how God could restore the years Becky and I would lose? Closing the book, I sat staring out to sea, searching for an answer. The white caps and rolling surf told me the sea was in the mood to argue, so I laid my head back and closed my eyes.

As I listened to the rain on the window, a shadow of a memory crept into my mind. It was something that Grandpa Jake had told me when I would cry for my mother after her death. "She's in a better place, Button," he'd said, cradling me against his heart. "She's moved beyond her pain. Your momma is in heaven, and that's a grand place, indeed!"

I wanted that for Becky. I wanted her to be free of the pain and to suffer no more. Rising, I tucked her blanket up under her chin. "Rest easy, Becky," I whispered. "It's almost over."

The next morning, Mussolini accompanied me as I retrieved the newspaper from its box beside the road. The headlines announced that the Baltimore Orioles were having their best season ever. Above, the sky still held the threat of more rain.

"It's hump day," I told Mussolini, as he led the way back into the kitchen. After filling his bowel with kibbles, I went to check on Becky. Finding her still asleep, Mussolini and I headed for the beach for our run.

After warming up, I set out at an even pace. I had only ten days left to train before the big day. By the time I returned from the second trip to the pier and back, I was catching my second wind. Checking my stopwatch, I gave myself a pat on the back. "Yes, I'm going to make it!" I shouted to the seagulls overhead, fists pumping into the air. "I'm going to run this 5K and not embarrass myself!"

Mussolini, fearing the worst, broke off chasing a small crab and ran to my side.

When I returned to the cottage, Becky was drinking a cup of tea at the kitchen table. I was surprised to see her out of bed. She was dressed in a pair of light-blue shorts and white tank top. She'd pulled her blond hair up into a ponytail with a blue bandanna. She looked ready for a day of fun and sun if not for the dark circles beneath her eyes.

"Well, you look chipper this morning, Becky," I said. Filling a tea cup with hot water from the tea kettle, I dropped in a bag of my favorite English breakfast tea. "You look as if you're ready for an outing."

"I am," she said, draining her cup. "I need you to take me into the flower shop on your way to work. Can you spare the time?"

"Please tell me you're not going to try to work today, Becky," I exclaimed, with true concern.

"Relax, my friend," she said, getting to her feet. "The shop will remain closed. I just want to go through a few things and close the books. I simply refuse to leave you my unfinished business."

There it is, I thought, recalling the words in the book Ann had given me. I surely didn't want unfinished business to be an obstacle for Becky at this time. "I can close the bookshop and assist you, if you need help," I offered.

"No, this is something I must do alone," she replied. "It should only take me a couple of hours. I hope to be done by lunchtime. How is your training progressing?"

"I'm ready," I replied. "I'm now running without getting too winded. I'm still walking for thirty seconds between sprints, which does help."

"That's great, Kat," she remarked, patting me on the back. "I'm so sorry to have abandoned your training after you volunteered to run the race for me."

"No worries," I said. "I'm finding this task challenging but very rewarding. I am determined to do this, Becky."

"Well, you're doing wonderful for only having started three weeks ago. I'm proud of you, Kat. Now if you can reduce your walk time to 'as needed,' you're on your way."

"Here's to our 5K run," I said, raising my teacup. "May the best man, or woman, win. Or at least finish before sundown."

"Here, here!" she said.

On the drive into town, Becky seemed preoccupied. I knew that her attempt to balance the books at the flower shop, was to ease the confusion when I took possession. After dropping her off at the Posey Pot, I headed for the bookshop, arriving with twenty minutes to spare until we opened. I was just eyeing up a box of books when the telephone on my desk began to cry for attention. Picking it up, the line sounded dead for a moment before I heard a far-off tinny voice amid the sudden crackling.

"Hello, Kathy!" the voice shouted from out in the middle of nowhere. "This is Marcus. I do apologize for the bad connection, but I'm in Torquay and stuck using a rather dreadful contraption right out of the 1940s. How is everyone back home?"

"We're well, my darling!" I replied. "You sound as if you're on the moon."

"I bloody well could be," he said. "It's early afternoon here, and Albert and I are in a pub enjoying a wonderful steak and kidney pie and a draft of good ale. How is Rebecca doing?"

"She's a real trooper despite her illness," I replied. "At this moment, she's at the flower shop closing the books. I miss you, Marcus."

"And I miss you, love," he said. Even over the crackling of the phone lines, he sounded forlorn. "This morning, I went to see the farm where I grew up. A new family lives there, of course, but they permitted me a look around the place. I felt like a kid again, Kathy. It brought back my memories of riding the Lindy bicycle, like the one in your attic."

"That's wonderful," I said. "Are you still hoping to be back in time for the auction?"

"That is our intention," he said, the crackling suddenly getting louder. "Kathy, may I ask a favor of you?"

"Of course, Marcus," I said, over the gathering noise. "Anything."

"I was wondering if you could—" was all he managed to get out before the line went dead.

"Marcus?" I shouted into the phone. "Are you still there?"

Silence. I'd lost his call. Hanging up the telephone, I felt like weeping. They say that absence makes the heart grow fonder, and I now knew what that meant. How hard it was to be apart from Marcus now that we'd declared our love for each other. I could, at last, share a little of my father's longing after my mother died. How he must have missed her joyful laughter and beautiful smile. He loved her so much that he mourned her until the day he died. It wasn't the same for me, of course. Marcus, I knew, was soon coming home to me.

"Oh, Pappa, now I know why you mourned for momma so," I whispered, feeling my anger toward him soften a little. "If I was to lose Marcus, I, too, would lose myself in my grief." When the bell above the door jingled to life, it brought me out of my self-induced sadness, and I went to greet my first customer of the day.

At noon, I closed the shop and made my way to the Posey Pot to check on Becky. She was just closing her business ledger when I walked in.

"I've left everything in place for you, Kat," she said, looking exhausted. "I've cleaned out the cooler and pitched the dead flowers."

Glancing into her empty cooler, a feeling of "this is it", stole over me. "Now what happens?" I asked her.

"Now it's up to you, girlfriend," she said, grabbing her purse from behind the counter. "I've left instructions for you should you decide to keep the shop going, and closed out the books should you decide to sell."

"I'm not sure what—"

"You don't have to decide now, Kat," she said, glancing around the shop. "There are no perishables and the utilities are paid through August. The apartment is just as I left it, I'm afraid. Except for a small bag of clothes, all I'm taking are a few mementoes from my years with Michael and my grandmother's Bible. I'll not require more than that." I was pleased to see her doll, Fiona, lying atop her suitcase near the door.

"Thank you, Becky," I said. "You're most efficient as always."

"This is for you," she said, handing me the worn green ledger. "This will tell you what needs to be paid and all the shop's accounts. Knowing that I'm putting the life's work of my entire family into your hands is comforting for me. I'm at peace with my decision."

"I don't know what to say," I said, feeling overwhelmed by it all.

"Just say you're taking me home," she said, with a weak smile. "I'm spent. I just want a hot shower and a nap."

I picked up her small suitcase, and Fiona, and waited on the sidewalk while she locked the door for the last time. Turning, she dropped the keys into my hand.

"It's yours now, Kat," she said, tears welling up in her eyes. "I feel as though I'm giving my child over into your care. Shall we go home?"

"We shall," I replied, helping her to the car. "I'll make you lunch."

Busying myself with soup and sandwiches, I thought about Marcus's interrupted telephone call. *The telephone service in England, must truly be medieval*, I thought. I wondered for the hundredth time what favor he was about to ask of me just before the call was lost. Perhaps he wanted me to check on his house for him. I knew where he lived. Surely, he'd arranged for a neighbor to see to that task, I concluded. It must have been important to risk a trans-Atlantic call just to talk to me.

When Becky emerged from the bathroom, she appeared pale and unsteady. The shower obviously did little to revive her, and after we'd eaten, I urged her to lie down. After she fell asleep, I returned to the bookshop to finish out my day. As I worked, I kept an ear open for the telephone in the hopes that Marcus would ring back. When he failed to do so by the time

I closed the bookshop, I found myself wondering if the world had somehow ended where he was. Surely, he wouldn't just give up after only one attempt if the favor was something important. Then I recalled that he'd mentioned it was early afternoon where he was. And noting that his time was now 10:00 p.m., I imagined he was now asleep for the night. With the mystery solved, I locked up and headed for home.

When I arrived home, Becky was sleeping, so I took Mussolini for a run on the beach. With so much to think about, my body didn't need my mind to go through its routine. My legs were getting stronger, although I was still a little winded by the end of my sprints. Before I knew it, I was back at the sea path and doing my cool down exercises.

Returning to the cottage, I found Becky sitting in my father's chair. As I drew closer, I was dismayed to find her in tears.

"Becky, what's the matter?" I asked, kneeling down beside her chair.

"Oh, Kat, I feel thoroughly wretched!" she exclaimed, losing her resolve. "I'm in extreme pain."

"I'll go and call Ann," I said, patting her hand. It felt cold and clammy. "She'll know what to do."

When Ann arrived twenty minutes later, I went to let her in. After assessing Becky's pain level, she gave her an injection from a vial in her bag. Within minutes, Becky was feeling better and drifted off to sleep. When I walked Ann to her car, I had a few more questions.

"The cancer is progressing, isn't it?" I asked her, feeling helpless. "I want to help her, Ann, but I'm not sure what to do."

"She's getting closer to the end, Kathy," she said, placing her hand on my arm. "At this stage, there's not much you can do but keep her comfortable. I've seen this many times over the years. All I know is that some hang on for reasons unknown while others go quickly. I believe it's the knowledge that their house is all in order that deems it okay to go. A few years ago, I attended the bedside of a dying mother, whose son was stationed overseas. That mother hung on for three days, waiting on him to get home. The moment she saw his face above her bed, she passed. Dying is a process that even the smartest of scientists still cannot figure out."

"I guess there are just some things that humans must trust God to handle," I said.

"I will say this, Kathy," said Ann, climbing into her car. "I think it's time you think about closing the bookshop and staying at home. Becky will need full-time care very soon."

"Consider it done, Ann," I said. "And, thank you."

On Thursday morning, I drove into town and placed a sign in the front window of the bookshop, informing the town that it would be closed until Monday. By that time, Albert would be home to take over. Pastor Kevin stopped me as I left Della's and offered his help with the auction.

"How is Rebecca doing this morning?" he asked, with concern.

"She's holding her own," I replied. "I'm afraid her time is getting short. I closed the shop until Albert returns from overseas. I just want to be there for her."

"God will be there for you both, Kathy," he said, softly. "The church is praying for you. Give Becky our love, and I'll see you on Saturday."

On Friday afternoon, the day before the auction, the town erected a large tent in the square, where the event was to be held. I hired a young man and his pickup truck to move the contents of my living room into town. Surely, there was a buyer in the market for "vintage" furniture.

Becky, although in terrible pain, begged me to take her into town to see the activities in progress. Unable to leave the car, she viewed, from the window, all the wonderful items that the good people of Cutter's Cove had donated to help her pay off her debts. The small sailboat, donated by Weber's Marina, had the attention of three young boys who now stood over it in deep discussion. Folks scurried about, filling the tent with colorful craft items and donated goods. Antiques of every kind, littered the grass, and folks were already looking them over and discussing their value. As the tent filled with bargains, I finally allowed myself to relax, with the knowledge that Becky's benefit auction was obviously going to be a huge success.

After supper, I left Becky sitting at the bay window while I made my evening run. After my warm-up, I ran my usual two trips to the pier and back. After doing my cool down stretches, my legs felt energized. Shaking the sand from my shoes, I called for Mussolini and went in to check on Becky.

"I was watching you run, Kat," she said, when I stepped into the sitting room.

"How did I look?" I asked, sipping a cold iced tea. "I truly think I'm ready, Becky. And, I want you front and center when I set foot to street."

"I had no doubts that you could do it, Kat," she said, proudly. "Hip hip hooray!"

"Please, save your cheers for the finish line," I said, happy to see her smile. "After my shower, we'll talk about tomorrow."

"I do hope Marcus makes it home in time," she said, stretching out on her bed.

"I haven't heard from him since Wednesday when he called to ask a favor of me," I said. "Losing his connection, I have no idea what he wanted. Oh well, he's due back in the morning. I miss him terribly!"

"You're in love with him," said Becky, smiling. "I can see that he returns the feelings. I can die knowing that you'll be taken care of."

"It feels wonderful to be in love, Becky," I said. "The magic of the sea stone, remember?"

"I do hope my wish comes true," she said, hopefully. "Your magic stone brought you true love and mine will, I hope, reunite me with mine."

Stepping over to the bay window, I swung open one of the side windows to allow the warm breeze off the ocean to refresh the air in the room.

"I love falling asleep to the sound of the ocean," said Becky, softly. "My bedroom window above the flower shop faces away from the beach."

"When I was a child, the sound of the sea was my lullaby," I said. When I glanced over at Becky, she appeared deep in thought.

"Kat, there are a few things that I want you to know," she said, after a moment.

"I'm listening," I said.

"After I'm gone," she began, "I don't want you to be sad. Oh, you can be so for a while, but don't dwell on my passing. And, I forbid you to wear black. Celebrate my life with cheery summer colors."

"I'll try, Becky," I said. "I'm afraid I don't own anything with that color description."

"Also, I've arranged for a small funeral, nothing flashy," she continued. "I have an insurance policy that will cover all my expenses. My attorney will see to that. I want to be buried in my blue-and-white sundress, as I was wearing it the day Michael and I drove up to Portland on our thirtieth wedding anniversary. We had such a grand time. He died three days later, you know."

"That sundress is an excellent choice," I agreed.

"I chose it because it was Michael's favorite, and I want to be wearing it when I see him again," she said. "You shouldn't have to deal with anything left over from my family, as I donated it all years ago. I'm no pack rat."

"My Grandpa Jake was a member of that species," I said, wanting to break the sad tone of our conversation. "Packis-ratis, I call it. And, I hope it's about to pay off."

"How so?" asked Becky.

"The attic trunk also contained three very old books. Albert believes they may be worth something."

"How much is 'something'?" asked Becky, now intrigued enough to abandon her earlier concern over her impending death.

"Albert is the expert," I said. "But, I'm thinking they could be worth, at least, a couple of thousand dollars."

"Oh, Kat, what will you do with your windfall?" asked Becky.

"Purchase new furniture," I replied. "I just gave it all away, remember? Oh, there was one more thing I found in my grandfather's trunk." Retrieving my mother's wedding dress from my closet, I held it up for her to see.

"Is that what I think it is?" she asked, with surprise.

"It is," I replied. "Who knows what the future holds, Becky. I may just get the chance to wear it."

"Marcus is your destiny," she said, smiling.

"I truly hope so, Becky," I said. "I truly hope so."

Chapter 14

Saturday, July 16, dawned clear with a brisk breeze off the ocean. *The perfect day for an auction*, I thought. After a quick run on the beach, Becky and I made our way into town. When I spotted a woman on a vintage bicycle, I suddenly remembered the Lindy bicycle still sitting in my attic. I'd planned to donate it.

"Well, it's too late now," I muttered, as I parked the car. I looked up to see Pastor Kevin making his way toward us.

"Good morning, ladies," he said, giving us his signature smile. "Becky, we have a place inside the tent for you with a bird's eye view of all the activity.

"Thank you," said Becky.

"We're ready for the bargain hunters to arrive," said Pastor Kevin. "And the ladies from the church have organized a lunch stand to feed the masses."

"You've been such a great help to us both," said Becky. "Thank you."

Although she'd slept through the night, she still appeared tired and unsteady on her feet. Knowing that she wouldn't want to appear helpless, I resisted the urge to take her by the arm as we entered the tent. Her efforts cost her dearly, though, and she quickly lowered herself into her seat. I had just stepped back outside the tent when Carl Whyndom approached me.

"Kathy, the auctioneer just called," he said, with a tone of frustration. "His wife had a heart attack last night, and he's unable to do the auction."

"Oh no!" I exclaimed. "What will we do, Carl?"

"Well, I can fill in, if you'd like," he replied, with a huge grin. "Auctioneering is how I worked my way through college."

"You're hired," I said, giving him a quick hug. "Now we have twenty minutes until show time. Break a leg."

After Carl hurried off, I rejoined Becky in the tent.

"I've prayed for a miracle today," she said.

"Well, we just had our first need for one," I said. "Oh, look at the time. Have you seen Marcus yet?"

"No," she replied, her eyes sweeping the crowd. "He was due back this morning. Perhaps he ran into trouble."

"Or, he's just running late," I said, hopeful. "Marcus is very reliable."

As the town hall clock struck one, Carl stepped up to the microphone and welcomed everyone to the Becky Porter Benefit Auction. As he introduced the guest of honor, Becky got to her feet and waved at the crowd. Shouts of excitement and enthusiastic clapping swept through the tent, and she looked slightly embarrassed.

"Okay, folks, shall we get underway?" asked Carl, raising his hand in an attempt to settle the boisterous crowd. Although the clapping died down, the feeling of excitement still ran high. "First item on the block is this vintage flintlock rifle that I'm told belonged to Bill Martin's great-grandpappy."

"He carried it during the Civil War," Bill announced, proudly. I knew what a sacrifice he was making by selling the gun. However, he was in his eighties with no family. And I knew of his fondness for Becky and Michael.

"Shall we start the bidding at $500?" asked Carl, hopefully. In less than a minute, the gavel came down with a crash as Carl shouted, "Sold to Nelson Dugger for $1,200. Next item up for bid, we have this beautiful handmade quilt made by the ladies of the Cutter's Cove Church of God. Who will open the bid at $100?"

As the afternoon sped by, Carl's voice grew hoarse. When the town clock struck three, he took a swig of his lemonade and announced the last three items of the day.

"Well, folks, we're just about to wind up this auction," he said. "We're down to a basket of goodies, a vintage 1963 Flexible Flyer rail sled and this small Chesapeake Bay sailing skiff. Don't put your money away just yet."

By now, everyone in the audience was holding on to at least one purchased treasure. Becky's auction was, indeed, a success. At first, I attempted to keep track of the proceeds but found myself, instead, watching the door of the tent. There was still no sign of Marcus. As Carl's assistant held up the basket of home-canned strawberry preserves and a loaf of honey-colored homemade bread, the bidders showed little sign of winding down.

Elmer Gussett stood up and shouted out his bid. "Twenty-five dollars!" he shouted. "I know who put them preserves up, and I'm a fixin' to enjoy every bite."

"Thirty dollars!" shouted another man on his left. "My wife doesn't bake, and that bread smells delicious!"

"Thirty-five dollars!" shouted Elmer, giving his rival a warning glare.

"Well, I do declare!" exclaimed a blue-haired woman beside us. "If Annie Durge's homemade jam hits fifty dollars, we'll never hear the end of her bragging!"

I was anxious to see if her prediction was imminent when the next bid drifted above the murmuring crowd.

"One hundred dollars!" a male voice, with a slight British accent, called out from the open door of the tent.

"Well, I'll be," said Becky, smiling. "Annie Durge will be the talk of the town for sure."

"Wait a minute," I said, jumping to my feet. "I know that voice!"

Carl's next words confirmed what I already knew. "Sold to Marcus Stone, for one hundred dollars!" he shouted.

Unashamed, I rushed past Carl and right into the arms of my true love.

"Oh, Marcus, you're here at last!" I said, as I felt his arms envelop me. "I've missed you so much!"

Nearby, several people began elbowing each other and snickering. I didn't care. Marcus was home.

"Come join Becky and me," I urged him, taking him by the hand. "We've a lot to tell you."

"Welcome home, Marcus," said Becky, winking at me. "Since you left us, Kathy has been moping around the house like a lost puppy."

"I wouldn't have it any other way," he remarked. "I do apologize for our tardiness. Albert and I ran into a bit of a delay at London's Heathrow Airport and missed our flight home. That forced us to grab a later one, which put us in late at Portland. Knowing you were at the auction, I rented a car. Poor Albert appeared all in, so I dropped him off at his house."

"Well, you're here now," I said. "That's all that matters."

"I'm afraid you've missed the biggest share of the auction," said Becky. "They're on the last couple of items now."

I could hear Carl taking bids on the vintage Flexible Flyer rail sled.

"Buggers!" exclaimed Marcus, glancing around. "I'd hoped to be back in time to bid on a certain item. Well, I've surely missed it."

"Well, you still have time to bid on the small sailing skiff," said Becky. "Of course, you'll have to bid against three young boys who have been standing guard over it since the auction started. Take heed, open your mouth and you could have a fight on your hands."

"I'm afraid it wasn't the skiff that I had in mind," said Marcus, looking disappointed. "Tell me, Kathy, what did the Shelby Lindy bicycle go for? And, please, don't tell me it went for some ridiculously low bid. It was worth a small fortune. I would have gladly paid at least two thousand dollars for it."

"Well, it's yours," I said.

"What?" asked Marcus, looking confused. "What did I miss here?"

"The bicycle never made it to the auction," explained Becky. "Kathy forgot to bring it. She was so engrossed in everything going off without a hitch that she failed to include her most valuable item."

"Becky is right," I said, apologetically. "Your vintage bicycle is still sitting in my attic."

"Excellent indeed!" declared Marcus, pulling my hand to his lips for a soft kiss. "You just made my day, Kathy. I phoned you from Torquay, to ask if you would bid on it for me should I, for some unforeseen reason, miss the auction. When my call failed, I tried several times to reconnect with no success. The phone service in South East England is painfully unreliable."

"So that was the favor you wanted," I said.

Suddenly a loud cheer erupted from the crowd, drawing our attention back to the auction. Three very happy young boys were pumping their fists into the air as two men carried the small sailing skiff away.

"Well, they're going home happy," I said.

"That's it, folks," said Carl, over the crowd. "Thank you for coming out today. Please pay at the door. Sarah will gladly take your money. And don't forget to stop by the lunch stand on your way out. I believe the ladies still have several pies left."

As the tent began to clear, I helped Becky to her feet. This time, she gave no protest. She looked exhausted. When Pastor Kevin approached us, I introduced him to Marcus.

"I'm glad to finally meet you, Marcus," said Pastor Kevin, shaking his hand. "I hear you've recently been to the UK. May I ask, was it business or pleasure?"

"A bit of both actually," replied Marcus. "I needed to settle the estate of my late uncle as well as pay a visit to my childhood home in Torquay."

"Is that so?" asked Pastor Kevin. "Is it true what they say? You can never really go home?"

"It's true, I'm afraid," said Marcus. "However, I spent a nostalgic afternoon walking the coastal moors of my childhood. I also had the pleasure of having tea with the family that now resides in Rose-Thorn

Cottage where I grew up. Later, I enjoyed a delicious steak and kidney pie in the Leapin' Lizard Pub."

"That sounds very right and proper," remarked Becky. "We're glad you're home, Marcus."

"Yes, welcome home," I said.

"Kathy, perhaps you should take Becky home," suggested Pastor Kevin. "I'll stay and help clean up."

"I will assist the good pastor," said Marcus. "It's the least I can do for I've done precious little to help. May I call you later, Kathy?"

"Please do, Marcus," I replied. "We'll catch up."

On the drive home, Becky dozed. Arriving at the cottage, I had to assist her up the steps and through the door. Exhausted, she stretched out on her bed to nap. While she slept, I took Mussolini for a run on the beach. By the time I finished, my legs were slightly shaking, but I felt exhilarated. With only one week remaining until the Founder's Day picnic, I couldn't start slacking now.

Marcus phoned a little after 10:00 p.m., and we chatted until after midnight. He sounded truly happy to be home. He related that Merlin, the black lab, and his young keeper, Douglas, were waiting on him when he returned to his house. Apparently, Douglas, preoccupied with a new computer game, had forgotten all about the auction.

"I guess Merlin and I were destined to be together," he said. "I'll donate to the auction fund and keep him. Of course, I'll have to lay down a few rules. He may be sharing my house with me, but he's certainly not sharing my favorite recliner. He simply has to get his own!"

"Do they have the tally for the auction yet?" I asked him.

"Pastor Kevin will have it in the morning," he replied. "There are still a few folks who simply want to donate money. I'll let you know the moment I hear from him."

"Thank you, Marcus," I said, with genuine gratitude. "At the moment, my only concern is with Becky's well-being."

"As it should be, love," he said. "Till the morrow?"

"Till the morrow," I replied, just before hanging up.

The following morning, Ann arrived and offered to sit with Becky while I attended church. The activities of the previous day had totally depleted Becky's energy, and she was forced to remain in bed. I was grateful for Ann's help and told her so.

As I entered the church, I found myself surrounded by a sea of cheerful faces. By now, I was a familiar part of the flock and no longer sitting in the back. When they inquired about Becky, I extended her regrets. As we found our seats, Pastor Kevin drew my attention when he spoke of forgiveness, and I found myself wondering if his sermon was God's way of nudging me in that direction. Only God knew how I struggled with resentment where my father was concerned. Was He telling me that the time had come for me to lay it all on the altar? After so many years, was it possible to just forgive and forget all the pain and anguish I felt toward my father?

"The altar is open for those wishing to give their burdens to God," said Pastor Kevin, stepping forward. "Come and allow Him to bear that heavy load that weighs you down."

As the organist played softly, several people stood and made their way to the front of the church. One by one, they knelt before a low, dark, ornate wooden railing and bowed their heads in prayer. Suddenly, a long-ago memory flashed through my mind and I was six years old again. It was raining that Sunday morning when Grandpa Jake and I knelt at this very altar to ask God to spare my mother's life.

"Pray for your poor momma, Button," he whispered, as tears filled his eyes. "Surely God will listen to your prayers and spare her. He simply must know how very much we need her."

I prayed as only a six-year-old could and simply asked God to let her live. When she died the next afternoon, I was heartbroken. As I watched the long black hearse take her away, my child's mind just could not understand why God failed to answer my prayer. Two days later, they held my mother's funeral here in this church, and the entire town turned out to pay their last respects. Immediately following final prayers, I watched the mourners file out of the church in low whispers. My father, without a word, stood and followed on their heels, leaving Grandpa Jake and me to witness the closing of the casket.

"Why did God let my momma die, Grandpa?" I whispered, as they closed the lid. I winced as her beautiful face disappeared forever from my sight. "Perhaps He didn't hear me."

"Oh, He heard you, Button," Grandpa Jake replied. Pulling his white handkerchief from the back pocket of his trousers, he wiped his eyes. "He will always listen to the prayers of His children."

"Maybe God didn't know how to save her," I suggested, feeling fresh tears on my cheeks.

"God is the Master Healer, Button," he said, leading me away from the casket. Taking his handkerchief, he knelt and gently dried my cheeks. "But, like any good parent, sometimes his answer is no."

Returning to the present, an overwhelming feeling of despair engulfed me. Glancing at the front of the church, my mind's eye saw not an altar of confession but my mother's open casket. I felt the tears threaten as the memory of losing her replayed in my mind. I was amazed to discover that the six-year-old who felt that God had let her down still hurt from His betrayal. Was I now willing to trust Him with Becky's life? Since her diagnosis, I'd spent hours begging him to heal her of her cancer. As it was with my mother, was I prepared for His answer to be no? Realizing that I was not yet ready to surrender my all just yet, I rose and quickly left the church.

After a short store stop for milk and kibbles, I returned home to find Ann chatting on the telephone.

"She just walked in from church, Marcus. Here she is." Handing me the phone, she whispered, "I hope you don't mind me answering your phone, Kathy. The thing was ringing off the wall, and I thought perhaps it was an emergency."

"Not at all, Ann. Thank you," I said, giving her a warm grateful smile. She gave me a knowing smile of her own and returned to Becky.

"Hello, Marcus," I said, warmly. "How are you?"

"Wonderful," he replied. "I just received a phone call from the solicitor in England with the final word on my uncle Hamish's estate."

"On a Sunday?" I asked, surprised. "It's not a workday."

"Over there, it's less a matter of whether the day is open for business," he said. "It's more of when the telephone service is available."

"I see," I said, kicking off my shoes and sliding into the nearest kitchen chair. "All is well, I hope."

"It is," he replied. "My uncle Hamish actually passed about six weeks ago, but it took the solicitors a month to track me down here in the States. My uncle, rest his soul, lived in a quaint little village called Chudleigh, and I don't believe they've progressed much beyond the 1940s."

"I'm so sorry for your loss, Marcus," I said. "Who was this uncle? Were you close?"

"We were close in my youth," he replied. "Uncle Hamish was my mother's only brother and a big influence on me as a lad. He was the salt of the earth and loaded with common sense. Since he never married, I was his only heir. He generously left me a quaint country cottage surrounded by a fairly large tract of land ideal for grazing sheep. I've listed it with a local land broker."

"You could probably sell it for a nice sum if you'd list it on the Internet," I suggested.

"Probably so," he said. "However, the internet will attract those wishing to turn it into a hotel or a tourist's golf course. If a local farmer, on the other hand, is the buyer, it will remain a quaint country cottage surrounded by a fairly large tract of land ideal for grazing sheep."

"Point taken," I said. "How did we do with the auction?"

"I'm happy to report, we raised enough to cover Becky's expenses," he said.

"That's wonderful!" I exclaimed.

"Thanks to you, Kathy, the auction was a screaming success," declared Marcus. "With the two thousand I'll contribute for the Lindy Bicycle and the last-minute donations, we're slightly over our goal with $10,500."

"Becky will be pleased," I said, relieved. "She'll be happy to know she will die debt-free."

"How is she doing today?" he asked.

"Not good," I replied. "Yesterday's outing wore her out."

"That doesn't surprise me," he said. "Oh, yes. Albert bids you to come and see him tomorrow. He has news of your old books. If you'd like, I'll come out and sit with Becky while you're out."

"That sounds wonderful, Marcus," I said. "Thank you."

After he rang off, I hurried in to tell Becky the good news.

Early the following morning, I left Becky with Marcus and drove in to see Albert at the bookshop. Since it was Monday, I found him busy at his desk. When I walked in, he was just finishing his breakfast sandwich and coffee.

"I'd like to explain why the shop was closed last week, Albert," I said, finding the chair across from his desk. "I need to take a short leave of absence. Becky will need me to stay with her now until she—"

"I understand completely, Kathleen," he said, quickly. "The bookshop will be here when you return."

"Thank you, Albert," I said. "I'm afraid Becky hasn't much time."

"I understand," he said. "You'll need to make every moment with her count."

"How was your trip to see Kathleen's family?" I asked, on a lighter note.

"Her Irish relatives are amazing folks," he said, with a smile. "I truly didn't want to leave them.

However, I still have a business to run here at home. Oh, by the way, I have a very pleasant surprise for you. I did a bit of research on the three books you found in your attic. They turned out to be quite valuable."

"How so?" I asked, in anticipation.

"They are in excellent condition for their years," he stated.

"That's welcomed news, Albert," I said. "I hope they're at least worth two thousand dollars. I just auctioned off all my living room furniture. If I should happen to have guests drop in, they'll be forced to sit on apple crates."

"Well, that was a very generous donation," he said, amused.

"Actually, what I really need the money for is to make repairs to Sea Breeze Cottage," I stated. "I have to admit that my father and I allowed it to fall into somewhat shameful disrepair."

"Well, your books were all valuable first editions," he said, trying to hide his smile. "The fact that they are signed by the authors makes them more so."

"That's a plus," I said. "However, you've always told me that a book is only as valuable as the collector's desire to own it. And that only 2 percent of the books that come into the market are truly worth any serious money."

"That is indeed true," Albert replied, taking a sheet of lined paper from his desk drawer. "Are you interested in some serious money?"

"Okay, Albert, now you have my attention," I said, sitting forward. "How serious are we talking?"

"My book broker did well in his research," he said, grinning at me over the top of his wire rimmed glasses. "The 1897 copy of Bram Stoker's *Dracula* is worth at least eight thousand dollars to a known private book collector." Hesitating for a moment to allow his words to sink in, he continued. "The good news is that a buyer in Houston has already agreed to that price. Your 1952 copy of Earnest Hemmingway's *The Old Man and the Sea* is a rare find in this condition. If we sell it at London's Sotheby's Auction Gallery, we could stand to profit at least eight thousand five hundred dollars if the mood is right. Shall I continue, Kathy? You look quite pale."

"I'm…just a bit overwhelmed," I said, finding my voice. "Please continue."

"Very well," he said, adjusting his glasses. "The 1937 copy of *The Hobbit* by J. R. R. Tolkien has to be one of my favorites. I found a buyer in London willing to pay nine thousand dollars. If we play our cards right and the collectors rally, you could be looking at around twenty-five thousand five hundred for your old books. Your grandfather left you quite a valuable legacy."

If only Albert knew the extent of that legacy, I thought. "I wish he were here now," I said, my hands shaking. "I would hug him for thinking of my future."

"Your grandfather was a wise man," Albert remarked, leaning back in his chair.

Marcus was right when he said that attics were a treasure trove. Not only did I discover a wealth of family photographs, but I gained a small fortune in rare books. I'd lived on a frugal budget nearly all my life, totally unaware that hidden away in my attic was the means to repair my beloved Sea Breeze Cottage.

"I'm speechless, Albert," I said, amazed at my good fortune. "I surely didn't see this coming. I'm not one to have such luck."

"Personally, I don't believe in luck," he stated. "My mother would have called this 'pennies from heaven.'"

"Your mother was a wise woman," I said, playing on his words.

Leaving Albert working at his desk, I hurried home to tell Marcus of my windfall. He was stunned.

"How extraordinary!" he exclaimed. "What will you do with your small fortune?"

"Sea Breeze Cottage is in need of a new roof and a coat of paint," I said. "And if anything remains, I want to buy a swing for the front porch."

"Excellent idea," he said, nodding. "They're a great way to spend a lazy summer's afternoon."

"My grandfather and I used to do just that," I said, wistfully. "I'm not sure what happened to it. I don't seem to remember a swing after he died."

After Marcus took his leave, I did a few chores around the cottage. Ann arrived just after dinner to check on Becky, so I slipped out to take my run with Mussolini. I was on my second return run from the pier when an image of Becky flashed through my mind, stopping me in my tracks.

"Something is wrong with Becky, Mussolini!" I shouted. "Forget the birds and let's go!" He had trouble keeping up with me this time.

When I came into the sitting room, I found Ann leaning over Becky's bed, a worried expression on her face. "Becky has taken a turn for the worse," she said, softly. "Her pain is now more than her regular medication can handle."

I found Becky in her bed, with tears running down her pale cheeks.

"Oh, Becky, what can I do?" I asked her, taking her hand in mine.

"I hurt," she gasped. Wrapping her arms around her abdomen, she rolled into a fetal position.

"Ann, perhaps we should take her to the hospital?" I implored.

"No!" Becky exclaimed, gripping my hand with amazing strength. "No *hospital*. I'll not have the last thing I see in this world be a sterile white room with an ugly curtain pulled around me."

"I'd say it's time to break out the big guns!" said Ann, opening her bag and pulling out a small glass vial and a syringe. "I've spoken to her doctor. He's authorized me to administer morphine. This should help her rest easier."

I watched in awe as Ann gently inserted an IV into Becky's right hand and injected the small tube with her medication. Within minutes, Becky relaxed and fell into a deep sleep. Ann, wearing a worried expression, monitored her breathing and vitals as darkness fell outside. I sat holding Becky's hand, praying silently for God to take it out of our hands. As much as I dreaded losing her, I hated seeing her in so much pain.

"I won't leave you again, Becky," I whispered to her sleeping form. "I promised to take care of you, and that's what I'm going to do!"

"She should sleep through the night," said Ann, wearily getting to her feet. "I'm going home to get some rest. I'll be back in the morning to check on her."

"What happened to her, Ann?" I asked her as I walked her to her car. "Becky was nearly her old self this morning."

"The pain comes from the tumor in her pancreas," replied Ann. "It's pressing against vital nerves. The morphine should help her to cope. She will need you more than ever now, Kathy. I'm afraid she's in her last days."

After seeing Ann out, I curled up in my father's chair and looked out at the sea. The bottom half of a moon hung low in the night sky above the water, leaving a sparkling white trail on the dark surface. My grandfather would say that the weather will be wet as the moon is holding water. Behind me, the sound of Becky's shallow breathing soothed my frazzled nerves. *How quickly life changes*, I thought. How many people in the world take their good health for granted? It was only a couple of months ago that Becky and I giggled like two teenagers as we pampered ourselves at the day spa in Portland. Just six weeks ago, we picked out my dress for my first date with Marcus. Becky and I had always treated life as if it would never end. Our friendship, now, was as familiar to us as a favorite sweater. Would we have done things differently had we known that death would claim one of us so soon? As the moon rose slowly in the night sky, I fell into an uneasy sleep filled with dreams of being tossed to and fro on an angry sea. When I awoke, it was after 7:00 a.m.

Spending the night in a chair was a bad idea, I thought, attempting to stretch the kinks out of my back and neck. The early morning sun on the beach below looked inviting, so I opened the windows. The sky held a mountain of high clouds announcing weather later in the day. Checking on Becky, I was dismayed to see that she was moaning softly in her sleep. When I heard Mussolini give out a low growl and then a rapid bark, I hushed him and went to let Ann in the kitchen door.

"How is she?" she asked, as she stepped into the kitchen.

"She's moaning in her sleep," I replied. "What can we do for her?"

"I'll administer another dose of morphine," she said, setting her bag on the table. "That should help her."

"Can I get you anything?" I asked, putting the teakettle on to boil.

"I'll take a cup of strong coffee," she replied. "Two sugars and light on the cream. I'll be in with Becky."

As I placed Ann's cup of coffee on the stand beside her, I watched as she filled her syringe and gave Becky her injection. As we sipped our coffee, Becky's labored breathing relaxed and she drifted into a deep sleep.

"I've seen to Becky's legal affairs," I told Ann, as she took Becky's pulse. "She's made me her power of attorney. She's leaving everything to me, so she'll have no worries when the time comes."

"I'm glad, Kathy," she said, dropping into my father's chair with her cup. "I've seen the chaos that a sudden illness can leave in its wake. Especially, if the dying has children and no one to turn to for their care. Same goes for owning a business, I suppose."

"I'm also her medical power of attorney," I added. "I'm now able to make any medical decisions for her if she's unable to do so."

"Then all is right with her world," Ann said quietly, sipping her coffee. "Becky will get very weak as her illness progresses. She'll need you to be her hands and feet."

"And, I am here for her," I said. "I've taken a leave of absence from the shop. I shan't leave her again."

After seeing Ann out, I returned to the sitting room. Afraid to leave Becky alone, I moved the old roll-away bed from the hall closet to the sitting room and made up a bed.

I watched over Becky the remainder of the day. Feeling anxious, I busied myself with the task of making a pot of homemade chicken soup. When I heard her call my name around dinnertime, I hurried in to her. She was lying awake and smiling at me, but the lines on her brow told of her pain level.

"Hey, you," I said, leaning over her. "How are you feeling?"

"Not well, I'm afraid," she whispered, her smile failing to reach her eyes. "I've been dreaming of Heaven. Do you want to hear about it?"

"Absolutely," I replied. Rolling her bed up to a sitting position, I sat on the edge beside her and leaned back against her pillow. "Tell me about heaven, Becky."

As she spoke, I released her into God's care. Heaven sounded like such a wonderful place, and I was happy for her. I felt my emotional grip on her slowly let go with the knowledge that her death meant she'd be spending eternity in paradise. As I lay looking out the bay window at the sea, the open window let in the sound of the waves hitting the rocks below. The fluffy clouds out at sea now held a tinge of gray.

"'Clouds are bringin' in rain,' my grandfather would say," I commented, when she, at last, grew quiet.

"Your grandfather was the salt of the earth," she said.

"He was," I agreed. "Are you hungry? I've made chicken soup."

"No, I'm not hungry," she replied. "However, I will take of sip of water."

"Are you in pain?" I asked, holding the cup to her lips. "Ann will be here soon to give you another injection of morphine."

"The meds make me sleepy, Kat," she said. "I'm afraid to fall asleep. What if I fail to wake up?"

"God has you in the palm of his hand, Becky," I told her. "Remember what Pastor Kevin told you? To be absent from the body is to be present with the Lord."

"And my Michael," she added. "If I'm in God's hands, then I've nothing to fear. I think I'll nap until Ann arrives."

Ann arrived around five to administer Becky her morphine injection. "Take a break, Kathy," she said, pulling out her small laptop computer. "I'll sit with Becky. I have a good two hours' worth of charting to do, and this is the only stop I have that allows me to enjoy the ocean while I work."

I seized the opportunity and took Mussolini for a run on the beach. I was now running full time and, as Becky suggested, only walking as needed. I still became slightly winded; however, walking for a minute or so usually helped me to recover quickly. I now felt myself ready to run the 5K for Becky. After stretching to cool down, I made my way to my father's rock to rest. *Too much is happening too quickly*, I thought. I was hoping to have weeks with Becky; however, fate was greedily whittling our time together down to days, perhaps even hours. I was deep in thought when I felt two warm hands upon my shoulders. Catching a whiff of my "assailant's" cologne, I leaned back against his body.

"Hello, Marcus," I said, smiling up at him. "When did you get here?"

"I just arrived," he replied, coming around to sit beside me on the rocks. "Ann told me you were on the beach. You enjoy it here."

"The sea is my balm," I said, wrapping myself around his right arm. "When I was a child, my Grandpa Jake would walk with me here and share his wisdom."

"And what wisdom did he share with you?" asked Marcus, giving my arm an affectionate squeeze.

"He shared his heart," I replied. "It was here on this very rock that my grandfather told me all about God and the story of Jesus and the cross. My grandpa was a very godly man, Marcus. Now I wish that I'd listened more closely to his words."

"Surprisingly enough, it was on a beach much like this that my own grandfather introduced me to God," said Marcus, with a faraway look. "I felt my grandfather very near to me in Torquay. My memories of him stirred within me as I walked in our old footsteps again. The roses my mother planted over the rock fence of my childhood home, still grow like a blanket of yellow sunshine. As I walked along the lane I played in as a child, I could feel the years fall away, and I nearly broke into a run. The only thing missing was my old dog, Shandy."

"I'm glad that you made the trip, Marcus," I said, feeling his closeness. "I must confess, though, I was worried that you would fall in love with it all over again and perhaps—"

"Stay in England?" he asked, reading my thoughts.

"Well, yes."

"Your Pastor Kevin is right. One can never truly go home again once you've grown up," he said, looking down into my eyes. "Although, it felt good to visit the haunts of my childhood, it also stirred up a loneliness that nearly consumed me."

"How so?" I asked.

"Well, I was pleased to find my old home much the same," he said. "However, it was missing my mother. The boy, within me, recalled the way her long raven hair played around the edges of her beautiful face as she called me in to the evening meal. Also missing, was my grandfather with his snow-white beard and wind-creased face. I half-expected him to step in from the barn and challenge me to a wicked game of checkers in front of the hearth."

"You sound as if you had a very happy childhood," I commented, thinking of my own filled with a daily struggle to gain my father's favor.

"It was indeed," said Marcus. "And it made me the man I am today. While in Torquay, I tried to touch the past without becoming emotional. I found it most difficult. Just between you and me, though, I did permit myself a few tears as I stood over the spot where my beloved dog, Shandy, lay buried these long years. No, Kathy, I'll not return. I've allowed my memories to have their day in the sun. My only solace was the thought that love awaited me back here in Cutter's Cove. I returned home to you, my sweet."

"Oh, Marcus!" I cried, falling into his embrace. "My love indeed awaited you here. And together we'll make new memories."

"That sounds wonderful," he whispered into my lips just before covering them with his own.

When Mussolini finally joined us, the three of us made our way back to the cottage. Ann was just finishing up with her computer work. Becky still lay sleeping, her breathing steady.

"I'll be off then," said Ann, gathering her things. "Becky should sleep comfortably."

As Marcus stood watching Becky sleep, I seized the moment to speak with Ann in private. Following her into the kitchen, I stepped close to her. "Ann, Becky's quit eating," I whispered, in frustration. "Should I be worried? How can she manage without food? She hasn't eaten more than a few bites in days."

"Walk me out," she whispered, motioning me out onto the porch.

Closing the door behind me, I awaited her answer.

"It's nearly the end for Becky," she said, leaning against the porch post. "Do you recall what you read in the book I gave you? Our bodies consume food to energize us. Becky no longer needs energy. Also, near the end, they have a surge of emotion and beg to share their memories or recite their last wish."

"She shared this with me yesterday," I said, sadly. "I just want to help her."

"At this stage, dear, Becky will require very little help," said Ann. "Just abide by her wishes and let her know how very much she is loved."

"That, I can do," I said, following her to her car. "Thank you, Ann."

"Call me if there are any changes," she said, climbing in her car. "No matter what the hour, I'll be here."

"I will, Ann," I promised.

Returning to the sitting room, I found Marcus standing in front of the bay window, looking out to sea. "The sea is busy tonight," he remarked, turning to join me beside Becky's bed. "It'll storm soon. Shall I stay with you tonight, Kathy?"

"I don't believe so, Marcus," I said, leaning into him. "I'll be here if Becky needs anything. Strangely, though, I think when the time comes, she'll have all the help she needs from beyond this world."

"That's how it should be, Kathy," he said, softly. "You'll call me if you need me?"

"I will. I love you, Marcus."

"And I love you, my sweet," he said, planting a kiss on my forehead. "I'll see myself out."

Exhausted, I showered and changed into my night clothes. The promised storm swept through just before darkness fell, lasting nearly an hour. Once again, the weather matched my mood as the emotional storm raged within me. When the storm's energy finally died down, my own waned as well. In the growing darkness, the small lamp beside my father's chair lent the room a soft light. I lay awake on my roll-away bed, listening to the sound of the sea and Becky's breathing. *Life is a funny thing*, I thought. *Becky and I have shared our lives with no thought as to how it would eventually end. Death, it seems, will claim her first.*

"She'll be with Me," whispered that still small voice within me. "It's okay to let her go. I'll take it from here."

"Thank you, God," I whispered, feeling sleep claim me.

I dreamed I was walking along a stone path that meandered its way through a beautiful garden. Although the hour was early, the light morning fog was just beginning to dissipate. I sensed that I wasn't alone but saw no one else on the garden path. Then from somewhere beyond the rising gray veil, I heard the sound of footsteps hurrying along the cobblestones. I halted, waiting.

"Kathy?" a voice called to me from within the mist. The familiar voice held a sense of urgency. "Kathy, are you here?"

393

When I opened my eyes, the soft light from the lamp beside my father's chair still draped the room in shadow. I lay still, listening, wondering if I were still dreaming.

"Kathy?" the voice called once again, this time from nearby.

Becky! Throwing back my covers, I rushed to her side. "I'm here, Becky!" I said, taking her hand in mine.

"I thought I was alone," she said, fear in her eyes. "Will you stay with me?"

"I'll not leave your side again," I whispered. Stretching out on the bed beside her, I pulled her frail body into my arms. "Are you in pain?"

"I'm not sure," she replied, relaxing against me. "I can't feel my body anymore. Kat, I had a dream."

"Tell me about your dream," I said, trying to keep the emotion out of my voice.

"I dreamed there was a beautiful golden ship with white sails moored just beyond our beach," she said, softly. "Someone stood waving from the railing, but I couldn't make out their face."

"Are you leaving me, Becky?" I asked her, my mind reeling from the realization that this was to be out last moments.

"Would you mind?" she asked. "I don't want to leave here, but I hear a voice calling out to me, beckoning me to join them."

"If you must go, Becky, then I'll not mind," I said. "I'll be right behind you very soon."

"Not too soon, I hope," she said, her voice wavering. "You've only just begun your life with Marcus. He promised to watch over you after I'm gone. He loves you, Kat. In Marcus lies that special kind of enduring love that I shared with my Michael. I bid you to live long and be happy, Kathy."

"I'll do that," I whispered, allowing my tears to fall into her hair. When she fell silent, I lay there holding her, willing myself to let her go.

"Oh, Kat, it's my Michael!" she said, stirring within my arms. "It is he that awaits me at the ship's railing. Oh, he looks wonderful. He's come to lead me home so I don't lose my way. He's calling to me, Kat."

"Then you mustn't keep him waiting, Becky dearest," I said, rising up to peer down into her face. Tears filled her eyes as she smiled weakly up at me.

"I'll see you soon, girlfriend," she whispered, her voice trailing off. As her body fell limp, she let out a long sigh as her last breath slipped from her.

She was gone.

We lay there in the stillness of the early morning, as the sound of my quiet sobbing mingled with the ancient song of the sea as it pounded the rocks below. Somewhere out there on the ocean, a beautiful golden ship sailed on the early-morning tide—a heavenly vessel sent to take Becky home. I was sure, had I arose and looked out to sea, I could have just caught a glimpse of its white sails disappearing over the horizon.

"Good-bye, my old friend," I whispered. "Smooth sailing."

With my tears finally spent, I rose and made my way to the kitchen to call Ann. I slipped off to get dressed just as the morning sun was hitting the bay window. When Mussolini gave off a warning bark twenty minutes later, I went to open the door. To my surprise, I found Marcus standing there, a concerned look on his face.

"Ann telephoned," he said, stepping inside.

"Becky's gone," I said, before slipping into his arms, my body wracked with my sobbing. I was still there when Ann arrived. Seeing that Marcus was caring for my needs, she quietly slipped by us to tend to matters in the sitting room.

Ann declared Rebecca Ann Fraser Porter dead at 7:35 a.m. on Wednesday, July 20, 2011. Since

Becky had prearranged her funeral, Dawson's Funeral Home, when alerted, arrived and whisked her away. As they left, I telephoned Calvin Dorset, her attorney, and he vowed to handle the legalities, putting my mind at ease. Before leaving, Ann tidied up the sitting room and left Marcus and me alone. What a comfort he was to me. At Mussolini's request, the three of us made our way to the rocks below the cottage, where Marcus held me as my tears fell afresh. I no longer needed to look to the sea for my comfort, for I now held all my soul required within my arms.

When we returned to the kitchen for tea, Marcus caught the telephone while I freshened up.

"That was Dawson's Funeral Home ringing up," he offered, as I walked back into the kitchen. "The funeral is planned for Friday morning at the Cutter's Cove Church of God with Pastor Kevin Diamond officiating."

"That sounds right and proper," I said, coming over to put my arms around him.

Later that afternoon, I sent Marcus home to freshen up, as he'd been with me since dawn. Alone, I put on my running shoes and headed for the beach. Running felt good for a few minutes, but I soon realized that my mind wasn't up for it. I decided to walk the distance to the pier as I tried to come to grips with the idea that Becky was truly gone. My heart was breaking as a lifetime of memories played in my mind, and I failed to recall a moment when she wasn't in my life. When my father died, I felt only relief that his ordeal of pain and anguish was, at last, over. Shamefully, I felt no loss. After years of enduring his anger and aloofness, I found I was unable to mourn him and cried no tears. Now I couldn't seem turn them off. Gazing out to sea, it looked like rain approaching. *Why not*, I thought.

Standing by the old pier, I watched Mussolini play happily in the surf, oblivious to what was happening in my world. How I envied him at that moment. As I glanced down the beach toward home, I spied a far-off figure sitting patiently on the rocks below the cottage. Marcus had returned. I knew he was concerned for me. Helpless in knowing what to do, he vowed to just "be here" for me. I found myself wanting to flee into his arms, where I knew I'd find the comfort and love that I needed to heal my wounded heart. He truly was my knight in shining armor.

"Come on, Pup!" I shouted. "Let's not keep Sir Lancelot waiting!" Setting off at a sprint, I set an easy pace as I made my way homeward. "I'm ready to do this for you, Becky," I said to the wind. "I'm ready to run your last race." I imagined her giving me an enthusiastic thumbs up.

As I neared where Marcus waited, he got to his feet. Slowing my pace, I ran into his arms. "Oh, Marcus, I love you," I breathed into his neck. "My heart needs you so very badly."

"Your love is what keeps my own heart beating," he said, tilting my head back to look into my face. "Are you sure you want to follow through with the 5K race? The townsfolk would understand if you're not ready. After all, you've just lost your best friend."

"This race meant a lot to Becky, Marcus," I said. "Therefore, it means a lot to me. No, I'll run for Becky."

"Then I'm here to support you," he declared. "The Founder's Day picnic is in two days. In the meantime, we have much to do."

"We do," I said, leaning into him. "I must say good-bye to a very old and dear friend."

Chapter 15

The day of Becky's funeral dawned filled with sunshine, and I had a sense that despite my heartache, all was right with the world. *It is just as it should be*, I thought, as I crawled out of bed and stumbled into the kitchen. After letting Mussolini out for his morning business, I put the teakettle on to boil. I longed to enjoy my toast and coffee in front of the sitting room's bay window, but I found myself still avoiding Becky's empty hospital bed. I was aware that I should call Greer Medical Supply and have it removed. However, I wasn't ready to do so quite yet.

After a quick shower, I stood in front of my closet, attempting to find *something* to wear to Becky's funeral. I was just settling on a dark forest-green blouse and black dress slacks when I recalled Becky's request, from a few days earlier, to "celebrate her life with cheery summer colors." To my knowledge, I didn't own anything that could remotely be described as a "cheery summer color." With my hair color, I was always drawn to dark and bold colors. I was just about to settle on the dark forest-green blouse when my eyes fell on a sleeveless, pale-yellow dress, trimmed in small white daisies. *Now where did this dress come from?* I asked myself. I didn't recall ever seeing it before. I was sure I had not purchased it, as it wasn't even my style. Shrugging, I pulled it from the closet.

Slipping it on, I stood before the oval mirror, amazed at how it looked on me. I was genuinely surprised to discover I looked good in summer colors. Its cheery yellow made me realize that the contents of my closet, over the years, had come to resemble my father's angry seascapes. When did this happen? Stepping into a pair of light tan sandals, I felt the sense of doom hanging over my heart, lift just a little. Becky had begged me to not dwell on her death but on our lifelong friendship, and I would do my best to honor her last wish.

I was just finishing my makeup when Mussolini announced that Marcus had arrived. When he stepped inside the door, his broad smile said it all. "Kathy, you look wonderful!" he exclaimed. "You look as if you're ready for a day at the beach. Yellow is your color."

"I'm honoring the request of an old friend," I said. "She forbade me to wear black."

"Black at funerals is overrated anyway," he commented. "I'm pleased to see times are changing. My mother was forced to wear black for a year after my father's death."

"Well, Marcus, shall we go and bid a fond farewell to one of Cutter's Cove's finest?" I asked, linking my arm in his.

"We shall," he replied.

"Oh, wait," I said. "I have to retrieve an old friend for Becky." Hurrying into the sitting room, I found Fiona propped up against Becky's pillow.

When we arrived at the church, it seemed like the whole town had gathered for Becky's funeral. As the organ began to softly play "Amazing Grace," Marcus and I stood looking down at Becky for the last time. Honoring her wish to be buried in Michael's favorite dress, I chose her blue-and-white sundress for the occasion. Someone had curled her blond hair, and it now framed her thin face like angel hair. In her hands, I requested they place her grandmother's small worn Bible and a tiny sprig of baby's breath. This I did to honor Becky Porter. As a favor to little Becky Fraser, I carefully placed Fiona into the crook of her left arm. "You'll never be parted again," I whispered.

Becky looked quite becoming for her long-awaited reunion with her husband. Ann stepped up beside me and linked her arm into mine. "She's quite beautiful, isn't she?" she asked.

"Thank you for coming, Ann," I said. "You know, she has no family left to mourn her. I, alone, was holding her hand when she died. How sad is that?"

"Becky had her closest friend beside her at the end," she replied, softly "What's truly sad is when it's the hospice nurse who holds their hand."

How I got through that day without falling to pieces was a miracle. Marcus held my hand throughout the service as Pastor Kevin told us how heaven's angels rejoice when one of their own comes home. After the service, we made our way to the Shores of Heaven Cemetery, where a small tent covered her open grave. Above the pit, Becky's white casket waited for this final step in her journey home. As we stood listening to Pastor Kevin's words of hope for us all, a small cloud slid in front of the sun, as if to emphasize our sadness. At the final prayer, all who knew and loved Becky, wept. Torn between the joy of finding Marcus's love and the grief felt over losing my best friend, I allowed my tears to join theirs. When they lowered the casket into the dark ground, Marcus held my hand within his own.

"I will live long and be happy, Becky," I whispered to her as she disappeared into the earth.

As Marcus and I passed through town, all was in preparation for the Founder's Day picnic planned for the next day. A large banner hanging over Main Street announced the next day's festivities, as well as, the 5K run for juvenile diabetes, planned for noon. Shops up and down the street took advantage of the event by announcing their Founder's Day blowout sales. Having avoided the event for years, I now looked forward to the laughter of the children and the sights and smells of the carnival-like atmosphere. I was sad that Becky was missing it, but I knew she was busy enjoying the sights and smells of heaven.

After a late dinner, Marcus took me home. The evening was warm so we decided to walk on the beach. As we strolled, I told him the history behind the friendship Becky and I had shared for fifty-five years. Later, as I lay in bed, I felt a great sadness steal over me, and I knew that Becky's wish that I not dwell on her passing, would be difficult to grant. I missed her. Despite her short stay, the house now seemed empty without her. Even Mussolini lay quiet tonight, as if he sensed his master's mood.

"It's time for sleep, Pup," I said, as I turned out the light. "I have a race to run tomorrow, and I need to be at my best." As I lay alone in the dark, I hummed "Amazing Grace" until sleep claimed me.

The day of the Founder's Day picnic and 5K run dawned full of sunshine and clear skies. *It's a good day to fulfill a promise*, I thought. Preparing for the race, I dressed in a pair of brown shorts, a white T-shirt, and my running shoes. I imagined the oval mirror in the corner of my bedroom, giving me its nod of quiet approval. Before leaving the room, I peered down at my sea stone collection displayed on the windowsill. There, lying unassuming and plain among the other stones, was my singing sea stone. The memory of the moment, when I'd first held it within my hand, still filled me with a sense of wonder.

Marcus picked me up at eleven thirty and we set off for town. Although I knew I was ready for anything, I still felt nervous.

"I've trained hard for this race, Marcus," I commented. "I just wish Becky were here to see me run."

"She would be immensely proud of you, Kathy." he said, reaching over to give my hand a reassuring squeeze. "As am I."

"I don't want to appear selfish, but I could use a miracle today."

"Miracles are over-rated, if you ask me," said Marcus. "Often it's simply our sheer will that gets us through a tough situation. You'll do your best and that is all God asks of us."

"I admire your ability to see the glass as half full, Marcus," I said. "Becky had that same ability. She was always looking for the silver lining in every dark cloud. Even when time was ticking away for her like an over wound clock."

"Speaking of clocks, I've news of the little gilded clock we discovered in your attic," he said.

"Really?" I asked.

"Yes. Do you recall my telling you that I was going to have a friend in New York take a look at it? Well, Wallace rang me last evening to say that he cleaned it up and found it to be in excellent condition for its age."

"How old does he think it is?" I asked, now curious.

"He estimates its age at around ninety years," replied Marcus. "It was made in Switzerland just after World War 1."

"Does your friend think it's valuable?' I asked, hopeful.

"He does indeed," replied Marcus. "He places its value at around twenty-five thousand. And, if you would be interested in selling it, he is confident he can find a buyer willing to pay that amount."

I was stunned! My little clock was yet another unexpected windfall that had, for years, lay abandoned in my attic. In addition to three valuable first edition books and the Shelby Lindy bicycle, that Marcus deemed worth its weight in gold, I now had my small gilded clock. I felt like the pirate, who upon deciding to retire from the sea, finds himself, at last, unearthing his horde of buried treasure. Of course, if the clock was valued at twenty-five thousand today, would it not be worth more in the ensuing years?

"Tell your friend, thank you for his assessment," I said. "However, I don't believe I will sell my clock at this time, Marcus. It can only increase in value, am I right? I am selling my grandfather's books only because I require the means to make a few immediate repairs to Sea Breeze Cottage. It is my thinking that my little clock shall be my rainy day insurance against the day I might find myself destitute and homeless. It will be my rainy day clock."

"Wise decision, my love," said Marcus, nodding his head in approval. "At our age, we all need that proverbial nest egg that we can hatch should an emergency arise."

"I agree," I said, thinking of Becky and her immediate need to settle her debts before her death. "And, with the knowledge of what Becky went through, I am now determined to never find myself in such dire circumstances."

"I would never permit that to happen, Kathy," said Marcus, his eyes meeting mine for a moment. "You now have me to watch over you."

"That is the rope I now cling to, Marcus." I said, as a feeling of warm gratitude washed over me. "Of course, I also have Sea Breeze Cottage and now a well-established flower shop to see me through my twilight years."

"And, there are the newly discovered paintings of your mother," added Marcus.

"There is indeed. And now that the famous artist, Ellery Jennings, is dead, his paintings will be worth a small fortune. Of course, they are not for sale for I shall enjoy them until I close my eyes in death. Then, I will have them donated to our local gallery."

"As you should, my pet." said Marcus, softly. "In the end, your grandfather's dark tale of a monster in the attic, though frightening, was his gift to you."

"And I have forgiven him his transgressions."

"What of your father?" asked Marcus. "Will you forgive *his* transgressions, as well?" I hesitated before answering.

"I must confess, Marcus, that I do now glean some comfort from my childhood. Some scrap of knowledge that my father once felt love for me. I have my mother's portrait and the painting of her and I enjoying a beautiful summer's day on the beach. In each, I believe, my father revealed his true heart. And, even though he left me emotionally bankrupt after her death, my paintings will bring me years of unspeakable joy. Having my mother with me again is giving me the closure I so desperately need. For that, I believe I can, at last, forgive him. I will fulfill my grandfather's last wish."

"Praise God." said Marcus, reaching for my hand. "Now, you can move on with your life. And today, you will fulfill Becky's last wish by running the 5k in her honor."

Thinking of the painting of my mother and I on the beach, I knew in my heart that I'd carried my anger for my father long enough. Turning my face towards the window, I closed my eyes and whispered the words that had eluded me for 54 years.

"I forgive you, Daddy."

Immediately, I felt the tears of joy fill my eyes as the weight of my terrible childhood released its long held grip on me. In my mind's eye, I saw my father's scowling face break into a huge smile that filled his face with light. How handsome he was when he smiled.

"Are you all right, Kathy?" asked Marcus, with a look of concern.

"Yes, Marcus." I replied, allowing my father's light to shine within me. "My father is smiling at last. I am ready to live again. And, as they say, today is the first day of the rest of my life."

We arrived just in time to witness Mr. Preston raising the flag at the town's war memorial in front of the courthouse. Surrounding him, veterans of all ages stood at attention, their right hand poised at their brow. Marcus and I joined the crowd as the national anthem blared its tinny notes over the town's ancient PA system. I knew the race was to begin right after the flag-raising ceremony, and I felt slightly nervous despite the fact that I was now a trained runner.

As the crowd dispersed after the ceremony, I made my way to the starting line. Feeling Becky's spirit beside me, I imagined her talking me through my warm-up stretches. Since the town closed Main Street for the day, the square wore the festive face of a summer carnival. Booths selling everything from scuba gear to sausage sandwiches lined the street. People filled the square, and I suddenly felt uneasy among such a large crowd. Sensing my apprehensiveness, Marcus squeezed my hand for encouragement. The event committee had strung a large blue-and-white sign over the street announcing the race's start and finish line. Off to one side was a table holding bottles of cold water and a sign-up sheet. I was surprised to see Albert approaching us.

"Knock 'em dead, Kathleen," he said. Removing his signature bowler hat, he gave me a slight bow.

"When you finish the race, I have some good news for you, Kathy," said Marcus.

"Wonderful," I said. "After yesterday, I'd welcome some good news."

"And now you must prepare yourself for the race, my love?" he said. "It begins soon. Focus on only that."

"I'm ready," I said. "I just need a number." After signing my name, someone handed me a white paper vest with the number 67 printed in large black numbers.

"That was my jersey number when I played rugby in high school," remarked Marcus. "I did very well." I took this as a good omen and joined the other runners at the starting line.

"It's noon, folks. All runners to the starting line," shouted the mayor. "The course has been laid out for you. You'll run all the way out to the cemetery, which is your halfway point. At the gate, you'll turn right onto Casterton Road. In one mile, make another right turn onto Sycamore Street. This will bring you back to Main and home. Watch for the white flags. The first to cross the finish line will win the trophy donated by Sam's Sport Shop located in the Sand Dollar Mall."

"We'll be here when you cross the finish line, Kathy," stated Marcus, leaning in to give me a kiss. "Good luck."

When the mayor raised the starter pistol, I followed the other runners lead as they stepped into position.

"Ready, set, go!" he shouted, as he pulled the trigger.

As the younger runners shot forward, I allowed my body to set my pace. After weeks of training, I no longer felt the burning and fatigue in my legs as I ran. Within a few minutes, I slowed to a walk, and my breathing grew steady. When a runner passed me on my left, I saw that it was old Mr. Thompson, whom I knew was in his seventies. I couldn't help but smile at the contrast between his snow-white chicken legs and his bright orange shorts and tank top. *Time to run*, I thought, picking up speed.

Twenty minutes later, I spotted the cemetery up ahead. I was halfway to the finish. Just outside the gate, two women handed out small cups of cold water, and I stopped long enough to down one. The other runners were long gone, so I continued on with Mr. Thompson.

"I didn't enter this race with any aspirations of winning," he declared, sounding breathless. "The fact is, I just turned seventy-four and I need to prove to myself that I'm not yet ready to quit living."

"Here, here," I said, matching his easy gait.

"There's Casterton Road, Missy," he announced, "We're almost home."

Slowing down to a walk, we both made our turn at the white flag.

"Time to run," I announced a moment later, setting off at a steady sprint. I was pleased to see Mr. Thompson join me on my left. When I spied the white flag announcing our next turn onto Sycamore, I slowed down for a quick walk. Mr. Thompson looked exhausted. Concerned, I hung back with him until his breathing improved.

"How are you doing, Mr. Thompson?" I asked.

"Don't you fret about me, Missy," he said, smiling. "I'll be right behind you. Now you go on ahead."

"Good luck!" I shouted, as I left him behind. Up ahead, I could hear loud cheering as the town welcomed the faster runners across the finish line. When the shouting died down, I knew there would be few remaining to cheer on the latecomers. I was beginning to tire out, and glancing down at my watch, I saw that my run time was approaching forty-five minutes. *At least I'm not in last place*, I thought, thinking of Mr. Thompson somewhere behind me. My body was calling for me to walk, but I refused to slow down. A slight stitch was developing just under my right ribcage, but I had to keep going. I was on a mission.

When I turned onto Main Street, I spotted the finish line ahead and felt a sudden boost of energy course through me. "I'll not walk across the finish line," I said, as I pushed my body to new limits. My legs felt like rubber and my breathing grew labored.

As I ran toward the finish line, I was pleased to see a small crowd lining the street ahead. When they spotted me, Marcus led the cheering. As I grew closer, familiar faces began to emerge. Welcoming me across the finish line was Della, her granddaughter Patty, Mr. Preston, Albert, and Carl Wyndom.

Marcus stood just beyond the banner, his arms open wide. "Come on, Kathy!" he shouted. "You can do it!"

"This is for you, Becky!" I shouted. Running the last few feet, I pumped my arms into the air. "Let's cross the finish line together, my friend!" Throwing myself into the arms of my true love, I allowed my body to collapse against him.

"Well done!" declared Marcus, pulling me close. "You finished the race!"

Leading me over to a nearby bench, he gently lowered me down. My legs were quivering from being pushed beyond their limit. When I felt my old friend Charlie attach himself to my left calf, I stood and shook him off with a few cool down stretching motions. Spying Mr. Thompson nearing the finish line, I joined the others as our cheers rang out, welcoming in the last runner.

"You made it, Mr. Thompson!" I shouted. "Well done."

"Thanks, Missy!" he exclaimed, slowing down to a walk. "You ran well. I better see you next year!"

Finished with my cool down stretches, I went to thank my welcoming committee. "Thank you, everyone, for your support," I said. "However, as you all know, I did it for Becky. This was to be her last race."

"And she would be proud of you!" declared Della, handing me a huge bouquet of white roses. "You deserve these, Kathy." Lifting them to my nose, I breathed deep, relishing their fragrance.

"Thank you, Marcus," I said, leaning into him. "They're beautiful."

"Oh, they're not from me," he said. "Read the card."

Reaching into the bouquet, I pulled out a small white card. Flipping it open, I felt the tears momentarily blur my vision when I recognized Becky's handwriting. My voice quivering with emotion, I read it aloud. "Thank you, Kat, for running my race for me. I couldn't have done it without you. Live long and be happy. Love, Becky." I felt unashamed as the tears slid down my face.

"Let's go home," said Marcus, taking me by the elbow.

As we made our way back to Sea Breeze Cottage, I held my roses in my arms, their sweet fragrance filling the car. I'd done it. I ran the race and finished. Arriving home, I declined Marcus's offer to help me from the car. I felt wonderful despite what I'd just put my body through. When we stepped up onto the porch, I noticed the beautiful white wicker porch swing gently swaying in the afternoon breeze.

"A porch swing!" I exclaimed. "When did you do this?"

"I have people," replied Marcus. Taking my hand, he led me to it and we sat down.

"I have fond childhood memories of a swing on this porch," I said, setting it into motion with my foot. Then I remembered the message Marcus whispered in my ear just before the start of the race. "Marcus, you said you have news to tell me?"

"I have good and bad news," he said, looking serious. "The bad news is that Albert is leaving us. He's chosen to return to Ireland, where he will spend his last days with Kathleen's family. That way, when his time comes, they will entomb him beside his wife."

"Albert's leaving us?" I asked, not at all surprised. "Well, if the shop is sold, I guess I'll just retire. And what is your good news?"

"I am buying the bookshop from Albert," he replied.

"Oh, Marcus, that's wonderful!" I exclaimed. "Wait, I'm the new owner of a flower shop. What will we do with two shops?"

"I've been thinking about that," he replied. "Perhaps we can combine the two businesses."

"What a great idea," I said. "A flower shop *and* bookshop. What would we call it?"

"How about 'Pots and Plots,'" he replied.

"Or, we could call it 'Weeds and Reads,'" I suggested, giggling. "A combination made in heaven."

"I've an idea for another combination made in heaven," suggested Marcus, looking deep into my

417

eyes. "What do you say we combine Jennings and Stone as well?" When his words hit my senses, I felt the blood drain from my face.

"Marcus, are you asking me to marry you?" I asked, hoping my question wasn't out of line.

"Would you do me the honor?" he asked, taking my hand in his. "Becky's last wish *was* for you to live long and be happy, remember? Will you do so with me, Kathy?"

My mind soared with the sheer joy of what Marcus was now asking of me. His proposal of marriage was proof that one is never too old to fall in love if you're willing to open your heart. Marcus Stone was that one miracle I'd waited for my entire life, and I wasn't willing to waste a single moment.

"Yes, Marcus, I'll marry you," I replied, happily. As his mouth covered mine, I again heard the song of my singing sea stone fill my heart, and I knew, at last, the real magic it held.

About the Author

Kathleen Martin calls herself a farm girl from Ohio. Her dream of writing a novel has lived within her heart since she was twelve. Retiring at sixty-one, she has finally achieved that dream. It will not be her last. She's retired and lives in New Philadelphia, Ohio, with her husband, Darrell.